EINSTEIN'S
MISTAKE

A NOVEL BY • WERNER KRIEGLSTEIN

ISBN: 1451576773
ISBN-13: 9781451576771
LCCN: 2010904552

contact: krieglsteinw@hotmail.com

Dedicated

to All Who Believe In the Power of Science
and the Force of *Magic*

On June 11th, 2027, at 3:33 Universal Time, a clandestine experiment, conducted in the icy waters of Lake Baikal, at the recently inaugurated Novotny Particle Accelerator, triggered a series of events that shattered the course of history and exposed the great Einstein in a critical error.

Acknowledgments:

I wish to thank my family and friends who have all tirelessly encouraged me in this project. My partner, Maryann, and my five sons, Robin, Mark, Daniel, Thomas, and Michael, helped me with endless discussions and often endured my creative absence. My special thanks go to three editors, who over the years helped develop and shape this project. Jean Caldwell guided me through the early stages. Her critical mind was like a creative mirror rejecting those ideas that did not further the story line. Mary Ellen Ugatz-Gonzales added a keen sense for developing the mystical, emotional aspects of the story. Last not least, Joe Latoria scrutinized the manuscript for redundancies and errors. Many logical and creative contributions came from my sons, my colleagues, and my students at the College of DuPage.

My very special thanks are directed beyond the limits of this, our three-dimensional existence. *Einstein's Mistake* would not have been possible without the inspiration of my mentor, Dr. Walter Gerstberger. While a young pupil at a German Gymnasium, this mystic and visionary instilled in me a sense of awe that propelled all my endeavors. My search for an ultimate reality would never have been possible without the seed this truly wise man had planted in my young mind. Like Jesse in my novel, Dr. Gerstberger boldly claimed to possess the ultimate formula explaining the secrets of the universe. His mystical journey began with an ecstatic vision of ultimate reality. Meditating into the magical drawings of the German nun Hildegard von Bingen, Gerstberger followed his inspiration. Tirelessly exploring the limits of science and the human mind, he finally came up with a mathematical solution, a true Theory of Everything. Put on the path of philosophy and science as a young man, I spent much of my life trying to disprove my mentor's theory. In *Einstein's Mistake*, the hero Jesse is in possession of TOE, the final theory of everything. But Jesse is afraid to publish it for fear of its potential abuse. Throughout this novel Jesse leaves clues as to the location of this ultimate theory.

Finally I must acknowledge two visionary educators and friends. Jon Butcher authored the original Lifebook seminar, an empowerment program designed to put you in charge of your life. While taking part in a Lifebook session I conceived of the Valley of the Clouds prophecy and the University of Self Design. My friend Brent Cameron wrote an inspiring book, appropriately called *Self Design*. Brent gave me the inspiration for the spiral ritual that became the centerpiece of the Communion Day Ritual. There are others who helped me along the way, too many to mention. Finally I like to thank my colleagues at the College of DuPage, especially Joseph Barillari and Keith Krasemann, and my friends Rebecca Fyffe and James Coddington for their support.

Part One:
The Unitary Crisis

If one puts in 100 GeV (billion electron volts), the theory goes haywire. The equation explodes in your face. In the jargon of physics, this is called "unitary crisis."

Leon Lederman, The God Particle

One

Jesse Barker woke up from a deep sleep and knew instantly that somebody had been reading his brain. It was dark in the bedroom. The digital numbers on his alarm clock next to his head blinked with an eerie glare: 3:33 a.m. Almost three hours of much-needed sleep left before wake-up time.

The frame of the door leading into the bathroom was barely visible. A nightlight was left burning there. Jesse heard the calm breathing of his wife next to him, sound asleep. He closed his eyes again. Once more he had the intense sensation that somebody was watching them from above. He cuddled up to the warm body of his wife.

Suddenly he saw himself and his wife from high above, lying there curled up like two prehistoric creatures keeping each other warm.

By now he was fully awake, sitting upright in his bed. A slight sweat covered his entire body. For a moment he wanted to laugh, but he was too frightened.

Was he losing his mind?

Jesse strained his eyes to look around in the dark. To the right he could just make out the large window frame barely set off against the sky. It was pitch dark outside—a *Stygian gloom*. Even in this situation, Jesse's mind had an encyclopedic function that turned everything into tangible concepts, metaphors, and words. This quality had a kind of survival function for him and had helped him out of many tight spots. Jesse loved this role of language: put a concept to an unknown situation and you are more than halfway there in mastering it. It was magic.

What he saw next made his blood freeze; no handy phrase came to his mind to conceptualize the image, and even his normally astute brain froze in horror. In the window frame, silhouetted against the dark night sky, he recognized the shape of a person. At first he thought the figure was floating in midair, but then he realized that the person must be standing on top of the rail that surrounded the small porch outside the bedroom.

Jesse shook his wife gently. "Mary...wake up."

"What's going on?" Mary finally asked in a sleepy voice.

"Look, over there."

"It's pitch dark. I don't see a thing." Mary said.

"Outside the window."

Mary gasped and bolted upright.

"Wait...stay calm," commanded Jesse as he set his right foot on the floor and lifted his husky frame out of bed. Years of academic deskwork had taken a toll on his fifty-six-year-old body. Weighing in at 220 pounds yet somewhat shy of six feet tall, he was painfully aware that he needed to lose some weight. Straightening his stiff back carefully, he turned back to Mary and whispered: "Let me take a closer look."

Seeing Mary's frightened reaction, he quickly felt more composed. *At least I am not losing my mind*. An old ghost story from his childhood flashed briefly across his memory. A sense of discovery and adventure suddenly rejuvenated his spirit and filled him with renewed energy.

"Who could it be?" Mary whispered, anxiously grabbing onto his arm. Jesse could feel her sweaty palms on his naked skin. Her long blond hair radiated elegance, draping loosely over her ivory nightgown.

"I don't know...wait here."

As Jesse slowly moved forward, Mary suddenly gasped. "Oh, my god, Jesse. It's Melissa! Do something, please!"

Jesse cautiously approached the window. His wife was right. The figure he saw floating in midair—or standing up on the rail of the balcony—was their teenage daughter. Melissa's fragile seventeen-year-old body was covered by a loose-fitting, long cotton gown. Her arms were extended as if flying. It looked like the gown alone was floating in the air. *What is she doing out there? Sleep walking?* Jesse's scientific mind began immediately calculating the options.

The rim of the veranda, which stretched along the entire east side of the upper level, was at least sixteen feet off the ground. Their daughter's room was right next to the master bedroom. A separate door led from there out onto the balcony. Jesse contemplated what to do next.

"Oh my god, she's sleepwalking," Mary whispered frantically. "You have to do something…" Jesse realized the danger their daughter was in. If Melissa was sleepwalking on the edge and she was to wake up suddenly, she could fall and get seriously hurt.

"I'll use the door in Melissa's room so she won't notice me right away when I come out," said Jesse, his voice barely audible. "Then I'll grab her."

Mary waited anxiously. While her eyes were fixated on the floating body out on the veranda, she sporadically buried her face in her trembling hands. Her slender fingers pressed hard against her temples. Thoughts shot through her mind, memories of events from Melissa's childhood she had never shared with Jesse. She saw a little girl acting out her dreams and strangling her own throat as if possessed by a spirit. Mary used all the force of her rational mind to push these thoughts back into the past and out of memory.

When Jesse entered Melissa's room the balcony door was wide open. A cool breeze blew in from the outside. Jesse slowly moved into the dark room toward the open door. He exited out onto the veranda. There she was, standing and swaying slowly, as if carried by the breeze, up on the edge of the guardrail. She had her back toward him and did not notice Jesse approaching. Her long black hair blew gently in the wind. Her livid body wafted in the twilight, effortlessly.

Cautiously Jesse moved closer. As he slowed down further, the term "poulticing" dropped into his mind. Poulticing: applying a poultice, putting a soft, moist mass of bread, meal, clay, or other adhesive substance, usually heated, spread on cloth, on an aching or inflamed part of the body.

Jesse felt completely in charge. His large hands, inherited from a long line of Irish potato farmers, reached out, ready to seize their target.

He leaped forward, grabbed his daughter in one quick swoop, and held her tight. Pulling her delicate body away from the danger and into his arms, Jesse moved back into the safety of the room. Melissa, at first tight and stiff, relaxed slowly in her stepfather's embrace. "Poulticing," Jesse mused and smiled with relief. His daughter's eyes were closed. She began breathing evenly as she rested in his arms. Jesse carried her into the bedroom where his wife was nervously pacing the floor. He laid Melissa's frail body on the bed.

"You scared me half to death," Mary said softly, stroking her daughter's pale cheek. Looking at her wide cheekbones, her slightly curved nose, and her dark complexion, she was reminded of Melissa's biological father, a Native American from the Hopi nation. Still shaking, Mary lifted her daughter's torso gently and laid Melissa's head into her lap. Jesse had turned on a lamp in a corner of the bedroom, which engulfed the scene in a warm light.

Stroking the girl's hair, Mary said, "She hasn't done this sort of a thing since she was a child."

"She's done this before?" asked Jesse, surprised. "Why didn't you ever mention this?"

From the deep grooves formed by his raised eyebrows, Mary could see that Jesse was upset. "I was convinced she had outgrown it. She had a few episodes when she was a child. She used to act out things in her sleep. The doctor called it night terrors. Real intense and scary. But then——"

"What do you mean, 'acted out things'?"

"I don't know, like in the movies. As if somebody else was there, strangling her, an invisible person. Her father said that this condition was not uncommon among his people. Spirit possession or something—oh, never mind. You probably think I'm crazy. That's why I never mentioned it."

"No, no, keep going. This interests me. I have a right to know, especially now. You know I don't entirely agree with the official line of thinking, even as a scientist. But as Melissa's father I think I have should know."

"I told you everything I know. John lived in a different world. When I think back, there was a lot about him that I didn't understand." Mary's eyes turned sad as her mind drifted far away. "And I was young," she added quietly.

"Well, we can't let her do this again." Jesse conceded. "We'll have to do something about the door, like fasten it shut so she can't open it at night, or secure it with an alarm. We'll have to do something."

Jesse watched Mary for a while cradling Melissa in her lap like an ancient Madonna. Mary's pallid face, her liquid blue eyes, and her blond hair were in stark contrast compared to her daughter's dark complexion.

Jesse had no intention in the world of increasing Mary's discomfort, but he watched the sleeping girl with worry. "Do you think we should have her checked by a doctor?" Jesse asked.

"I don't think that'll be necessary—at least not right this instant. She'll be all right. I think you can take her to her bedroom now," said Mary.

"Maybe we should have her sleep with us, so we can keep an eye on her. What if she gets up again?"

"Jesse," Mary began, raising her voice ever so slightly. "Like I said, she'll be all right. I'm her mother, and I should know. She and I have been down this road before. Let's go back to sleep now, please."

Jesse wanted to say more, but by the reaction of his wife he knew that it was better to give in. He was a little upset that Mary felt it necessary to remind him that Melissa was not his child.

Next to him Jesse heard the even breath of his sleeping wife. Restless and worried, he got up and took a last look at Melissa. He was satisfied that he had been able to undertake such a difficult rescue mission for her. Undoubtedly Melissa was the daughter he had always desired but never could have on his own. Living together as a family, Jesse had made every attempt to introduce his young daughter to some of the more esoteric practices he cherished. He taught her yoga and meditation, and often talked to her about the wonderful secrets of the universe. Jesse desperately tried to gain her confidence and trust, but still, Melissa had remained somewhat of a mystery to him. At least this is how he saw it. Melissa's biological father was a Native American, presumably from the Hopi tribe. Mary had been married to him until he died in a car crash when Melissa was only two.

For various reasons, Mary had not been willing to share the story of that period of her life with Jesse. As a consequence, Jesse knew virtually nothing about Melissa's birth father. After Jesse married Mary, nearly fourteen years ago now, he had been waiting for the right occasion to start a conversation with her about her past, but it never seemed to be the right moment. Over time he had given up thinking about it.

As Jesse crawled back into bed next to his wife, he embraced her warm body gently and stroked her rich blond hair thinking about how lucky he really was. He was married to a gentle and kind woman who dearly loved him, and they both shared a deep commitment to giving their daughter the best possible education and the most fulfilled life imaginable.

Besides, at last he had a job he really liked. Jesse enjoyed teaching. Perhaps he had convinced himself of this. After many years working with the National Foundation of Science in research, with a specialization in particle physics, he had asked to be reassigned to teaching, mostly because more recently his views had often been at odds with the powerful Science Council. When the One World governing board began instituting a new set of laws to regulate all levels of life and of research, he was eager to leave his top position and disappear into virtual obscurity.

His present situation allowed him the right combination of teaching and private research. His deep interest and unquestioned success in basic physics had once earned him a Nobel Prize nomination, but the turbulent times and changes in world attitudes had prevented the once-famous committee from even gathering, much less choosing any winners. Nevertheless, on a private level, Jesse kept himself informed about the newest discoveries in physics. He was familiar with all the latest experiments that were arranged to reveal the most intimate secrets of the material world. In his time, Jesse had conducted his own investigation into the connection between the smallest particles of nature and the geometry of the universe. As far as being on the cutting edge of science, Jesse still felt he was there.

More recently, Jesse had succeeded in making some astounding discoveries, which he believed would one day revolutionize human life on earth. He even had developed an intricate mathematical algorithm to prove his far-reaching theory, challenging one of Einstein's major assumptions. His newest calculations proved beyond a doubt that the great master's speculations about the nature of the fourth dimension were false. For Einstein, the fourth dimension was merely an extension of our physical world into time. But Einstein also believed that time was a fundamental quality of the natural world. If space and time were intricately involved in the process of primal creation, how could it be possible that there were three dimensions dedicated to space even prior to evolving into a fourth dimension of time? No, time could not be an adequate explanation.

Jesse hypothesized that the fourth dimension was neither space nor time, but some kind of a mysterious field. The fourth dimension, his research indicated, was mind, pure and simple. Instead of being just another extension of our well-known three-dimensional material world, the fourth dimension comprised an enormously large, quite possibly infinite field of pure consciousness.

Jesse now feared that if this powerful field was ever made available to technological manipulation, some tyrannical power could establish ultimate mind control. Knowing that his intricate calculations could provide such an access, Jesse was determined not to reveal this powerful secret to anyone, especially not to the current scientific board, comprised of a dogmatic, narrow-minded, and often ruthless group of scientists. So he kept his breakthrough to himself, hoping to someday safely unveil this knowledge to a society that would be mature enough to handle the evolutionary advance that his discovery entailed.

Just before he fell asleep again, Jesse remembered the intense feeling he had when he awoke before, the feeling that somebody was watching him, that somebody was reading his brain. Was there any meaning in this at all? He put the question quickly out of his mind and fell asleep.

Two

The engine of Richard's jet hummed evenly and vibrated seductively through every fiber of his body. Looking out of the cockpit window at the deep blue sea beneath him, he could see a ship plowing through the current, leaving a trail of white ripples behind. The body of the vessel was a tiny dot in the vastness of the emerald ocean.

Richard could hardly contain his joy and his sense of accomplishment. Everything was working exactly as expected. All the hard labor was going to pay off. He was nearly ready to interrupt his experiment, to call Joe and share the news with his friend. But then again, he was anxious to see how far this new application would take him. He quieted his excited mind and let the software take control.

Suddenly, in front of him, he saw a tropical paradise on the horizon. Skillfully, Richard dropped his single engine aircraft down until a small landing strip appeared beneath him. Following a sudden impulse, he pulled the plane back up. Just when he reached a height of nearly ten thousand feet, he ejected across the open horizon. Thoroughly enjoying the freefall, Richard watched with open eyes as his aircraft plunged into the sea even before he released his parachute.

A jolt went through Richard's body as he landed next to a lagoon filled with crystal clear water. He stirred with excitement when he noticed a gorgeous blond bathing in the middle of the lagoon. She waved to him invitingly. Richard got up, untangled himself from the cords of the chute, and quickly stripped off his clothes. When he came nearer he recognized the girl: Wendy, his girlfriend. He jumped into the water, which was less than three feet deep and comfortably warm. He felt his body touching hers. Her lips were hot. Wendy's vibrating fingers caressed his wet skin until he was thoroughly aroused and hard. Richard closed his eyes and let his senses take total control. And yet, even underneath his growing lust, he could not hide the joy over the success of his new application.

Wendy! Love! Excitement! Richard did his best to suppress his thoughts and enjoy the event until his body became one with the warm liquid that surrounded him, and he finally relaxed. Richard reclined comfortably and soaked in the soothing music that now filled his headpiece. After a while he took off the elaborate laser-to-retina projection gear. The remote control for one of the most powerful multi-processors was in easy reach.

Richard wondered if Joe would still be awake. It was almost three in the morning now. Then again, Joe was a night owl just like him. Even though he was only in his early twenties, Richard had made a fortune in developing software applications for virtual reality fantasies. The son of a successful business man and a regional beauty queen, Richard had learned early in life that the only values worth living for were connected to unlimited carnal fulfillment. His engaging mannerisms complemented his handsome appearance and his blue eyes and blond hair, which he wore in a neat tail down his neck, were the attraction of any female interested in a short-lived acquaintance.

In the past few years Richard had cooperated with several global hardware producers to develop consumer-friendly instruments. He was proud of his accomplishments and always willing to share a good time with a circle of friends.

Richard activated the remote phone and asked to dial Joe's ID. Joe was Richard's best friend and business partner. Joe was a whiz in computer animation, but his first love was deciphering the mysteries of the human brain and turning his theories and insights into usable machines. After they had produced a series of breakthrough computer games, both Joe and Richard had dropped out of college and started their own company: Fantasies Unlimited, Inc.

Richard was interested in virtual reality right from the start. As a mere child he had been involved in the development of this new interactive medium when it first became popular back at the turn of the century. He had read every book he could get his hands on. Once he had mastered the programming technology he began inventing his own interactive games.

"You gotta come over as soon as you can, Joe!" Richard's voice was filled with mysterious promise. The digital videophone carried his enthusiasm through the airwaves. "I'm telling you this is out of sight fantastic. It works impeccably. Everything is right on the mark, temperature controls, goggles, vibrators, everything. I am telling you, you gotta feel it for yourself."

"How about the PVP unit?" His friend's voice came back. "Does it work satisfactorily?" The video image on the screen showed the plush art deco furniture of Joe's deserted living room.

"Man, Joe, it was like the real thing, like being there. Being with Wendy. She was right there, and I made out with her. It was absolutely real. By the way, why am I communing with an empty room again? Where are you?"

Joe was just tying his bathrobe around his waist when he finally appeared on the screen. Joe was an equally handsome young man with a well-groomed appearance except for the onset of a little belly that indicated his insatiable appetite for gourmet foods. In recent months, Joe had grown a little beard that complemented a carefully kept thin mustache covering his upper lip. His slender nose bone skillfully hid the nose job he had had performed a couple of years ago that gave his face the looks of a Greek god.

Joe now was putting on his own smile of success as one puts on an outlandish necktie. He had been working on a new and improved PVP unit for many months now and felt that he had a real blockbuster.

"I'll be over to give your machine a spin. But wait till you try my piece. It's a revolution. It does hot stuff, baby. Nobody, I tell you nobody, has done this before."

"Get out. What do you mean nobody? Give me some more."

"You know $E = mc^2$?"

"Sure, Einstein's formula. Don't keep me in suspense."

"All I can say now is, cube it."

"Cube it? What do you mean? Mass times the speed of light cubed? What are you trying to say?" Richard was genuinely puzzled.

"It adds a whole new dimension to reality. That's why I call it the Cube. See?"

"A new dimension? The Cube?" Richard did not see.

"I'll come over and give you a demo. It's exciting stuff, I tell you. I can't get away for about another hour or so. And then I might need a few hours of repose. How does noon tomorrow sound to you?"

"Sounds fair, compadre." Joe had a way of using big words. Richard often tried to imitate him, but never hit it quite right. "Let's meet in the usual place."

"Don't forget to bring your own PVP unit. You say you're all wired?"

"It's all hooked up, if that's what you mean."

"Just keep your adrenaline pump handy and the vibrators oiled."

"I'll keep the tub warm for you, all right. But bro, don't forget to bring your own girl. I won't let you do Wendy, dig?"

"No problem. Wait till you see old Joe's little gadget. I'll give you one more hint. I am one giant step closer in creating a true mind-link. Get the impact? The Cube opens the gate to a whole new field."

"A new field? What do you mean? Like ether or the magnetic field?"

"Yes, do you see why I'm excited? It's big. Real big."

"So what's the new field?" Richard insisted.

"That's all I can tell you. Okay, I'm signing off now. See you at noon tomorrow."

Richard stretched back into his lounge chair and slurped his iced tea. His mind was reeling.

I can't wait to get the demo package ready, he said to himself. *I just know Fat Benno is gonna be the first one to buy a unit. With his bad luck with women he certainly could use a Personal Pleasurizer, but then who couldn't?*

Still relaxing, with his feet dangling in the hot tub, Richard raised his voice as if making a commercial announcement: "Ladies and gentlemen, the PVP revolution is about to begin. A Pleasurizer in every household. No, a PVP in every bedroom. Let the machine take control of your soft spot. Pleasure in every home."

Reveling in all the rich possibilities, Richard leaned back into the soft, neatly manicured grass, letting his creative mind soar. Only the sky seemed the limit.

Three

Jesse was used to getting up early in the morning. He lived a disciplined life. After eating a light breakfast of juice, yogurt, and some crackers, he went to his study and meditated. With his eyes almost closed, the fair, freckle-faced professor focused on his large, gray cat sitting in front of him on his desk. From a distance one could have thought the professor was sleeping, but a careful observer could see his blue-green eyes piercing attentively through the slits of his eyelids, which were buried beneath a pair of bushy, auburn eyebrows. In intellectual discussions, Jesse liked to compare his encyclopedic mind with some of the great thinkers that his ancestral country had produced in the past. Frozen now in front of the equally motionless animal, Jesse himself appeared like a supernatural being, the earthly presentation of some pagan deity cast in stone.

The eyes of the big tomcat were focused sharply on Jesse's eyes. Anybody observing this stare-down might have thought that man and beast were involved in an intense, non-verbal conversation.

In his youth, Jesse had spent a summer with tribal people deep in the taiga of Siberia, where he had his first lesson in communication with animals. Ever since, he had been fascinated by this unorthodox passion and soaked up any theoretical explanations in scholarly journals while pursuing his own practical research into the subject. Significant progress had been made lately to unlock and understand the minds of animals, underestimated by science for millennia. But now these inane scientific purity laws accepted standard human language as the only means of communication and strictly forbade any other attempts, even on an experimental basis.

Jesse made sure nobody would see him in this exercise, not even a member of his own family. Such an activity would be viewed as a transgression of the scientific purity laws—something not to be taken lightly. Staring into the cat's dark eyes, he saw a human reflection within them watching him intently. *Melissa?* He briskly turned around. For a moment he thought his daughter was standing behind him. But the room was empty. Gazing back into the cat's eyes again, he saw nothing but darkness and emptiness. He quickly wiped the impression from his memory and got ready to leave the house.

On his way out the door his wife stepped in his way and looked at him expectantly. Planting a quick kiss on her face Jesse noticed that she was hiding something behind her back.

"What's that?" he said curiously pointing at the parcel behind her back. "Am I..? Oh, no…I forgot—again."

"I've gotten used to it. Remember the first year of our marriage? I played 'Happy Birthday' for myself on the piano until you noticed," Mary said with a sweet and sour smile.

"I'm sorry. How could I," Jesse began apologetically. "How can I make it up to you?"

"Here, take this and hand it to me." Trying to avoid an extended apology, Mary quickly handed the package to Jesse and then held out her hands to receive it back as a gift.

"You embarrass me.," Jesse said shyly, handing her back the package. "Happy birthday, my love." He gave her a warm hug.

"What's in it?" he asked curiously.

Mary laughed. "You should know! It's your birthday present to me."

"We'll celebrate when I get home. I promise."

"Would you wait just a minute?" Mary said. She quickly opened the package and took out a beautiful new dress she had gotten herself for her birthday. It was a black dress with an unusual deep red design in the front that looked vaguely like an eloquent orchid filled with life and beauty.

"Do you like your gift?" she asked while slipping on her new dress.

"It's beautiful—really. Looks great on you." Jesse was overwhelmed with how wonderful she looked. He was almost too embarrassed to speak. "I'm so sorry."

"No worries, honey," Mary reiterated. "I'm used to you. Nothing can surprise me. By the way, I'll be going out for a while later. I should be back home before you, though. I'll take you up on your offer."

"What about Melissa? Have you seen her yet? I wonder if she remembers anything—from last night?"

"She's still sleeping. She had a rough night."

"I have to run. Now I'm really late. We'll have to talk about this when I get back." Jesse quickly left for the office.

Four

Ten minutes before class, Jesse arrived at Frankfort College. He rushed into his office. A note was pinned to his office door. Without reading it, he crunched it up and threw it in the wastebasket. He figured it was probably a reminder that he had missed the scheduled morning awareness session again. This was a mandatory assembly provided by the college for faculty and staff. It was designed to keep every employee in proper working spirit and good health, a method all United World schools had adopted from a highly successful cognitive experiment. The professor had his own ways to keep up his spirit. He left his office in a hurry to go to his classroom.

The students were already exercising on their walkers and trampolines when Jesse entered. He mounted his own walker and began lecturing immediately. Jesse had gotten used to this new teaching style, which had recently become popular. Hardly anybody taught the old-fashioned way anymore. This interactive method did keep students alert. While listening to the professor's lecture, they got a good workout for their bodies. There was nothing wrong with that. Lecture notes were prepared for them by a voice recognition system placed in every classroom.

Some of the new applications Jesse did not mind at all. They added a lot to the experience and made life easier. And admittedly, even those who got nothing at all out of his lecture left the classroom with a sense of accomplishment: they got a physical workout if nothing else. *Mens sana in corpore sanu*, a healthy mind in a healthy body. In many other ways, however, Jesse was one of the last representatives of the old school. Jesse knew that he could get away with some of his idiosyncrasies because at the highest government levels he was respected for his insights into the nature of matter. But few here at the college were aware of the extent of Jesse's involvement in particle physics earlier in his life. It was a period of his life he did not speak much about since he had distanced himself from the ruling scientific elite.

After the lecture, a crowd of students surrounded the professor asking all kinds of questions. They slowly cleared out, and Jesse was finally ready to leave the lecture hall when he noticed a woman a few feet away from the podium looking at him expectantly. She was in the middle of her life and a little plumpish. Her opalescent eyes stood out against the slow and deliberate movements of her body. In contrast to most other students, who generally wore light exercise outfits, the woman in front of him had donned a dress with old-fashioned embroidery that could have been of Russian or Siberian origin. Her hair was covered with a scarf typically worn by immigrants from that region.

"Can I help you with something?" Jesse asked politely but without any real interest.

"Did you get my note? I left a note pinned to your door. Did you read it?" the woman inquired eagerly.

"Sorry," Jesse muttered. "I was kind of busy this morning. What did the note say?"

"It was a message, just for you. You must come to our meeting."

Jesse looked around, a little uneasy to see if anybody had heard her. When the woman spoke she had a strong foreign accent and a strange blaze in her dark eyes. It surged through Jesse's mind that she looked familiar. Somewhere he had seen those eyes before.

"Meeting?" he asked. "What kind of meeting?"

"Please, we must speak in private. It's a secret gathering. Much depends on it. Can I meet you in your office, please?"

Secret meeting? Jesse was apprehensive and nervous. This woman's request sounded like trouble.

When Jesse hesitated she said, "Are you mad at me because I didn't jump around on those silly things? I am too old-fashioned for this. I do enjoy your lectures, regardless."

Jesse remembered vaguely that the woman before him was one of the few who had not participated in the calisthenics exercises during his lecture. Being somewhat of a dissenter himself, he had never paid much attention to whether his students all participated as required by academic procedures. But secret meeting?

Jesse said sternly. "You are aware that any assembly must be approved by the authorities. So please, …"

The woman now had a thin smile on her face. Jesse's sobering attitude had in no way discouraged her.

"But you are different. I must speak with you in a more private setting. Please, Professor."

"No, I cannot oblige, under no circumstances." Jesse looked around again to make sure that nobody was watching. This was against all protocol, but something told him to give this woman a hearing. Quickly and nervously he scribbled a few words on a little piece of paper and handed it to the woman. "Come to my office. I'll be there this afternoon from four to six."

"Thank you," the woman said, visibly relieved. Her hand sank down on the professor's hand for a short moment. Jesse looked into her dark, feral eyes. He felt her hand trembling. He was suddenly overcome by a strange feeling of kinship, a feeling he had known this woman in a far-away place and a distant time. Suddenly out of nowhere Jesse said: "Are you a rebel?" He didn't know what made him ask this question.

Still holding his hand, the woman smiled calmly. "Every woman is a rebel and usually in wild revolt against herself."

"Oscar Wilde," Jesse said, smiling now as well. "I'll see you in my office, then. But now I must go."

"Oh, thank you," the woman replied. "I am so appreciative that you will see me. And by the way, great things are happening this very moment, great things. But it is you who is holding the golden key, Professor. You hold understanding. You must join the force."

The woman's voice was filled with excitement.

Jesse pulled away from her and walked off swiftly. The woman remained behind in the empty lecture hall.

Five

Melissa entered the kitchen. She was showered and dressed, and all ready for school. She wore a pair of tightly tailored blue jeans made entirely from hemp and a white peasant blouse, accentuating her swan-like neck and youthful tanned skin. Her long black hair flowed freely down her back.

Melissa looked briefly at her mother and noticed her inquisitive look. "What? Why are you looking at me like that?" Melissa sounded irritated.

"Nothing. There's your breakfast." From her mother's closed expression Melissa could easily tell that she had something on her mind.

"Come on, something's wrong. I can tell," Melissa insisted.

"Maybe I should drive you to school today," her mother said conciliatorily.

"Don't be silly. Everything is fine. I'm almost eighteen."

"I'm worried. I guess that's my job. Did you sleep well last night?" Mary tried to act casual. She wanted to see if her daughter had any memory of the episode.

"Fine, I slept fine." Melissa attempted to be composed even though deep inside dark and unknown emotions were gathering.

"You don't look fine," Mary responded. She lovingly stroked her daughter's hair. *Could it really be that my daughter remembers nothing of that terrible episode?*

"Mother," Melissa said, raising her voice ever so slightly. "I'm fine, really."

As much as Mary tried to contain her worries about her little girl's safety, she knew these were strange times. Melissa's sleepwalking incident was now overshadowed by more general concerns for her daughter's safety. Recently people had started disappearing in broad daylight, and many had yet to be found.

"I prefer you to take the boulevard to school instead of driving through the park. Another young woman disappeared just a couple of days ago, a friend of the Degas. You know them. Don't ever stop for anyone or anything. Sometimes they even disguise themselves as police."

"Maybe they are police." Melissa said and then added quickly: "I promise I'll be careful, mother." She was done with her breakfast and gave her mother a quick kiss. Melissa was ready to leave when she spun around. "Stupid me. I knew I was forgetting something." She hugged her mother and yelled, "Happy birthday, Mom! I've got something for you." She quickly went back to her room and returned with a small packet, neatly wrapped in violet paper.

"Open it," Melissa said." I made it for you."

"How beautiful!" Mary exclaimed and gave her daughter another hug as she looked at the little painting in her hand. It was a picture of a young Native American man, probably in his late twenties. He stood underneath a blooming cherry tree as if casually posing for a photo. His proud demeanor was accentuated by his wide cheekbones and chiseled features, including a slightly bent nose. He wore turquoise and silver jewelry around his neck, and he wore his hair in two tightly braided tails that came down by his chest. Wearing a brown shirt and a long cotton skirt, the young man looked stately. In a wide hip belt slung around his waist, he carried a small leather pouch adorned with brightly stitched embroidery.

As Mary stared at the picture, her face suddenly turned pale.

"Cha'risa Catori," she whispered. Her voice was hardly audible.

"What did you say?" Melissa asked.

"Nothing, never mind. It's beautiful. The picture is beautiful. I'll cherish it always. You need to hurry now or you'll be late."

Melissa quickly threw on her jacket and left the house.

Long after Melissa had left the house Mary still stared at the picture in her hand. *How could my daughter have painted this?* She was only two when her birth father died, and even during those two short years of her young life, Cha'risa was seldom home. As a truck driver, he had spent most of the time on the road. Could she have seen a photo of him? Mary was sure that she had no photo of him around. As she looked closer, she detected something even stranger. The man in the picture wore a familiar necklace around his neck. It was a piece her first husband wore only on rare occasions. She remembered him wearing it for their wedding ceremony, which took place on an Indian reservation many years ago. To Mary it seemed an eternity had passed since then.

Six

Melissa's high school was about five miles away. On her way there, she would normally drive through a wooded area of about four acres—an overgrown suburban park. She liked this little spot of wilderness. It was the closest to nature she could get. She felt a strange sense of peace there. In the evening, she often lingered here to watch the sun set and an occasional deer step out into the meadow.

Halfway through the park Melissa spotted a black limousine parked between the trees off the road. She suddenly sensed danger and accelerated. But before she could pass the limousine, it rolled onto the road and blocked her way. She slammed the brakes and immediately threw the car into reverse.

At 8:44 a.m., a police patrol discovered a clearly abandoned yellow Roadstar TX. The car was parked on a side street off the main drag. Officer Rowley had spotted the vehicle during a routine drive through the park. The driver's side door had been left open, and the flashers of the car were blinking. Curious as to the where-abouts of the driver, the officer got out of his car to investigate. Before entering the vehicle, he scanned the license number into his computer and instantly verified ownership.

At 9:02 a.m., high school counselor Sebastian Redgrave made a missing student report. Four minutes later, a call to the Barker home was processed through official security lines. But before the parents even received the message, the police had established a link between the vacant car in the park and the missing girl. Mary Barker's personal communicator was off, so police left her a message to return their call. Seconds later the voice communicator in Professor Barker's office rang off the hook, but no response.

Jesse was on the videophone with an old friend from the Ministry of Science. When an urgent report of a missing person appeared on his video screen he was busy listening to his former friend's request.

"We need you, Jesse. You know I wouldn't say this if I didn't mean it. What do you say?"

Jesse's mind reeled. What did Carlisle want? He hadn't talked to him for over three years. Back then they had been working on a secret government project together. *Science is calling? What a joke. Doesn't that guy know I'm not working in his type of science anymore?* The man on the other side of the video monitor tried to read Jesse's reaction.

"Come on, Jesse," Carlisle said again with a beseeching tone. "You're the only one who can help. You're uniquely qualified. I can't give you any details about the project over the phone, but we need you, our country needs you. Goddamn it, the world needs you. You know what that means."

Carlisle's voice carried a tone of finality as if the decision had already been made, and there was no room for negotiation. Jesse knew well what that meant.

"I'll be at your place in an hour," Carlisle continued. "I'm taking a chopper, and we'll head straight to the airport. I know this doesn't give you a lot of time to prepare, but you'll be away only for a couple of days, I promise."

"Wait a minute, Carlisle. There's…at the very least, I'll have to gather a few things together and…inform my family…"

"You don't need to do anything," Carlisle interrupted. "Everything is taken care of. You'll be our guest. I repeat again, this is one of the most important government missions you've ever been asked to take part in. Do I need to say more? Do you understand that time is of the essence here?"

The tone in his voice made it clear to Jesse that he really didn't have a choice. If the Ministry of Science called, one could not refuse. It was that simple.

"See you in, let's say, sixty minutes. We've already contacted your school and informed them about this. Your lectures for the next two days will be arranged over teleprompter. With telepresence you won't miss a thing, and your students will hardly know you're gone. So just meet me at the landing pad and I'll pick you up. Oh, and by the way, don't worry about the message regarding your daughter. As I said, everything is taken care of. She is in good hands. Signing off now."

The picture on the monitor faded, leaving Jesse behind with a hundred questions.

"Wait!" My daughter? What did Carlisle mean? A moment later, a missing person news snippet flashed across his screen. How did this report end up on his prompter? He had all nuisance messages screened out before they got to him. He suddenly realized that this must be a personalized communication sent to him by the news bureau or some other government agency. *Something terrible must have happened to Melissa*, Jesse thought. The event from last night flashed before his mind. Anxiety overtook him.

Jesse called home immediately. There was no answer. His wife didn't respond either. On the other hand Jesse expected Carlisle to be punctual. In the Ministry of Science, every minute was accounted for. Even though his mind was spinning and he wanted to have some answers about the whereabouts of his daughter, he couldn't afford to be late for this appointment. So he slipped on his overcoat and left his office on the way to the heliport on top of the Science Tower.

Just as Jesse stepped out into the fresh morning air—it was five minutes before eleven—he could hear the hum of the chopper in the distance. Within minutes the aircraft had landed, Jesse jumped in, and they were back in the air again. Jesse looked at Carlisle; his former friend's face resembled a worn mask. The vitality he remembered was gone as well as the energetic sparkle in his eyes. His hairline had receded and the few strains of the formerly brunette hair had turned gray.

Jesse had not met his old friend for several years. Ever since he had spontaneously deserted his research position at the Science Foundation he had been avoiding contact with Carlisle. Jesse had met Carlisle during his student years, and they had become best friends. But when Carlisle moved up to become one of the leading brains of the recent scientific revolution, Jesse first criticized and later outright rejected some of Carlisle's well-known practices of control and manipulation. As the chief engineer of the new scientific purity laws, the One World government under Carlisle's direction began restricting personal freedoms and even went as far as to completely outlaw love marriage. In Jesse's eyes, Carlisle's reputation was tainted but his power was unrivaled.

"You know I don't appreciate this. I've no obligation to the ministry. That was our deal," Jesse mustered his sternest voice.

"I could say that I'm sorry to disturb you in your seclusion, but that's not really the point, is it?" Carlisle came back with a cold, almost cynical voice. Years of working for the ministry had made him an uncompromising negotiator.

"Then what is the point?" Jesse asked, squinting his eyes skeptically. He refused to be intimidated by Carlisle's arrogant demeanor. "You know, this always amazed me about you, even back in Tallahassee. You are so…goal-oriented, so…I don't know how to say it…practical."

"That's the only way I can be who I am," Carlisle said icily.

Jesse did not need to be reminded of his former friend's powerful position in the Ministry of Science. He was second only to the president in his ability to get things done. Some even believed that he and his men were at times more powerful than the highest officials in the country. The top jobs at the Ministry of Science were immune to the mood swings of the people. Carlisle's position was secure for life—almost. Science could do things that no other department was able to accomplish. Next to God, there was the Ministry of Science, or better yet: the Ministry of Science had replaced God. Once science had shown its true power, the United States of the World had fully subscribed to the Church of Reason. Cool thinking minds everywhere had come to agree that science was the only hope for the world to stay clear of total chaos.

Jesse had to be extremely cautious. He had to find out what they wanted from him—why they had asked him to go on this mission. He could lose everything if he refused to cooperate with what they believed to be a reasonable request.

"Nothing much has changed, my friend, since those early days," Jesse said. "I'm practical, yes, but I'm still committed to the cause of world peace, just as we both were back then. How can you hold it against me when I'm only trying to realize our dreams? But I have to be a realist." Carlisle had noticed his friend's hesitation. He sounded almost conciliatory.

"Sure, especially in the line of work you're in now." Jesse tried unsuccessfully to hide the cynicism in his words.

"What do you mean? You're not implying...?"

"Let's be straight-forward, Carlisle. I know your position at the ministry, and I know that when you called I had no choice but to comply. But I can still let you know that I don't like it." Jesse tried to suppress his agitation.

"That's certainly your privilege. But please, no emotional outbursts. When you compose yourself, I'll brief you on the mission." Carlisle was just as serious and, as usual, extremely formal.

Jesse took a deep breath. "Go ahead. I'm ready—I can't wait."

"In a few minutes, we'll board a plane to Moscow. We'll arrive there in two and a half hours and then connect with another flight to Irkutsk."

"Irkutsk?"

"Yes, we'll be there in three hours. The connection is a little slower, a regular supersonic. From here to Moscow, we'll be taking a Stratojet."

"Spare me the details, please." Jesse could not avoid the impression that his friend was bragging.

"Sorry to bother you. By the way, this was the second time I said sorry to you. It's not my usual style, as you know. So I hope you realize that I'm being as patient as I possibly can be."

It sounded like a warning.

"I understand," Jesse replied curtly.

"You know about the supercollider we recently completed in the Baikal Sea?"

"Of course," Jesse replied, looking up in expectation. "It's built entirely underneath the water to utilize the cooling capacity of the arctic ice. How is it working out? It's only been in operation for less than six months. I haven't heard of any tangible results, no accidents either. I suppose that's good news."

Jesse was beginning to get interested. Particle physics had remained his primary interest, even though he had left experimental science for philosophy when he bailed out of the government project in Tallahassee.

"A month ago the collider was fired up at full energy for the first time. We'd done a few test runs earlier, but we had no chance to run it at full 1000 GeV."

"And?" Jesse could not hide his curiosity.

Jesse and Carlisle had hardly noticed that the helicopter had approached the airfield and landed right next to the Supersonic III Stratojet bound for Moscow. The silver lining of the jet betrayed the fact that the whole aircraft was constructed of a new super-light alloy material, assembled on one of the moon stations. This nano-engineered material had the capacity to repair itself in emergencies within seconds. When used in fighter jets, a hole caused by enemy fire could essentially fix itself in midflight.

The pilot had unlatched the gate of the chopper and indicated that they should get ready to dismount.

Carlisle turned to Jesse as the two men climbed up the staircase of the gigantic aircraft. "At the end of the day, my friend, you'll thank me for getting you involved. This is cutting-edge science. I can't wait to hear about your discoveries. Rumor has it you are out to prove the old man wrong. As I said, I can hardly wait."

Seven

Around 11:30 that morning, Mary Barker returned home from her meeting with the Sisters of the Thousand Lights. The sisters were a worldwide service organization dedicated to assist children in need. For a while this group had been under investigation for illegal spiritual activities, but more recently the government had given them a stamp of approval.

Mary noticed a green and yellow police car waiting in front of her house. It was a Special Forces vehicle from the Ministry of Science. A patrol officer, dressed in a green and yellow uniform matching his car, walked over to Mary. He politely informed her that her daughter Melissa was missing from school and that her car had been found on a deserted stretch of parkway in Villa Stream Park.

Mary was understandably shocked. *I should have followed my instincts. Why didn't I drop her off?* She could not help but blame herself. Her frustration and her real worry for the whereabouts of Melissa brought tears to her eyes.

"We informed your husband's employer, Mrs. Barker. Professor Jesse Barker is your husband, is that correct, ma'am?"

"Of course," Mary answered. *Why does he ask such stupid questions? I'm sure he already knows everything about me.*

"Your husband is out of town on a government mission. That's all I could find out."

"What? My daughter disappeared and my husband is 'out of town'? How long will he be gone? Where is my daughter?"

"Negative to both questions," the officer said, but when he realized by the look on Mary's face that she didn't understand, he added, "In both cases I can only say we are sorry, but we don't know." The young officer seemed truly apologetic. He tried to put a little smile on his face, but it froze when he realized the desperate condition of Mrs. Barker.

"Can I do something for you? Do you want me to get a medic unit? If you wish, I could drop you off at the nearest public comfort center."

"No, thanks, I'll be fine. I knew I should've dropped her off at school this morning myself." Even though Mary said this last sentence almost to herself, the policeman picked up that she might know more than she was willing to say.

"Did you make any observations that could advance our investigation in any way? Any irregularities in your daughter's behavior?" the officer inquired.

"No, of course not. What do you mean?" Mary sounded defensive.

"Between me and you, Mrs. Barker, if your daughter materializes, you should keep a close eye on her. We have reports that she's been keeping sensitive, if not illegal, acquaintances, if you know what I mean."

"No, I do not know what you mean," Mary shot back.

"Just trying to be helpful. By the way, why was your communicator disabled this morning?"

Mary mumbled something about the batteries being dead. The officer smiled knowingly and said, "I can only advise you, Mrs. Barker, to be on guard. But I've already said too much. I shouldn't even have shared such sensitive information with you. I must be on my way."

The officer was ready to leave the house, but then turned around and added, "We're presently doing a routine inspection of your daughter's car. It's in police custody at the town center garage. When we are through with it, you may pick it up. But we do need your permission in writing. Procedure, sorry. Please sign here."

"What about my daughter?"

"You can pick her up as well, as soon as she materializes." The policeman had a faint grin on his face.

"You talk about her as if…" Mary was upset and offended by the rude behavior of this official.

"Mrs. Barker, people disappear all the time, especially teen-agers. I told you that we'll bring her back as soon as we find her."

Mary did not know what to make of this man. One moment he seemed genuinely compassionate, only to make the most cynical remarks in the next instant.

"Isn't there anything I can do?" she asked helplessly. She was upset and confused.

"We'll send an investigator out later today. He'll ask all the relevant questions, and we'll do an extensive computer search as well. Perhaps something will show up. But don't get your hopes up. As I said, people disappear all the time."

Minutes later Mary was sitting in her large, empty house, with both her daughter and her husband gone. Her worst fears had come true, though she had never really thought it could happen to her. True, you heard stories about missing people and people disappearing all the time. They did not even bother putting it on the news any more. It was best to keep the bad news out of one's own four walls.

But people sometimes still talked to each other. A plumber was missing here or a beautician there. You got used to someone, and suddenly he didn't show up for work anymore. Nobody could do anything about it. Since the Ministry of Science had become so powerful, human life had become an expendable commodity.

The policeman was right: people disappeared all the time. However, nobody dared to voice discontent. You were just happy to be left alone and to be alive.

Mary wiped the tears from her face. Her husband's cat silently entered the room and lay down on the little black carpet he liked so much.

The phone rang.

Back in his vehicle, Officer Green filed this report: "Suspected activities verified. Both subjects, mother and daughter, involved in underground assembling. Recommend arresting Mrs. Barker as well. End of report."

Eight

It was eerily silent in the cabin of the Supersonic Stratojet bound for Moscow. Flying at an altitude of sixty thousand feet, the jetliner had reached its traveling speed of Mach 5. At that speed, the sound of the engines fell behind in the distance.

Jesse had taken his seat next to Carlisle in a luxurious private cabin. There were only a few other passengers on the plane. Carlisle mentioned that this was a special plane owned by the ministry. A stopover in Moscow would be necessary because the airport in Irkutsk was not equipped to handle Mach 5 supersonics, but Carlisle assured him that work to build such an airstrip would be completed soon.

Jesse was ready now to continue his briefing. He was curious enough about the test results. Were they ready to reach this energy for the first time now or had they already achieved it and were calling him to interpret the results? Only eight years ago, Jesse had made dire predictions should this enormous energy ever be reached. In a widely echoed speech to the Science Academy at their annual convention in Buenos Aires, Jesse had addressed the question of possible catastrophic consequences when reaching 1000 GeV.

"Ladies and gentlemen," he had said at that convention, "1000 GeV is a magic threshold at which our mathematical predictions simply collapse. I remind you of the words of one of the greatest physicists in the world, Nobel Prize winner Leon Lederman, who once predicted that at the energy of one billion electron volts all theories go haywire. We reached 100 GeV many years ago, and the world has not come to an end. Science moves on. This time it may be different. We do not have a good idea what will happen. Reaching this intensity can only be compared with one event the universe has seen in the past, the Big Bang itself. Here, too, the laws of nature collapsed. With the Big Bang, nature and its laws were born and the material world was created. What will happen at 1000 GeV? We simply don't know. This is why we scientists have come to call this unique situation nothing less than the Unitary Crisis."

Jesse's speech was rudely interrupted by a young man in the back of the auditorium. He looked more like a graduate student than a scientist.

"I heard the same doomsday nonsense when we reached 100 GeV!" the young man shouted. "They called it a unitary crisis back then and it turned out to be much ado about nothing."

There was some laughter in the assembly and voices of agreement. A clerk handed Jesse a slip of paper. A quick glance confirmed that it was a note from his boss at the Science Foundation, who was in the audience. It simply stated: "Stay on message." Jesse knew that the purpose of his speech was political, not scientific. As much as his scientific mind was compelled to address the possible dangers connected with high-energy exploration, his assigned mission back then was to sell the project to the public. These two objectives simply contradicted each other. But Jesse swallowed it, took a deep breath, and continued:

"For those of you from the political arena, let me explain this in more detail. One thousand GeV is the energy with which two or more particles collide—that is, if we ever reach this kind of energy. The highest level we have been able to produce so far is 600 GeV. We understand quite well the physics up to 900 GeV. Our computers developed adequate models. But at 1000 GeV, our formulas simply disintegrate. In plain words, they become nonsensical. There is no predictable data. At 1000 GeV, nature will either reveal her secrets or—? Ladies and gentlemen, take your pick. We just don't know. But as always, we must know. We must find out. We—humanity—is committed to the promise voiced by the legendary Odysseus who, faced with the unknown, once said, more than two thousand years ago, 'We must explore it. Why? Just because it is there.' Therefore, ladies and gentlemen, I urge you to fund the proposed Supercollider Arctica in Irkutsk. Needless to say, this global cooperative venture will solidify our longstanding friendship with the Russian and the Siberian republics. Thank you very much for your attention."

Jesse's speech had failed to produce the desired effect, and funding of the collider project was initially denied. But within less than a year the Science Council had consolidated power and issued strict guidelines for research and exploration. Work on the collider began soon thereafter. Deeply disappointed by the authoritarian direction of the world government and the tendency to curtail every aspect of people's lives, Jesse withdrew from his position in spite of his interest. He put in his resignation and applied for a teaching position in philosophy at an obscure school in Frankfort, Illinois. But privately he had continued his passion and had come up with some astounding results. Now he was curious whether the current experiment in Irkutsk would verify his calculations.

Nine

A hostess tapped Jesse on his shoulder and brought him back to the present.

"You have an appointment in the communication booth, sir. Your home office requests your presence; please, come along. I will seat you for the conference."

Jesse followed the air hostess to a communication cabin and sat down in a comfortable chair. His image would instantly be beamed in a three-dimensional holographic projection to wherever his presence was requested. From a distance of only a few feet, it would be hard to recognize that he was not present in person. This new technology actually manipulated each molecule separately to adjust the image to the original in such a way that even sophisticated detection devices could not discern a difference from reality. In fact, the only thing missing from the appearance was consciousness. It was a near perfect reassembly of the original material unit.

First the image of his secretary appeared in the cabin before him. "Professor Barker! You have an appointment this afternoon."

"Oh, do I?" Jesse could not remember. Too much had happened since he had left his office.

"There is a lady here who wants to see you."

Probably some student in need of advice.

"You can let her in," Jesse replied. But the very moment the visitor's likeness appeared before him, Jesse realized his mistake. He immediately recognized the visitor as the woman he had encountered in the morning. Remembering her mission, Jesse was suddenly quite uneasy about this visit, now even more than in the morning. But turning her away was not an option.

When the woman entered his office, she saw Jesse sitting in his armchair behind his desk. This kind of projection had become commonplace. He had to keep her at a proper distance, though, in order for her not to violate his image.

"Professor," the woman said eagerly upon entering. She rolled the r's on the tip of her tongue. "I am so glad you let me speak to you in private. You must listen to this, Professor. Are you sure we are alone?" She lowered her voice and looked nervously around the room. "You see," she continued, "I can see things that other people don't see. I was sent to you to bring you a message."

"A message? From whom?" Jesse asked.

"I bring you a message from the Golden Lady." The woman said, moving closer.

"The Golden Lady?" Jesse's jaw dropped. He abruptly remembered the story of the Golden Lady. It was half a lifetime ago, on a trip Jesse had taken with the Boy Scouts to a jamboree in Siberia. There he developed an intense interest in an ancient tale that had fascinated explorers and adventurers from the Vikings to the German fascists. Jesse had learned that, in ancient times, the Golden Lady was a spiritual being, some kind of a light creature. In Sanskrit, the oldest known written language, the word for gold and light were one and the same. Over time, the spiritual part was forgotten and the Gold Lady was believed to be a statue of solid gold, a prized trophy, desired and chased after by many adventurers.

The woman moved still closer and whispered with the voice of a snake. "I was told that you have the key. I am bringing you a message from the Golden Lady. You are non-Mlecha."

With that, the woman moved across the large desk, extending her arms. She had come so close that she was in danger of touching his image.

"Are you out of your mind?" the professor shouted. "Move back. Now!"

In an instant, a message flashed over the screen in the conference boutique: IMAGE VIOLATION! The connection had broken down.

For a while, Jesse sat alone in the silent cabin. Only a slight vibration reminded him of the present while his mind wandered deep into the past. Images of a dark-eyed taiga girl, a wild wolf, and an old shaman appeared in the fog of his memory. It was a time when he had first learned the secrets of communicating with animals, a time of great discovery and a time of first love. He remembered an old shaman calling him a non-Mlecha. Be he had never been able to find out what this meant, not even whether it was a good or a bad thing to be non-Mlecha.

For a moment Jesse contemplated to reestablish communication but quickly realized that this was out of the question. His mind was filled with hazy memories, when he finally made his way back to the cabin.

Ten

When Jesse returned to his seat, he noticed that Carlisle had set up a game of chess. As soon as he sat down his friend invited him to a game.

"What do you say? For old time sake, how about a round of chess?" Carlisle said.

"I am still waiting for a detailed briefing, you know." Jesse grumbled.

"Relax. We have plenty of time. Remember how we used to challenge each other? A game of chess can't hurt. Here, pick your color." Carlisle held out his two hands.

"I don't believe you, but alright then, I accept the challenge."

After only a few moves Carlisle said, with just the slightest smirk in his face: "Friend of yours?" He pointed with his head to the communication booth.

Jesse was already quite frustrated about the misguided communication and the many questions it had left unanswered. Now he could no longer contain his irritation. "What's wrong with you people?" he barked angrily. "Must you have your nose in everything?"

Carlisle looked at him silently. His friend's lack of a response made Jesse only angrier. Carlisle now kept staring at Jesse with piercing eyes.

"You expect my cooperation in whatever matter I can be of use to you. Yet you grant me not the least bit of dignity. This is outrageous. Forgive my disgust."

Carlisle showed not the slightest emotion, but calmly said, "When you're done, perhaps we can continue our game."

"Go ahead," Jesse said gruffly. He took a deep breath and forced himself to calm down. Jesse knew well that in the current situation anger and resentment would get him nowhere.

"Do you remember when we first met back in 2004 on the campus of Grand State?" Carlisle said casually after making another move. "We were both young and inexperienced. You invited me for a beer in that tavern. Jimmy's they called it, the only drinking hole on campus. You remember what we talked about, the very first time we met?"

"I was in the midst of a game with an old high school buddy when you barged in."

"We got into a discussion about climate and global warming."

"You made me lose the game. The same strategy is not going to work again," Jesse said, moving his bishop into place to attack Carlisle's queen.

"You had all the facts. I was thoroughly impressed by your knowledge. But more importantly, we both had the same goals. Do you remember?" Carlisle asked, eying his friend with expectation.

"You tell me, I honestly don't know what you're talking about."

"We wanted to change the world. Save Mother Earth." Carlisle sounded somber. Jesse noted the deep wrinkles around his friend's eyes. His stressful occupation had taken a toll on him.

"Saving Mother Earth? Well, it's still a noble idea, isn't it? Who didn't want to save the earth, the environment, and all that back then? Indeed, who wouldn't want it now? But it looks as if the world is in a pretty hopeless mess now in spite of all efforts. Wouldn't you agree?"

"Since when is your glass only half full, my friend? " Carlisle tapped a passing attendant and asked for a drink. "Back then I admired you for your idealism and your resilience. It was quite rare, actually. Most people I knew were into sex, cars, and power. But you were different. That is what impressed me about you. You inspired me. Did I ever tell you that?"

"So what has changed? Why can't I still inspire you? Is it because you went for power, and I did not?" Jesse moved his knight to protect his king from Carlisle's advance.

"Come down from your high horse, Jesse, will you? You, my friend, are the one who has changed. You seem despaired, no longer willing to take any risks."

Carlisle moved his castle back to a safe location. "Give me one good reason why you are not on our side?"

Jesse could hardly believe Carlisle's audacity. "You want me to be on your side? Take away people's liberties? Tell them who to be friends with, how to behave, how to think? How and when to have babies? What happened to the old dream of privacy and personal freedom? No, truly, I can never agree with your policies. They've put the world into a permanent state of terror, worse even than the terror you claim to fight."

Carlisle paused to take a sip from his drink. Holding his queen suspended over the board ready to make his next move he shook his head and continued slowly, as if weighing each word. "The terror we had to contain, my friend, was the distinct reality of total annihilation of the human race." Carlisle crunched an empty juice can in his right hand while moving to take Jesse's bishop with his left. Carlisle seemed frustrated, but then immediately caught himself. He continued, cool and collected, but with an unquestionable passion in his voice. "We at the Ministry of Science had no choice. As the world's supreme governing body, we have a responsibility to everybody. We chose life over mass extinction. If some of those ideals, you and your outdated friends call personal freedom, had to be sacrificed, so be it. Call it the lesser of two evils. Do you think I agree with all the policies? I love freedom and independence as much as you do. But everything changed after the Year of the Horse. You know that. Whole communities accepted collective suicide as a legitimate way to pass over. This is unacceptable. Mass suicide, inspired by religion, this makes a travesty of all life. Why stay in this world when the other world promises you eighty virgins—or whatever attraction it holds out? By the way, your queen is in danger."

"I completely agree with you." Jesse turned his head away from his friend and looked out the window. Somehow he wished this conversation was over. Deep underneath him he could see a blanket of white clouds covering the blue planet.

"I am glad you can see it my way." Carlisle did not let go. "Suicide is a disease we must counteract."

Suddenly Carlisle could see a sarcastic smile on Jesse's face.

"What?" Carlisle quipped. "Why are you smirking? I don't see any humor in any of this."

"I had to think of an old tune from our youth. These ideas are not new, you know. Here, listen to this. I wonder if you remember." Jesse whipped out a little pocket communicator, pushed a few buttons, and handed it to Carlisle. The communicator played an old song. "Imagine there's no heaven, it's easy if you try, no hell below us, above us only sky."

Jesse hummed along with the tune. "Nice, isn't it?"

"Poetry is not the answer," Carlisle said. "It's part of the problem, not the solution. We finally have unlimited access to energy, limitless consumption is in reach, and, nevertheless, humanity clings to ancient deceptions and even invents new ones. With all the material needs fulfilled, there is talk again about higher realities. It inspires folks to forsake the here and now and escape to a better place in the sky. Even some scientists encourage this nonsense. Science only deals with the things we can measure, touch, see. Everything else is false and must be forbidden." Carlisle stopped abruptly and looked at Jesse as if expecting a response. Jesse stared at the board and realized that he was cornered.

"How will you ever know the true nature of the universe if you limit research, if you control each and every thought? The communists tried that back in the twentieth century and failed miserably. And they were infants compared to your sophistication."

"I resent you comparing us with such monstrosities of the past," Carlisle said. He was moving his knight in position to take Jesse's queen.

"Science needs philosophy to give it value." Jesse moved decisively to protect his queen.

"Our science is deeply involved with value, the value of life, the value of sustainable ecology, the value of material advance. Don't tell me these are not proper values. What else can you philosophers add to this? Faith? Mystery? The unknown? You're not naïve, Jesse. You've never been. Irrational inclinations start in the human heart, or should I say brain. Religious fanaticism has brought us all to near-extinction."

Carlisle had just moved a whole army of knights to attack his very existence. He had to stay his ground firmly.

"It's the one-sided arrogance of you people that will ultimately bring you down. Science seldom teaches humility, does it? Nor does it know anything about wisdom."

"Nonsense. Philosophy has become all but useless. Philosophers stand in awe and stare at the beautiful construction that science erected, from the outside. Philosophy has nothing to add. Check mate." Carlisle had a satisfied grin on his face.

But Jesse was not ready to give in. "Then why did the Ministry of Science call on me?" Jesse countered Carlisle's move by moving his queen in front of the king.

Carlisle smiled, conceding. "Good move. One score for you. I could of course say that we called on you for your expertise in particle physics. But I know and you know that more must be behind us contacting you. The ministry has plenty of experts available, especially in this particular field."

"So what is it? Why me?" Jesse wanted to bring the game to a swift conclusion.

"All right, let's level with each other right now, Jesse." Carlisle became very serious. "When you left the project in Tallahassee, remember what you were working on then? Of course you do. Your discoveries were the reason you left. Not some speculation about values, and so on. Am I correct?"

"I left because I disagreed with government policies."

"You left because you had made discoveries about the inner composition of the material world, far beyond what anyone else had discovered—far beyond even the discoveries of the great Einstein. But you, you felt you did not want to share your discoveries with the rest of us."

"That is nonsense. As you know, I gave up research. I would have never—"

"We found evidence of your research on a backup file you failed to erase. What else is it you discovered? Why didn't you disclose everything?"

"The whole thing is pure conjecture. It's utter nonsense."

"I could've had you arrested back then."

Jesse had the distinct feeling of imminent danger. What was his friend indicating? He tried to sound as casual as possible: "Why don't we stop these accusations, and you brief me on the mission at hand?" His face was slightly pale and his hand, picking up a can of soda, trembled ever so slightly.

Carlisle smirked. He seemed visibly satisfied. "All right then. Now you're talking sense. I mentioned already that we need your expertise."

"And I'm asking again. Why me?"

"We've reached 1000 GeV."

"And? This is exciting news, indeed, but why do you need me?"

"We need you to interpret the results."

"Then show me the protocol. Let me have the numbers."

"It's not about numbers," Carlisle said quickly. Jesse sensed a strange hesitation.

"Then what is it about?"

"We decided it's best to have you on location for the next test. Then you can judge for yourself."

"I don't understand," Jesse said coyly. "Are you asking me as a philosopher or as a scientist?"

"As both. We need your scientific and your philosophical expertise. Besides this, there is really not much more I am at liberty to tell you. We need you as unprejudiced as possible. This way we hope to get an unbiased report."

"Since when has the unbiased report of one observing individual had any scientific significance?" There was obvious cynicism in Jesse's voice. At least he wanted to make one more move before concluding the game.

"Let's just leave it with that!" Carlisle said decisively. He obviously had finished his briefing.

After a few minutes in silence Carlisle said, "Let me just add one more thought. We have reason to believe that your discoveries in regard to higher dimensions can, in some way, illuminate the events in Irkutsk. You'll see for yourself. We'll expect your full analysis."

Jesse bit his lips and said nothing. Having lost all their pawns, both kings stood silently opposite each other like two intellectual giants engaged in a mythical battle, which neither one was ready to concede.

Eleven

Richard sat comfortably in a small café enjoying a latté while waiting for his friend Joe. But Richard was also on a mission. Occasionally he contracted himself out to a government agency to "collect data," as they called it. In fact, he did the age-old work that any tyrannical system requires to sustain its power. He spied on people.

Richard enjoyed this line of work. It paid well, and frequently he was able to use the data he gathered for his own purpose with Fantasies Unlimited. For this reason (and many other testosterone-related ones) he especially preferred it when the observed subject turned out to be an attractive female.

This morning he felt less than lucky. The girl he was paid to observe did not show at the time he expected. The bar was nearly empty. Even if another pretty face had shown he would have had to ignore her because no one would pay him for observing a random victim. Richard sat and waited. After a while he tapped the screen on his recorder, bringing back a clip he had taken a few days earlier when he first shadowed the pretty face he later found out was called Melissa. Richard had actually been contracted to shadow the girl's father but he found the daughter far more attractive. When he first spotted her she was deeply absorbed reading an electronic book. Now Richard stared at her on the screen and visualized her attractive body in his mind. The black-haired teen wore a turquoise windbreaker that was opened and hung loosely about her shoulders. Under this she wore a pair of straight leg jeans and a peasant blouse of varying pinks and oranges. On his first encounter, a few days ago, Richard had followed her every move, occasionally taking video images. Now watching the recording he was reliving this memory and relished every moment.

Richard liked to live in his own thoughts, and hence he paid little attention to the voice coming from a giant monitor that covered the entire wall at the opposite end of the bar. President Viswamitra, scientific patriarch and leader of the One World government, was giving one of his typically long-winded speeches:

"My dear friends, I am happy to report to you: our world is finally improving. Our indicators show a decisive upswing in activities, especially in the economies of the Pacific Rim. This is due to the reforms we successfully introduced only two years ago. More importantly, however, the social climate around the world is improving. The single most decisive factor that has contributed to the overall humanization of social life can be found in the introduction of the One World Act, which put arranged marriage into law. This act above all has helped to stabilize the fragile human psyche. The institution of arranged marriages has been a resounding success. Our polls indicate beyond doubt that the abolishment of love marriages has widely contributed to the freeing up of millions of hours of social time, and general productivity has soared.

"In the not-too-distant past, I might recall, precious resources were wasted in the pursuit of courtship and the unstructured and unguided enchantment by the opposite sex. Men and women have finally outgrown their animalistic instincts, which for centuries, even millennia, contributed to the creation of an emotional wasteland populated with tragic figures, such as Romeo and Juliet, or worse yet, young Werther, that fictitious German fellow, who inspired thousands of lovers to tragic suicide. I am happy to pronounce that these times are over. Human beings can finally focus on their true mission on earth, living happy, content, and rational lives, and producing good things for generations to enjoy."

I can't believe this nonsense, Richard mumbled. He turned to catch his friend Joe, who was approaching him from behind. Joe tapped his friend on his shoulder.

"Welcome, compadre," Richard said, recognizing Joe. "Am I glad to see you! How's your work coming? Did you bring the tools?"

"Sure thing. Busy as usual. What are you up to?" Motioning toward the giant wall monitor, Joe said. "I can't believe you listen to that garbage."

"I'm not." Richard pointed at the screen on his recorder. "Check out my latest client here. Her father's a professor. It's actually her father, the agency pays me to shadow."

"And?" Joe said with a question mark in his face. "Why are you prusuing her?"

"Wouldn't you if you had a choice?"

"But, you don't have such a choice. Didn't you say the agency asked you—"

"Yes, of course, it's her dad they're interested in; still, she'll lead me to him."

"And? May I ask where she is?"

"She didn't show. But I swear, my intelligence said she would be here unless…"

"You lost her."

"I guess you are right. That's so depressing."

"Didn't you just say her father was a professor?" Joe said in an attempt to cheer up his friend.

"Yes, and?" Now it was Richard who did not understand.

"A professor has an office, a professor gives lectures. If you are supposed to collect data on the professor, you go to his office or sit in on one of his lectures. You're wasting your time doing it this way."

"Not at all. I have different plans for her," Richard said.

"So instead of doing your job, you're pursuing your animalistic instincts?" Joe said and continued. "If the authorities get wind of this you could be risking our entertainment license. We don't want to lose that precious piece of paper after all the hard work to get it."

"Don't lecture me. This animal pursuit, as you like to call it, is perfectly legit. Well, almost, if you think about it. After all, my goal is not libido," Richard replied confidently. "My animalistic instincts serve a higher purpose," he said with a grin in his face. Then he bent over to his friend and whispered into his ear. "When I first got on her trail, it might have been base instinct. But as I followed her I found out a few things the science people were quite interested to learn. I tell you, this pretty outfit is in trouble, deep shit trouble, if you know what I mean. I recorded her attending an underground assembly—positively illegal. Smoking illegal substances, spiritual séances, face painting, and wild tribal dances. You get the picture. For all we know they might have picked her up already. What do you say, Joe?"

"Did you turn her in?" Joe asked in disbelief. "You did, didn't you? You… I don't even know."

"I did my job." Richard waited for a reaction. But Joe suddenly refocused his interest. He had a way to stay out of politics.

Joe's interests were less focused on the physical bodies of people, and more on their minds. He would soon find out whether his newest invention would make it possible to see inside a person's mind.

Joe quickly scribbled some sketches on a tablet while the voice of the president continued to provide a background in the empty hall. The they both left the empty bar.

Viswamitra's speech went on filling the deserted hall with propaganda even after Joe and Richard had left. Nervously blinking automatic juice machines provided a silent audience.

"On another front, my friends, great progress can be repor ted. Our scientists have finally perfected the process of cold fusion. Limitless energy supplies are now at hand. This will put our earth on a completely new course of recovery. We will immediately begin to replenish the broken ozone and counteract the devastating results of a century of pollution. Scientists all over the world are working to rescue the ailing patient. With the help of science, peace and prosperity is at hand."

Twelve

Joe and Richard drove straight to Richard's house ready to try out their inventions.

"You said you brought your own clip, right, bro?" Richard said anxiously. "Remember, you can't have Wendy, even though it's virtual. I am not possessive about her or anything. But I do have my plans, with Wendy, I mean. So, did you?"

"Okay, okay, I got the drift. Don't worry, I didn't forget. My personal assistant actually offered me a sample. She practically forced me to take it. Sacrifices you have to make for science, that's how she put it..." Joe handed his friend a small chip.

"Let me activate her then." Richard was excited to show off his gadget.

"I hope it's not a problem" Joe remarked with a sly grin. "But my assistant, you know, she is a robot."

Joe seldom grinned. Ever since one of his many female acquaintances had pointed it out, he was always aware that the two dimples that appeared on his face when grinning distorted his classical looks. Richard had a question mark in his face.

"I mean, I am asking: will your contraption still work if it's a robot?" Joe asked innocently. "But to tell you the truth, she looks so human that I myself often forget the difference."

"You're not serious? You're kidding, right?" Richard's face dropped, and he almost looked like he was near tears. He had his machine ready and was about to ask his friend to submerse in the hot tub—but not with a robot.

"No way, not with a robot." Richard was adamant. "That would be total desecration like—like—" He was desperately searching for a suitable image. "Like dressing up in a tuxedo and—"

Joe, who was always better with words, quickly continued: "— taking a ride on a donkey."

When he saw his friend looking at him with an empty face he quickly continued, "Can we do this perhaps some other time? I don't think I can get into it."

Richard looked at his friend in disbelief. He always suspected Joe of having a case of erectile dysfunction. Defeated, he began packing away the body gear and turned off the machine.

"May you never again have wet dreams in fantasy-land," Richard said cynically.

"Is that a curse or something more serious? Sorry I spoiled your surprise. Now let's find a suitable name for your invention."

"I already have a name," Richard said coyly. "Besides, you don't even know what my invention is capable of doing."

Joe laughed. "I have a pretty good idea. So what do you call it?"

"I call my invention the Pleasurizer. Very simple and straight forward. It will revolutionize sex, and in a way the science people can't even object to."

"Pleasurizer, hmm, that works." Feeling a little guilty, Joe made it a point to recognize his friend's creation of a new brand name. This was almost as important as the gadget itself. Usually it was Joe who invented new words and Richard who tried hard to use them. Now Richard basked in the praise. No matter how much he tried, Joe always seemed to be a nose length ahead of him. Well, it was probably more like an elephant's nose.

Concerning the Pleasurizer, Richard was banking on the idea that recent restrictions on sexual relations would ultimately help him sell his new gadgets. Under the strictly enforced scientific purity laws, all procreation had to be arranged in specifically authorized labs in order to guarantee quality production. Because of strict registration requirements and enforced controls that extended into every corner of society, illegal procreation rarely happened. When it did occur and when such intercourse resulted in a pregnancy, government-certified doctors were required to ensure miscarriage of the unwanted fetus, which in fact amounted to enforced abortion. Even though many disagreed with this measure, few dared to voice dissent.

Virtual intercourse, however, would not fall under these limits. The government was less interested in restricting the personal enjoyment of ordinary citizens, but rather to ensure high-quality offspring. In developing his new gadget, Richard was convinced that his version of virtual intercourse was as close to the real thing as anybody was permitted to entertain. And this kind of activity was actually encouraged. Research had shown that pleasure was positive. Studies confirmed that human beings, just like their chimpanzee relatives, were far less likely to engage in hostile activities when their sexual urges were not restricted. On the other hand, real sex on a mass scale was likely to produce countless pregnancies, many of which would result in lesser grade offspring. Even when counting in all available methods of birth control, the risk of disease also remained high.

The government clearly separated the process of human reproduction and the enjoyment of sexually active adults. But until now, technology had been lagging behind. Richard's invention finally promised to provide an exciting alternative. With the help of his Pleasurizer, virtual sex in an electronic, clinically clean environment would become indistinguishable from real sex.

Richard had already forgotten his friend's refusal to actually try out his machine, but now he insisted in explaining every detail. "My application works like this. If you were sexually attracted to a mate, you would acquire a few minutes of video from that person. We could set up an agency for that purpose, similar to a private eye. For a small fee, a 'detective' would go out and do the filming. Current technology requires at least half an hour of decent video to make the machine work properly. With the advancement of this technology, it could be cut down to a few minutes of actual footage. The video would then be transferred into the Pleasurizer."

The beauty of the transponder, as Richard explained, is its lifelike reenactment of the person but within the virtual environment.

The ultimate pleasure would now be available anytime, and it would be clean, efficient, and highly personalized.

"A time will come when average people will know nothing but your Pleasurizer," Joe chimed in. "Most people won't even remember this primitive custom of bodily procreation. Real physical sex will go out of style just like the old typewriter or the use of natural teeth in your mouth. Pain-free, clean, and sterile, but highly efficient—that's the wave of the future."

Richard beamed with pride as his friend described the final vision of a society shaped by his very own invention. Now he had the feeling that his friend could wait no longer to present his own creation. Richard was not insensitive. Politely he encouraged Joe to demonstrate his gadget.

"As a matter of fact, in order to demonstrate the power of my invention, I would like to do a little experiment," Joe began with a broad grin. "I will let you choose your subject. Who would you like to inhabit?"

"'Inhabit?'" Richard said, not quite sure what his friend was getting at.

"It means you will be inside your subject's mind. You'll see the world through her eyes, have her feelings, everything. Get it?" Richard still looked confused. Impatiently Joe continued, "Seriously, why don't you see for yourself? So who is it going to be?"

"I know what you're getting at. No, it's not going be Wendy. I can't do Wendy. That would feel wrong. You know that I am somewhat serious with Wendy. I care about her."

"Honestly, that must be a new sensation for you. But so what? Why not Wendy? Don't you think it would be kind of interesting?"

"It just wouldn't feel right, okay?" Richard said. He was a bit irritated. "I guess I'm more traditional than I thought."

"Then who? Who is it going to be?" Joe asked again.

Richard thought for a while. "If I understand you right, it's similar to a hypnotist getting into your mind. So it shouldn't be someone

I know real well, like somebody from my family. It wouldn't be right to know their deepest secrets. Don't laugh. Maybe I am old fashioned. But what if I find out that a person I think loves me, really hates me? Or someone I believed was straight in reality is gay?

"It's got to be someone you don't really care about."

"I know," Richard's face lit up. "How about using the girl I recently shadowed, Melissa? I don't really care about her."

"Great idea, let's see what she's up to. What do you say?" Joe was excited. But there was still hesitation in his friend's face. "Now what?"

"What about if she is in prison? Would that still work? Remember, I told you?" Richard bit his lip and played embarrassed.

Joe just shook his head. "I don't see where this would really make a difference. But, seriously, you really had to turn her in, did you? You are such a prick."

"I take my job seriously." Richard said defensively. "Will she know that I'm, like, inside of her? That's what will happen, right? It could be kind of embarrassing." Richard still wasn't sure.

"According to my calculations, she shouldn't even know at all. She'll have no awareness of your presence."

"Are you positively sure?"

"Why? What does it matter?"

"I'd be uncomfortable. That's all."

"Come on. All I need is a few minutes of footage. My GPS fills in the details. The clip you showed me the other day would be fine."

"I've got plenty. How many hours would you like?" Richard tossed him a chip.

"Let me see what we got. I upload it, and then you can take her for a spin. But first let me see if I can make contact. Get ready for a new experience?" Joe said confidently.

Richard was more than ready, and within seconds of putting on the elaborate headgear, the virtual environment took over. Momentarily Richard found himself in a strange place indeed.

He was surrounded by hundreds of people, young and old, each one distinguished by a very original outfit, a strange hat, a multicolored jacket, and pants that were totally out of style. This was a scene Richard only vaguely knew from watching old movies. What he witnessed was obviously an illegal gathering of some sort.

Before Richard could reflect on his new situation he heard himself speak, but it was the voice of a woman, the youthful voice of a girl.

"So where do we go from here, can anyone tell me?" he heard the voice asking.

"We must be patient," replied an older gentleman with a long beard who stood nearby. "Instructions will come in time. In fact, there is Oxana now. She has been receiving the messages most strongly. She will guide us. Let's listen to what she has to say."

The colorful crowd grew silent. They all focused their attention on the woman the old man had called Oxana. She stood on a pedestal in the front of the vaulted space. She wore a colorful robe over a flowing wide skirt. Her weather-beaten face bore two sparkling blue eyes. Her head was covered with a thin cloth. Her thick white hair was braided into a tail that fell down to her hips. Some unsuspecting observer could have taken her for a pagan priestess or some ancient goddess. She was around fifty years of age.

Richard looked around and took notice of the strange architecture of this place. Huge pipes ran across the ceiling from one end to the other. There was very little light and everything was painted in a monotonous gray. Richard had the feeling that he had been in this place before.

"Friends and seekers," the woman started to speak. "We can all rejoice today, because our wishes have come true. Or let me say, they are going to come true in a way we are sure to celebrate. Strong signals have reached me from the other side of Mother Earth. A bright light shone up to the sky and into the far reaches of the universe. So powerful was the message that no one with an open heart could have missed the signal. Didn't you all receive the message? Isn't that why we are all here?"

The colorful crowd responded with enthusiastic applause. Richard felt the excitement in every fiber of his body, but he was also aware that these were not his feelings, that he was an observer in a strange body.

Oxana continued: "Spontaneously, you have all congregated and found your way to this secret meeting place. And in just the same way, the light will guide us to unite with our brothers and sisters at the epicenter of conscious union. Deep in the icy fields of Siberia, a new light has been born; a powerful union has merged the physical world of our bodies with the eternal mind. A new age is dawning. We have all felt the vibrations of the event, and that is why we have come together."

Suddenly Richard remembered where he was: this meeting was taking place in a basement underneath the Great Mall of America. In his youth, he had liked to hang out there with other teenagers. Sometimes they stayed there overnight because the mall security forces somehow had an incomplete plan of the property, and this underground vault was not listed on it. Richard had eventually outgrown his youthful ways and began following different passions. Living among peers in the mall was no longer one of his joys.

Returning to the present moment, Richard was jolted back into this strange double existence. Like a multiprocessor computer, he was at the same time Richard, with his own memory banks intact, but on the other hand, he also owned the consciousness and memory of the young girl whose mind he inhabited. Her mind appeared like a subroutine of his own mind, or better yet, his mind and her mind were both a subroutine of a higher mind that controlled them both. He felt her excitement about being here and listening to the passionate speech of their leader. He not only knew the girl's feelings, but he actually owned them. She was excited and so was he. He was expecting to go to Siberia and to leave everything behind, to be united with all those like-minded people. Promise Seekers, as they called themselves, were evidently coming together from around the world to create a new force. It was a force directed against the scientism of the current world government, revolutionary and extremely explosive, but peaceful at the same time. It was a force that would bring about a new order for the universe.

Richard suddenly felt himself rapidly withdrawing from his host body. Within a fraction of a second, he was back in his own body looking into the face of his friend in utter amazement.

Thirteen

"So? What do you think?" Joe looked expectantly at his friend as Richard took off the headgear and untangled himself from the cords.

"How was it?"

"Quite a program you put together, I must admit. Felt damn real." Richard was impressed, but at the same time he wasn't sure what exactly he had experienced.

Joe laughed. "It *is* real. Didn't you get that? This isn't a program, it's reality."

"What do you mean?" Richard was even more puzzled. "You mean to tell me that… this is the real thing? —No, totally impossible. You almost had me fooled."

"No, really. I didn't fool you. This is real. It's a true mind-link— at last."

"It's not possible." Richard was adamant.

"What do you mean? How can you be so sure?" Joe almost begged his friend to believe him.

"So, wow, you're telling me I really was in her mind? That's unbelievable, insane, intense, and voyeuristic." Richard was scrambling for words. Suddenly he stopped again and shook his head.

"Impossible." He said.

"Now what?"

"We must be missing something."

"What? What bothers you? Tell me?" Joe asked nervously.

"It couldn't have been her."

"Why not?"

"She is in the SuperMaxRobomate. No one escapes from that."

"Hm. You're right. That would be difficult." Joe admitted.

"And where is she now?"

"That's the point. She's not in the SuperMax. Definitely not."

"There is a first for everything. She must have escaped?"

"Have you ever heard of anyone who escaped from the SuperMaxRobomate? I haven't. They use every technology under the sun to keep people secure. I should know; I applied for a job with them once. They pay real well."

"Now you're putting a real damper on my success. Here I thought I had invented the first telepathic mind-link machine, and I can't even convince my best friend."

"Don't get me wrong, Joe." Richard had a soft heart. He really did not want to disappoint his friend. "Maybe she did escape. As you say, there is a first for everything. In fact, she must have gotten away. How else would she have ended up in this weird place? Let me get this straight: You say you can link up to any mind you want and read that person's thoughts, his feelings, have all the experiences of the other person."

"Not only that," Regaining confidence Joe continued his friend's thoughts, "you can be there with the other person. No more walls between me, you, anybody. This is the end of isolation, Richard. All you need is a few minutes of recording of a person and you can socialize whenever you want."

"That's fantastic, Joe. No, really, it's a revolution. I mean it." But Richard realized the true impact of what he had just said. What sounded at first like a great idea suddenly struck him as ominous. Just as quickly as he agreed to celebrate his friend's invention, he now recognized its limits.

"So wait a minute. You mean privacy is forever a thing of the past?"

"Privacy, privacy, an illusion of the twentieth century," his friend said with exuberance. "We are heading with lightning speed into a new era, the era of collective advancement, and this machine represents a giant step. It will be the sensation of the year, the number one invention of the twenty-first century." Joe was excited and had no doubt about his invention.

Richard in turn still appeared troubled.

Joe finally nudged his friend and said, "Come on, Rich, cele-brate with me. What's the matter with you? Where is your sense of adventure? What happened to your enterprising spirit?"

"What do you mean?"

"Come on. I really don't get you." Joe suddenly had a thought. "No way. You're not jealous, are you? Of course, we share the profit and the fame."

"No, that's not it at all." Richard was a little offended by his friend's lack of trust. "It's more that I'm concerned what the science people will say." Richard added cautiously.

"Are you kidding? I think they'll jump at it. No seriously. I think they'll love it. How much do you think they'll pay for being able to peek into anybody's mind? I have already drawn up plans to offer my invention to them. So tell me, what did you see? Did she get undressed? Was it just weird normal? Or was it weird weird? What was she doing?"

"There was this strange assembly of characters, weirdoes all right; they all seemed to be from the last century, you know what I mean. Individualists, dreamers or poets, or something weird. I think they called them hippies, free spirits, dead heads, or something like that. It's of course all perfectly absurd and absolutely illegal."

"And those are the people she associates with? No wonder they took her into custody."

"The only question now is how did she get out?"

"Perhaps they let her go on purpose. So she would lead them to her bosses, the ringleaders of the conspiracy. Perhaps she is bait." Joe tried hard to contribute to Richard's line of thought.

"No, not too likely," Richard said. "But you know what—maybe we can use your machine to search through her memory. She must know how it all happened."

Joe shook his head. "Can't do it. At least not yet. So far I've only developed an algorithm to inhabit the present. If you could get her to think about the past, and thus bring the past to the present, then there would be a possibility. But honestly, just a little more fine-tuning, and we can turn this into hard cash."

Richard suddenly had an idea. "I know. The girl's mother must be worried to death. I bet she would pay a good price to know the whereabouts of her daughter."

"Isn't that like blackmailing her?"

"Are you kidding me? All we're doing is providing a service. We didn't create the situation, did we?"

"Do you know how to contact her mother?"

"I would be a lousy investigator if I didn't know that. Collecting data on a subject's relatives is rule number one. Of course I know her mother."

Fourteen

Arriving at the airfield in Ust-Kut in Siberia, Jesse was surprised how busy the little provincial terminal was. Ust-Kut is a small town at the confluence of two rivers just east of the Baikal Sea's northern shore. Ever since the nuclear disaster that destroyed most of the vegetation around the great sea, once known as the Pearl of Siberia, few visitors ever came up to this region any more. Jesse had expected a deserted airfield in the endless Russian taiga, but what he encountered was a jam-packed terminal filled with thousands of odd-looking people. It reminded him vaguely of one of the music concerts he had attended in his youth. Jesse smiled when he thought of those times.

The people Jesse now observed wore long, baggy, and color-ful clothing. Most of the folks were young, each of them in their appearance making a statement of individuality. By the way they were dressed, one could hardly distinguish their sexes.

Before Jesse could get a better look at the crowd, he and Carlisle were whisked away by two officials who had been expecting them. They boarded another helicopter that chauffeured them for the last two hundred miles across ice fields to the central administration building of the Novotny Accelerator at the eastern shores of the lake just fifty miles west of Nachangarsk, a little fishing town that now lay all but deserted.

Jesse did not know that the helicopter had orders to avoid the normal flight route over the southern plain, but took the northern corridor instead. He was not supposed to witness the millions of people that had assembled all around the southern shores of Lake Baikal.

As far as the eye could see there were people who had come from all corners of the world. And they all gathered for one pur-pose: they all believed that they had received a message, to assemble somewhere here in Siberia for a great revelation. It was by far the largest assembly of Promise Seekers ever, and certainly the largest of its kind since the world government had outlawed such organizations.

The Promise Seekers were a loose organization of individuals who embraced spirituality, but rejected rigidity and dogmatism. They had sprung up in the early part of the twenty-first century as a response to the so-called Promise Keeper movement, an organization of evangelical conservatives whose radical branch made attempts to replace secular world governance with a conservative Christian rule. Seeking communion with nature, Promise Seekers embraced poetry, creativity, and a mystical way of life. Their favorite emblem was the "Sacred Wheel," which they saw as a symbol for ultimate unity in diversity. The spokes, many of them believed, represented the different spiritual expressions, while the hub had to remain undefined.

As the helicopter trailed along the blue coastline, Jesse admired the beauty of the lake that was in sharp contrast with the utter desolation still visible along the shores. After the nuclear meltdown that had destroyed everything around the lake for thousands of miles, new vegetation had finally taken hold again. Right beneath the aircraft, Jesse could make out a dark blue line running perfectly straight through the water along the ragged coast. It was the pipeline of the Novotny Accelerator project. It ran about forty feet underneath the surface of the lake for its full length of twenty-eight kilometers.

Jesse remembered his first stay here at Lake Baikal: a pleasant memory. In his youth he had been a Boy Scout and later a decorated Eagle Scout. At the age of sixteen, in 1995, he took part in a Siberian Scouting Symposium, a meeting of American and Siberian Boy Scouts right here on Lake Baikal. Back then people had great hopes for the environmental future of this beautiful lake, one of the world's largest freshwater reservoirs and easily the world's deepest lake. After the demise of Communism in 1989, there was a short period in which industrial giants tried to exploit the lake for its natural resources. The newly elected Russian government declared the lake and its surroundings a national park and a protected area. It was during those days that Jesse visited here. He had the fondest memories of the natural beauty of the Russian taiga, the sprawling forests, and the rugged hills of the Barguzin Mountains. Hiking among the ancient trees, swimming in the crystalline blue waters, and bathing in the ice-cold waterfalls had been an unforgettable adventure of his youth.

Once the main camp had ended, Jesse was invited to spend some time with a Russian friend in his native village. Memories of first love were vivid before his mind's eye. He recalled now how, deep in the Russian wilderness, he had his first lessons of shamanism, magic, and communication with the animal world.

These pleasant memories were clouded many years later, after Jesse had settled into his job as a researcher and scientist, by the news that Lake Baikal was again opened up for industrial exploitation. A nuclear facility was build right at its shores. Little was known about the safety of the installation. In 2016, the news traveled around the world of a terrible meltdown at the Baikal facility. Soon it became obvious that the meltdown was the result of terrorist activities spurred on by religious fanaticism. When a well-known religio-fascist group took credit for the attack, the world was thrown into World War III. This man-made disaster became the trigger point for ancient emotions to fully explode into all-out war. Years passed and the world settled into an uneasy peace, trying to make the best on top of the ruins of civilizations.

The small group traveling with Jesse had arrived at the main science hangar of the Novotny Accelerator. He was greeted by a delegation of distinguished scientists. Rested and refreshed, Jesse found himself in the observatory alongside some of the world's best-known experts. Doctor Ping Wong, a Chinese particle specialist who had received the Nobel Prize for the discovery of Gravitational Unification, welcomed Jesse and offered him a seat in front of a large observation screen.

"I am glad you could join us, Professor Barker," she said with an engaging smile. Jesse had met Dr. Wong briefly at a conference in Beijing many years ago. In spite of the time that had passed, he recognized her immediately by her short, cropped hair, her black-pearl eyes, and her pale but perfect skin.

"Ah, well, the pleasure is all mine. Carlisle should have told me that I'd meet you here. He could have spared himself some arm-twisting," Jesse said.

"Then you remember me?"

"How could I forget?"

"Twenty years change a person's appearance."

"Time must have passed you by. How did your new assignment work out?"

"You remember this as well?"

"How could I forget? You were contemplating leaving research and joining the service. Am I correct?"

"Your memory is astounding. After I left I worked as a field agent for almost ten years."

"But now you are back in research. In fact, you are one of the leading experts."

"Too much flattery, Professor. That title belongs to you." In spite of the friendly exchange, Jesse could not get free of the feeling that they were sizing each other up like two peacocks interested in the same mate.

"Why don't you join us so we can begin," Dr. Wong began. "I trust you had a chance to freshen yourself up after the long journey?" Jesse found a seat in the underground observation hall and made himself comfortable. After giving some quick orders, Dr. Wong turned again to Jesse and affirmed, "We are ready to begin the experiment momentarily."

"Yes, of course," Jesse said. There were about thirty scientists gathered in the room, all dressed in professional uniforms, mostly men.

"How did it go the first time? Will I be able to see the data?" Jesse asked somewhat impatiently.

Dr. Wong smiled. "We would rather not give you any detailed reports. You should see for yourself, Professor. I am sure Carlisle supplied you with the necessary information, even though, considering your knowledge and background, no such briefing is needed, I am certain."

"This truly flatters me. But as you and the ministry know, I no longer deal in these matters. I have left—"

"We know. We know." Dr. Wong smiled again, conciliatory. "Of course we are fully aware, but as the project director I specifically requested your presence. I admired your earlier work, and in my humble opinion, Professor, it is a pity that you have withdrawn. However, I must ask you now to refrain from any further questioning until the experiment is completed. I am absolutely convinced that you will fully understand our position once we have run the experiment."

"But can I at least see the input data? What are we working with? What is being propelled?"

"Believe me, Professor, you won't need any briefing. It is the subjective results we are interested in." Dr. Wong put a strange emphasis on the word 'subjective.' "I am certain you understand the meaning of my words. Now let's concentrate on the experiment. I have already spoken too much."

Subjective results? Jesse wondered. *This is science, isn't it?* He was puzzled and mystified, to say the least.

Before Jesse could ask another question or say anything else, the countdown for the experiment began. Everyone in the observatory seemed unusually silent. Most of the scientists stared at the overhead screen, but some had their eyes closed, as if in meditation. Others cast inquisitive glances over to where Jesse was sitting. As the accelerator began its work, the stillness grew even more ominous.

The numbers on the screen indicated the speed of the particles and next to it the corresponding energy numbers: 600, 700, 800, 900, 995, 996, 997, 998, 999…1000 GeV. A flash of light wiped over the screen and darkened it momentarily.

Jesse strained his eyes to see. Just then a violent jolt went through his body that darkened his mind. Suddenly he had an intense feeling that someone from high up was watching him. His head turned around to look for the shadow of his daughter in the window. Before he realized the absurdity of this move, his mind spiraled out of his body. For a short moment, he observed the scene in the observatory from high above—but only for the briefest moment. Then he was taken away even higher. He saw the Baikal disappear beneath him. Now he was floating freely in empty space, above Earth, which he knew must be visible somewhere in the distance. As he focused closer on the blue planet, he saw an intense light emanating from its northern hemisphere, somewhere around the area where he knew Lake Baikal was located. The light beam extended all the way up to where he was.

As the light from the giant beam began to touch his body and totally immerse him in brilliant energy, he felt an energy going through him. A powerful attraction moved him down the light beam and plunged him back to Earth. But being immersed in light, he did not feel the force of the plunge: he felt as if he had become light itself. Jesse recognized the waters of Lake Baikal and quickly found himself back in the room with all the scientists.

Next Jesse had the distinct awareness that his mind had merged with the minds of all the colleagues in the room. He was looking at himself through their eyes. There he was, sitting, still staring at the monitor, but at the same time he was everywhere, he was many minds, not just one single mind looking out from one body at all the others, he was many minds looking in on his own singularity. Before he could grasp the situation, he found himself back in his own body looking around in the room in utter disbelief.

Fifteen

"Quickly, get this Barker woman. I have contact with her daughter," Joe motioned to his friend. Richard quickly left the garden area and ran over to the house where Melissa's mother was waiting.

Mary had hesitated at first to accept Joe and Richard's proposal. When the two young men came to her house and promised her they could get her in touch with her missing daughter, she was filled with suspicion. But then, seeing that this might be her only option, she quickly agreed to the deal. Assuming that the government would do little to locate Melissa, Mary held onto any straw she could find. Even though in the back of her mind several cautionary signals had told her to be on guard, she figured that she could not lose more than she already had by giving this a try. Mary now questioned her own involvement with the Sisters of the Thousand Lights, not because they were illegal—they were not. But in hindsight she felt she had set a bad example for her daughter. Looking back she blamed herself for ignoring signs that could have indicated that Melissa had been involved with illegal underground activities. She had left home quite frequently without telling her where she spent her time. On several occasions she had brought items home such as incense, a mask of an animal, or a feathered headpiece, which could have innocent explanations, but taken together could likely be signs of illegal cult involvement. Mary, of course, did not want to stifle her daughter's interest in Native American culture, but she knew that Native American spiritual activities were among those forbidden by the Scientific Purity Laws. In spite of her suspicion Mary never had enough evidence nor did she have the courage to confront Melissa. But she often felt that something more powerful than her was pulling her daughter away, alluring her into a trap.

"Quickly, Mrs. Barker, come along. We established contact again. You can see your daughter now," Richard bellowed when he entered the room where Mary was waiting.

Mary Barker looked doubtful in spite of the hope she nourished inside.

"See her?" Mary said. "Do you mean you're holding my daughter captive? Are you blackmailing me?"

"No, not at all. I didn't mean to imply that you'll actually see her…at least not directly."

"Then what did you mean, young man? I'm not in the mood to play games." Mary's face was filled with a determination and toughness rarely seen in her.

"I'm sorry for any misunderstanding, ma'am. I didn't mean to say see her, not physically meet her," Richard said. "How shall I explain? This is actually even better than seeing her." Richard grinned. For a moment, Mary felt as if she was the center of some kind of hoax.

"All I'm concerned about is whether she is safe. Is she okay? Where is she? Who's holding her hostage? What are their demands?" Mary peppered Richard with questions. She had reconsidered her position and was no longer interested in what they had to say. Richard could feel the prospect for a sale slipping away.

Maybe I should have trusted the authorities to bring back my daughter, Mary thought as she relented to their request and rushed out the veranda door, entering the elaborate garden area that contained the hot tub with Joe's virtual reality mind-link machine. With Joe's assistance, Mary put on the helmet.

Not sure what to expect, Mary looked bewildered at the scene before her eyes. She found herself momentarily in a rather strange environment. Women with black hoods covering their hair were rushing about in front of her. There was a long dining room table filled with bread, soup, and water jugs. The women spoke in a strange language that Mary did not understand. Suddenly one of them approached Mary directly, said something to her and then stroked her face. Mary felt the sensation of the strange hand on her cheek, but when she reached there with her own hand she could only feel the metal bars of the headgear. It was as if she was two people at the same time, or one person split in two. The whole thing seemed utterly confusing and frightening. Mary panicked and ripped the strange contraption from her head.

"Where is Melissa? Where's my girl?" Mary was frantic. *What kind of weird trick are these people playing on me?* "All I see is a bunch of women in a dining room." She looked at the two men in frustration.

"Mrs. Barker. Keep it on, please. We are offering you a once-in-a-lifetime chance here. You can be inside your daughter's mind."

"I have no desire to be inside my daughter's mind, do you understand? And I don't even know what that means."

"You see what she sees. You are where she is."

"What good will that do?" Mary shrieked.

"Wait a minute. Hear us out, please," Joe chimed in, using all his salesmanship.

"This contact can lead us to valuable clues about where we can find her, don't you see?" offered Richard. He tried to speak in a scientific tone, detached and objectively. At the same time, he wanted to communicate a sense of urgency. He realized that the current case would be a brilliant test for the power of their machine. But Mary had the distinct feeling that she had fallen prey to the cunning of a clever salesman. *But what in the world are they trying to sell?* she wondered, convinced that the whole thing was nothing but a new kind of sophisticated video game.

"This is insane," Mary screamed. "I want to go now. I don't have time and energy to waste with some second-rate video game. My daughter is missing, and you people are playing games. Please show me the way out."

"Please, Mrs. Barker. What do you have to lose? Give it one more try." Joe practically forced the helmet back on her head. Suddenly he saw Mary's face turn pale white. "Melissa, that's my daughter—in the mirror. Melissa."

Melissa was looking at herself in a bathroom mirror, and Mary was seeing her through her daughter's own eyes.

Sixteen

"Professor Barker! We request answers."

Jesse slowly became aware of Dr. Wong staring at him. *Answers? What answers are these people looking for?* Jesse did not dare to voice his thoughts aloud. He knew he had to be extremely careful.

"The ministry requests a full report of your experience, your subjective experience. Secondly, we request a scientific evaluation of your experience. Nothing more and nothing less." In stark contrast to her earlier demeanor, Dr. Wong's attitude now was intense and uncompromising. After all, this was to be expected in an interrogation conducted by the High Ministry of Science.

"I should inform you, Mr. Barker, that President Viswamitra himself has expressed interest in the results of this investigation. So you understand, this is an operation that involves the highest levels of government. I hope you realize the urgency of this matter."

Jesse was well aware of the severity of the situation. Hallucinations such as the one he just encountered were strictly prohibited. The Sub-Ministry of Rational Enlightenment had issued a special communiqué on this. Visions and hallucinations, especially those that tended to occur as a result of the practice of yoga and certain forms of meditation, had been declared absolutely unscientific. Generously labeled a Category V mental disorder, such conditions were treated with medications, electroshock, and isolation. Severe cases had often resulted in the accidental death of the patient or in suicide. Jesse understood the implications. He had to bargain for time.

"Can you show me to my room, so I can...?"

"We completely understand you must be tired after the flight and the stress of the experience. If you wish we can supply you with a dose of regenerative DBC. Nevertheless, we need some answers, now."

Perhaps they somehow know what I'm thinking. I'll try not to think about it at all.

Jesse put on a disinterested demeanor. As if attempting to comply, he said, "Thanks, but I'm a bit old-fashioned. After a few hours of rest, I promise I'll be in a much better condition to give you a complete report. I'll be one hundred percent at your service."

Dr. Wong whispered for a short while with a tall, blond scientist who was waiting nearby. Then she turned back to Jesse.

"Well, all right then. Mr. Barnward will show you to your room. You will arise punctually at seventeen hundred hours. We must go to work. Ah, by the way, there is a voice recorder in your room, in case you would like to record your impressions, lest you forget what happened here this evening. Have a pleasant rest."

On the way to the sleeping quarters, the tall Scandinavian-looking man at first walked silently next to Jesse for a good fifteen minutes. They proceeded through long and well-lit underground corridors. On several occasions, Barnward opened security gates by staring briefly into an eye recognition machine. Then they walked again in silence.

Typical Scandinavian mentality, Jesse speculated. When they finally had reached their destination, a comfortable underground suite with a gurgling water fountain as its center piece, Barnward pulled Jesse into the bathroom. He suddenly held Jesse's arm and whispered, "You must be on guard, Professor. Something mystical happened when they reached that energy. It does not fit in their worldview. They need you to explain it to them and then, once they understand what actually happened, they would do anything to deny it. That's how things work around here. Don't you think, Professor? This here is your room. Have a good rest, Professor, and—be careful."

Jesse did not respond. This could be some sort of trap to find out his real thoughts. He just mumbled a short "thank you" and locked the door behind him.

Even as he readied himself for bed, Jesse avoided reflecting on his experience. He could never be sure.

Seventeen

Completely exhausted, Jesse fell immediately into a deep sleep. In order to help him not to think about the events of the evening, he concentrated on the phrase "catching forty winks." Counting and catching "forty winks" guided him gently and mercifully into the land of forgetting. But Jesse's stressed mind could not let go. He could not forget. Instead Jesse slipped into a dream as if it were some kind of a super-reality.

Jesse found himself walking through a snow-covered forest. He looked down and saw that he was wearing snowshoes. The brilliantly glistening snow was newly fallen. He would have surely sunk in down to his waist had he not been wearing these Siberian shoes, intricately woven from brown wicker wood. He noticed that he was wearing a gun over his shoulder, one of those old rifles hunters used many decades ago. In front of him, a path stretched up a gently inclining slope through a pine forest. The forest itself stretched as far as he could see. Looking back now, he noticed that someone was following him at a distance. He slowed down to see who it might be, but the person slowed down as well. From the distance it appeared that it was a woman dressed in heavy animal fur.

The woman was motioning to keep going. He heard her voice shouting: "Keep on your course, you will see. You will see. You must keep going."

Compelled by the sound of the woman's voice, Jesse followed her advice and kept going. Crossing Jesse's path, a young deer galloped in the clearing. It was a beautiful animal, more beautiful than he thought a deer could ever be. The fawn stopped and stared at him, motionless. Jesse returned the stare. He slowly took the gun from his shoulder and aimed at the animal. He suddenly sensed the deer's curiosity and fear. Overcoming his hesitation, he aimed again and pulled the trigger. A loud bang pierced the air and the deer fell to the ground. The bullet had gone right through his head and had torn out half his brain.

Jesse walked over to where he had seen the animal go down. In the snow, he saw a big pool of scarlet blood, but the body lying there in the snow was not that of a deer, it was the body of a woman. Shaking and trembling, he turned her lifeless head to see the face. He stared into the blood-soaked face of his wife, Mary.

Jesse awoke suddenly and shot upright in his bed. The darkened room around him did nothing to dispel his horror. Suddenly he heard the metallic voice of a monitor. "Professor, are you ready now to give your report? We are anxiously waiting for details."

Eighteen

Before Jesse could get his thoughts organized, the door opened and within minutes the Scandinavian escorted him to a large conference room where he was offered a place around a big oak table. A group of about a dozen scientists looked at him with expectation. Jesse promised himself to do his best to avoid the issues. When asked again, he gave a report of his scientific opinion of the experiment. He passed out ample praise for the accomplishments and assured them how utterly impressed he was that one had indeed reached this memorable energy and that great technological advances would surely come from this. The progress of international cooperation and of science was unsurpassed.

On first impression, he said, none of the dire predictions, including his own, had come to pass. As to the specifics, Jesse said, he would have to wait for detailed testing results, photographic images of the smoke chambers, mathematical calculations, et cetera, et cetera. But surely, a detailed computer analysis would clear up all questions. One could only be happy that nothing completely unexpected had happened as a result of this experiment.

Dr. Wong, who had been listening emotionless, suddenly interrupted Jesse. "Professor Barker, let's spare ourselves any further commonalities," she said with piercing fire in her eyes. "We have not invited you here to give us a scientific lecture and laud our accomplishments. We don't need a smokescreen. My colleagues and I are perfectly capable, as you might imagine. We have asked you to be here and attend these sessions for your insights."

"Insights?" Jesse asked with feigned surprise. Wasn't this a scientific conference? Every flag in his mind went up telling him to be vigilant. He had heard of colleagues disappearing for having the wrong thoughts.

"Yes, your subjective observations. This and this alone is what we are interested in. We quite simply want you to tell us what you experienced."

"Subjective experiences are for psychologists and such," Jesse replied firmly. "I believe that psychology has been delegated to the past. I believe that we deal with objective science and with science alone. Am I not correct in assuming this?" Jesse was agitated. He had to be extremely cautious. Then again, he remembered what Barnward had told him about the present predicament.

"Of course, of course, you are correct. Since the establishment of the Scientific Purity Laws, the world has become a great deal more objective. Thanks to the foresight of President Viswamitra and the wise acts of the Science Council, we no longer have to rely on murky science to deal with the human mind. As I said, you are right, of course; psychology, the humanistic kind, is a thing of the past."

She even gave Jesse a thin smile.

"Then why, why should you be concerned with my subjective experience?"

"Let me say it plainly, Professor Barker. What happened here last night, and what happened two times earlier when we reached GeV1000 is phenomenal. Do you understand? Phenomenal. I am not saying this lightly, and I am not using this old philosophical terminology without reason."

"Phenomenology has been outlawed along with psychology," Jesse quipped back. "We all know this and are aware of this. What used to be called phenomenology is mere speculation. I personally resent and reject the implications." Jesse felt he had to sharply distance himself from such pre-scientific subjects.

Dr. Wong's face appeared almost motherly. "Jesse, you are among friends here. We in the scientific community have to work together. We have known about your interest in, how shall I say, paranormal phenomena for some time now. Your dabbling in interspecies communication is no secret to us."

"I must reject…" Jesse was close to erupting, but tried to conceal his true contempt for this kind of interrogation.

As if reading his mind, Dr. Wong countered, "We are not bringing this up to embarrass you, quite completely to the contrary. We need your help. We know you have been meditating."

"Meditating?" Jesse interjected.

"And you have been attempting to communicate with a feline."

"Don't be ridiculous."

Without reacting at all to Jesse's protest, Dr. Wong continued, "we also know that you are a first-class scientist. We don't need to mention the loss to the scientific community when you left us and went into teaching—philosophy of all things. But we have been following your development, and now we are in need of your specific expertise. We need explanations. Not explanations of a scientific nature; we are quite capable of supplying these for ourselves. We have all the numbers. What we need is your analytical brain giving us a breakdown of your personal experiences during this experiment. Let me rephrase this. We request an analysis of our private histories, a first-person account, so to say. Do I make myself clear?"

"Are you telling me that everyone in the room…" Jesse quickly stopped himself from finishing the sentence. This was absurd. But Dr. Wong continued staring at him. "Yes, everyone who attended," she added quickly. "Your suggestion is absolutely correct."

Flabbergasted, Jesse said, "And why, why would this be of any importance?" Jesse was now genuinely curious himself. He was well aware of the strangeness of his experience during the experiment. Was she saying that all of these esteemed scientists had similar out-of-body experiences? Could that be possible? As a scientist, Jesse understood the gravity of this. There would simply be no logical, scientific way to explain it. In fact, it would contradict much of what the scientific world council stood for and enforced. Such an event, on a mass scale would be an embarrassment, to say the least. Before he could finish this line of thought, he heard again the sharp voice of the woman:

"Let us be in charge of importance. For starters, why don't you simply give us a narration of your subjective input?"

"Subjective impressions of an objective event are fictions of one's misguided imagination and therefore to be considered illusionary. I have nothing to report." Jesse repeated this like a mantra. He decided to remain firm even though he no longer was sure in which direction this investigation was proceeding and what the real nature of this event was. Jesse did not want to believe for a second that they actually were in need of his expertise.

"Is that all you have to contribute?" Dr. Wong was definitely not pleased.

"I believe this is all I have to contribute, yes."

"You are excused then until further discussion is necessary. Perhaps you will change your mind. Why don't you take a look at these protocols? Perhaps this will help you understand. Escort him to his suite."

Nineteen

At nightfall, Joe, Richard, and Mary had reached the shores of the Black Sea in what used to be the country of Ukraine. They had been traveling for nearly three weeks now. In the ruins of ancient Odessa, a raggedy group of locals welcomed them enthusiastically. These people had survived World War III in the underground caverns of the old city. These caverns were used by the resistance during World War II against the occupying fascists. Now they were of use again to escape the ever-present radiation that made permanent surface living dangerous, if not impossible. Most people, therefore, chose underground living to minimize exposure. Others had given up caring and arranged a new way of life in the midst of the rubble. Such people, known as Exposurists, often suffered from a genetic deformity or mental illness and had a general life expectancy of less than thirty years. The war had taken a terrible toll on the bodies and souls of people.

After Mary had found no satisfaction from the government, she had decided to pay the price and follow the young inventors. Following the trail of her daughter had become a single-minded pursuit for her. Whenever possible, she used Mind-link to connect with Melissa.

Richard and Joe were happy to see that electric power was available in the cave they had been assigned. They hooked up Mind-link for Mary to give her some time alone with her daughter. This link helped nourish the hope of eventually catching up with Melissa and being reunited.

When Mary finally was connected, she was mortified to find herself inside her daughter's body, resting—on a stretcher. As she looked around, she first noticed a burning sensation in her eyes. The place vaguely looked like an old-fashioned sanctuary in an ancient chapel. She was surrounded by dimly lit icons. Hundreds of candles spread a pallid light over the scene. Melissa's rest was uneasy. Her eyes opened momentarily, but then kept falling shut. She was breathing heavily and her body was burning up from an internal fire. Mary was aware of this as if it was happening to her own body, but simultaneously she knew that it was her daughter's fate. Her motherly instincts overwhelmed her instantly. She remembered her little girl's fragile condition. Images of Melissa floating in midair swelled vividly in her mind. She still trembled recalling the frail body hanging limply in her arms. Now she was overwhelmed by the fear that her daughter was gravely ill.

A deep sense of helplessness suddenly overcame her, and this feeling was even more aggravated by the one-directional nature of this Mind-link device. She ripped off the head gear in frustration and looked around desperately for help. Richard and Joe were nowhere in sight. For them, it was mostly about proving the effectiveness of their invention. Pursuing the search for Melissa had the importance of a global video game for them. The poorly lit cavern was empty.

I only wish I could talk to you, my darling. What is happening to you? How can I help you? Mary quickly slipped on the headgear again only to find herself surrounded by darkness. Through her daughter's feverish eyes, she stared at the barely visible shape of a black Madonna. Melissa's mind began to churn. The candle-lit icon in the old church danced in magical circles. The images in front of her began to whirl as she entered into deeper and deeper dimensions of oblivion.

Melissa's vision suddenly disappeared from Mary's mind. Dazed and amazed, Mary woke up. She had the painful recognition that her daughter must be terribly ill or, worse yet, that she was going insane.

When Joe and Richard returned they found Mary horribly distraught. The two were loaded down with food and travelling supplies they had bought in the black market.

"What's wrong?" Richard asked innocently.

"My child's ill, and I can't do anything to help her," Mary said faintly, holding back tears. "Your machine, it just went black." Mary looked around the primitive cave.

"Just give us a minute. We can try to reconnect."

Joe and Richard tried multiple times to connect again with Melissa, but even after hours of trying they had to concede to Mary that they had lost the signal. They helped Mary to prepare a place on the floor. In the corner they found a stack of mattresses filled with straw.

Early the next morning, the small group broke camp and left the burned-out city. The big stairs in the center of town that once were crowded with lovers, fortune-telling gypsies, and with average people enjoying the fresh air or a rare ray of sunlight on a late autumn afternoon now were deserted. Out on the pier, once the home of a luxurious high-rise hotel, only a pile of stones and rubble reminded of pre-war opulence that had returned to this city in the wake of a capitalist building spree that had followed almost a century of socialist neglect.

Just as the group was leaving the city, they heard the thumping noise of a helicopter approaching.

"Looks like a GY chopper," Richard shouted. "Let's take cover." They started running toward an empty building, but it was too late. The small aircraft hovered for a few seconds right above them. The blue and green stripes were clearly visible.

A commanding voice blared, "Don't move. You are under arrest." In the next moment an impenetrable wall of sound pierced their brains, closed in around them, and froze every muscle in their bodies, making any movement impossible. Minutes later the chopper landed and armed guards surrounded them. Without explanation, they were taken into custody.

Twenty

Deep inside the underground compound of the Novotny Accelerator, Jesse had fallen into a dreamless sleep, but after only a short while he was woken up once again. The Scandinavian politely asked Jesse to follow him. He announced that members of the council had reconvened and wished to see him.

When Jesse entered the room, six council members in business suits were waiting for him. None of them looked familiar and none appeared to be a scientist. Right behind them, at the far end of the hall, Jesse noticed a protective enclosure that looked like a cage. Behind the metal bars he saw two young men who, in their slightly worn suits, looked vaguely like travelling salesmen. Next to them was a woman. She had her head bent so Jesse could not see her face. Unexpectedly she looked up, and immediately Jesse recognized the woman.

"Mary!" he screamed with full lungs. "Mary! How did you get here?"

The woman inside the cage was his dear wife. Jesse immediately wanted to run up to her but was forcefully stopped by two guards. *How did you get involved in this mess?* he wanted to ask her. Jesse saw a shock wave crossing Mary's face when she heard his voice and recognized her husband. She ran up to the bars and pressed her body against the metal. She grasped the bars with both hands, but a guard pulled her back and forced her down on a chair.

The Scandinavian who had caught up with Jesse mumbled: "Sorry. No contact. Protocol."

"Professor Barker! Please!" One of the council members, a slightly fat and bearded man with a French accent, motioned Jesse to take a seat. "Do we have your attention?" the Frenchman said with an almost cynical expression on his face.

"May I address the tribunal?" Jesse asked in the sternest tone he could muster. He noticed that none of the council people were present who had interrogated him before. *This is not a good sign.*

"Though highly unusual, but yes, you may." The Frenchman consulted with his neighbor and added quickly, "Let me assure you, this is merely an exploratory meeting. You are not under investigation—yet. You may voice your concerns, of course, which we believe are more than justified."

This apologetic tone is outrageous. Jesse noticed a smirk on the councilman's round face.

"Why am I treated like a prisoner? What do you people want from me? I need explanations, especially now that you quite obviously have dragged my wife into this. What is my dear wife doing here? Why can't I talk with her? How did she get here?"

Jesse asked these questions in quick succession, but made sure to leave a short pause, to see if anyone would offer an explanation.

Finally the Frenchmen said, "Professor Barker, all your questions will be answered at the appropriate time. Let me fill you in with some details."

"That would be much appreciated," Jesse snapped back.

"Your wife was detained for obstructing an ongoing investigation into the disappearance of your daughter. When she placed herself on a strange journey to the Altai Mountains somewhere in Siberia, we saw no choice but to take her in. Can you tell us what she was planning to do in Siberia?"

What are they talking about? Jesse let out a thin laugh, but it did not sound convincing. "Why don't you ask her? Ask her, I am sure you did already. I have no idea. Why she—I? What did you say? Where in the world are the Altai Mountains?"

His strange dream flashed through his mind. His vision of Mary's bloody face in the white snow was harshly interrupted by the sharp voice of the interrogator.

"We believe these events are all connected: your unwillingness to share information, your daughter's disappearance, and your wife's journey to the Altai!"

So she's under investigation as well, Jesse contemplated. "Ask her how she got there. How should I know? People travel." Jesse seriously had no clue. *What was my wife doing in the Altai Mountains?*

"I told them everything I know!" Mary let out a desperate howl. "They forced me to come here or they said I'd never see my daughter again. I'm worried sick. Melissa's been gone since you left that morning. I didn't even know you were gone either until they told me."

There was suddenly a lot of commotion in the tribunal. One of the officers tried to quiet Mary, without success. Two guards proceeded to drag the screaming and struggling woman out of the room.

The two young men who were detained along with Mary now joined in the turmoil. They took turns speaking and, at times, spoke simultaneously, as if their minds had some strange connection. "We had nothing to do with anything, Professor. We are computer scientists. When your daughter went missing, we tracked her down, electronically, you see. We built this device, a machine-to-human mind interface. We call it a mind-link."

"Suddenly we got a signal from a strange assembly, somewhere underneath the mall, the Mall of America."

"I recognized the place because I've been there, not recently, of course. But then they all started on a huge trek. From what I gathered, their goal was a mysterious mountain chain somewhere in Siberia. We just followed the signal. Honestly, that's all we did."

"And then we discovered this new field."

The guards tried to silence them as well and pull them out of the room.

"Professor Barker," the councilman suddenly interrupted the commotion and turned back to Jesse. "At the moment there is no need for your presence. You may retire."

"My wife? What about my wife? Can I at least spend some time with her?" Jesse said, but nobody was listening. In spite of his protest, the Scandinavian led Jesse by his arm back to his suite, much like escorting a prisoner.

Twenty One

"We've arrived!" Richard declared, stretching out on the cashmere-covered couch in the luxury suite they had been assigned. They both felt that they had played a great hand in selling their device to the powerful Science Council. Already during Jesse's interrogation the two entrepreneurs had skillfully whetted the council members' appetite. As soon as Jesse was dismissed they immediately turned to Joe and Richard to strike a deal. The eminent usefulness of their invention was never in doubt. When they finally left after an hour of intense negotiation, the deal had not been fully sealed yet, but there was no doubt in their minds that the ministry was definitely interested. A suitable offer was soon expected. From the science compound they had been chauffeured in a limousine to a guest-house nearby where they now settled in, waiting for an offer.

"Let's get to work!" Joe called to Richard as he bolted up, clapping his hands.

"Work? I thought we finished our work and reached our goal. Now let's enjoy life and reap the fruits of our labor. Getting rich is easy." Richard fingered for the remote to turn on the old-fashioned plasma screen. "I wonder what's on the tube here. Probably only reruns from the war. Maybe we should take a dip in the pool and soak in the tub."

"I said let's get to work. Set up Mind-link." Not waiting for his friend to react, Joe started opening his suitcase and retrieved the PVC.

"What's that for? Don't you think the Melissa project is over? She's most likely lost somewhere in the mountains. No, she probably got herself arrested again, and this time for good. It gets boring after a time, don't you agree?"

"While you were busy negotiating a deal for us, I was busy securing the background information we might need. Check this out." Joe waved a little microchip and dropped it into the PVC. "I've got a sample of the head honcho of the council."

"Get out! You don't say." Richard jumped up from his bed. "I don't believe you. What's up your sleeve now?"

"I sampled the Frenchman. I got enough to listen in on him. This way, any deal they propose we'll know in advance and we'll have the upper hand. Let's get to work." Joe was triumphant.

"Now you're talking," Richard agreed. "I'm sure curious to know what those guys are cooking up. You go first. It's your idea."

Joe attached the head gear and tuned the PVC. After a few moments of spinning and whirling, Richard could see just by looking at Joe's face that he had contact.

After a minute of intense listening, during which Joe closed his eyes, he exclaimed, "Incredible! This is incredible."

"What's incredible? Are they trying to steal our invention? They won't get away with piracy, because that's what it is. I know they'll have a million ways of using it. I could see it in their eyes how eager they were. We're not gonna let them just take it."

Joe motioned his friend to be quiet and after listening intently for a few moments he beamed: "They are hot. They need us big time, more than you can possibly imagine."

"Why's that?" Richard asked curiously.

"Those rumors we heard are right on. You know how they're obsessed with surveillance? Well, now they have a situation where thousands, perhaps hundreds of thousands, millions of people have simply disappeared from their radar. All those travelers we met back in Odessa, they can't see them. Their instruments, cameras, global surveillance, satellites and all that stuff, they don't work. They are completely in the dark. Get it? They need us. And they know it. Since our device operates in a completely new medium it might work for them. Wow. Who would have guessed? This is phenomenal. Here, check for yourself."

Joe took off the gear and secured it on Richard's head. As soon as Richard was tuned in he saw himself inside the mind of one of the council members. They were gathered in a room not unlike the one they just had met a short while ago. He saw the three other council members sitting across from him, looking as if they expected him to make a statement. Just then a door opened and a woman with Chinese features entered the room.

"Ah," Richard heard the councilman with the French accent say. "What an opportune moment for you to return, Dr. Wong. We have incredible news. We believed you had left for India, no?"

"We arranged a teleportation conference instead. It eliminates the empty flight time."

"What happened at the meeting?"

"Things turned out as expected. Carlisle carried the day. That's all I am at liberty to say. The details are classified."

"And what is our role here?"

"We have orders to determine the exact coordinates of the event. Our satellites have failed to penetrate the clouds over the Altai region in question, strange as this may sound. In fact, we are unable to track their movement. This leaves us in an unacceptable position. It's embarrassing."

"Dr. Wong, you will be pleasantly surprised when we tell you our accomplishment here." The Frenchman had been patiently waiting for a break in Dr. Wong's speech. "We got hold of an invention that just might solve our problems." As Richard heard the councilman praising their invention, he felt an immeasurable sense of pride growing, both in himself for having been part of the invention and in the mind of the person he inhabited for securing it for the Science Council.

"I can hardly wait," Dr. Wong said skeptically after she listened to the Frenchman's report.

"While you were gone we apprehended two most curious fellows. A little naïve, I must say, both of them, but quite useful."

"What the fu—" Richard was about to say, but realized that this might not be a good time while inhabiting the Frenchman's mind. He couldn't be sure whether his host wouldn't be able to sense his presence.

"As I said," the Frenchman continued unconcerned, "to make a long story short. These two fellows have come up with a quite remarkable invention, which might well help us out of our predicament."

"Go on, let's have the details." Dr. Wong became rather impatient.

"Their contraption, which they call Mind-link, is capable of transporting a person's mind into another person. I mean this quite literally. Seems like they invented a genuine mind-link machine."

"Aha, quite interesting," Dr. Wong said with a cynical smirk on her face. "Let's assume this Mind-link actually works, how do you propose it can help us in our present dilemma? How can it accomplish what all our scientific marvels have failed to do?" Dr. Wong asked even as she imagined a multitude of uses for such a machine.

"This machine works on a frequency unknown to current science. It penetrates where our current technology has failed. So for starters, we could send someone on the journey, someone we know could lead us in the right direction. Then, quite simply, with the help of the machine, we would be guided to the place in question. We could define the coordinates and boom."

"How can we arrange a test?" Dr. Wong wondered. She was not comfortable with the idea that the Frenchman had actually guessed their classified plan.

"We should first ask them for a demo. These people are eager to show off their gadget, but I reckon they will want some assurances from us. They are talking compensation."

"Damn right we're talking money," Richard mumbled under his breath, so only his friend could hear him.

"We will make them a generous offer, provided the gadget really works, of course. Where are they now?" Dr. Wong was ready to pay them a visit. Her interest was aroused.

Richard pulled off his head gear. "We better get ready. They'll be coming for us momentarily. They want a demo."

"We are ready for them, whenever they come."

A few minutes later there was indeed a knock at the door. Without waiting to be invited, Dr. Wong and the Frenchman entered briskly.

"Gentlemen," the Frenchman said, "may I introduce you to Dr. Wong, the director of this facility. Dr. Wong is eager to observe a demonstration of your machine. Are you ready?"

"We sure are," Richard said with a grin, "as long as you're prepared to make an offer."

"I am authorized to sign a deal right now. Don't you worry about anything. But first let's see what your apparatus can do."

Richard was content. He was convinced that their invention would more than persuade them. Pointing to Joe, he said, "This gentleman will give you a demonstration. Ladies first. Would you like to have a demo, Dr. Wong? I know you'll be pleased with our invention."

Joe looked at Richard questioningly. Richard pointed at the councilman and said, "This gentleman here, whose name still eludes me, happens to be uploaded into our system. Dr. Wong, you will not only have the exceptional honor of seeing what is on his mind, but also you will be *in* his mind. Would you like to share his thoughts, Dr. Wong?"

Dr. Wong was eager to comply and began putting on the headgear. But the Frenchman hesitated.

"Why me?" he stumbled, looking a little confused. "Don't I have to give my permission to let someone enter my mind?"

"His name is Blanchard," Dr. Wong mentioned. Then she turned to the Frenchman and said with a smirk on her face, "No, my friend. If this machine does what they tell us it does, I do not need your permission. But if it makes you feel better, can I have your permission to share your mind? I promise I won't pay attention to anything inappropriate. Then you can have the same privilege with me. I don't care. I never think of anything inappropriate, do I?"

"You may not," Blanchard said, still hesitating. "They say a man has sixty sexual thoughts an hour or something like that. That's one sexual thought per minute. For a Frenchman, you can easily make it sixty dirty thoughts per minute."

Dr. Wong laughed. "As long as you think about me, I won't mind at all. If this machine is for real, it could be a powerful tool, don't you think, Blanchard?"

Blanchard was still skeptical, but Dr. Wong was already gearing up. As soon as Richard had activated the controllers, Dr. Wong saw herself watching herself from the outside, through the Frenchman's eyes.

She really is fucking sexy, Blanchard thought, and Dr. Wong listened in on it. *I wonder how she is in bed?* With that Dr. Wong suddenly saw herself undressing, her blouse opening, and breasts bare. But to her surprise, she saw the breasts of a much younger woman.

Dr. Wong ripped off the head gear. "Wait a minute. Turn off this machine. This is preposterous."

Blanchard acted even more embarrassed and said, "What is it? You didn't just hear what I thought, did you?"

Dr. Wong caught herself quickly, smirked lightly, and turned to Joe and Richard. "Gentlemen, your invention is fabulous. I can see a million uses for it. I only hope it comes with an instruction manual."

Richard assured her that they would give them detailed instructions. Dr. Wong then turned to Blanchard and said, "By the way, Blanchard, I am outraged—no, actually, I am flattered that you look at me that way. Even for a Frenchman this is commendable, especially for a Frenchman. That dirty fantasy of yours, my friend. Some day it will get you in trouble."

Privately Dr. Wong was utterly intrigued with this new invention and wondered about its exact nature. It had not escaped her that there were distinct similarities in the experience between the way this device had enabled her to observe herself from the outside and the way she had experienced looking at herself and her colleagues during the GeV 1000 phase of the accelerator experiment. Perhaps there was a simple scientific explanation for these events after all.

Twenty Two

Hours later, alone in his suite, Jesse nervously paced the length of the room when he heard a knocking. He opened the door cautiously. Barnward, the Norwegian scientist, stood outside and indicated that he wished to enter. He was a man with broad shoulders, a full head of blond hair, and animated blue eyes that often had a tendency to gaze sadly into empty space. Barnward quickly shuffled inside and nervously shut the door behind him. He looked around rather uneasily and motioned Jesse to step into the bathroom area.

"These rooms are equipped with remote monitoring devices," he whispered, "but the bathroom is safe." Barnward lowered his voice to where it was almost no longer audible. "I was present during the initial phase of construction, so I am completely informed about the installed securities. For whatever reason, the engineers' panel did not believe it proper to spy on bathrooms. Bathrooms are magnetically protected from remote intrusions." Barnward had a sly look on his face.

What is it he wants? Jesse's mind was on highest alert.

"I have good news for you," Barnward said.

"My wife? Where is she? I must see her." Jesse had only one thought.

"That's just it. That's my proposal. I can put you in touch with your wife." Barnward was eagerly looking for Jesse's reaction.

"You have my attention," Jesse answered cautiously. This man had his interest, even though Jesse was skeptical. "Let's just say I agree. How would it work?"

"You will be able to share information with her," Barnward said, again waiting for Jesse's reaction.

"What do I have to do?" Jesse said.

"There is one hitch," the Norwegian said. "It goes only in one direction. Unfortunately, kind of a one-way conversation."

"What do you mean? A one-way conversation?"

"Hear me out. I had a chance to speak with your friends Richard and Joe."

"You mean the two individuals that for some reason attached themselves to my wife?"

"Precisely. They are willing to set up a session on their unique new machine between your wife and you, just as soon as they get a moment alone with her, which we expect to be this afternoon. But as I indicated, your wife will be able to be with you and she will know everything you think and feel. That is what their machine can do, you see. At this point that is the best they can do. It's not possible to make it a two-way presence."

The Norwegian noticed Jesse's hesitation but continued with increased weight. "Maybe someday in the future, two-way existential cohabitating will be available. Quite a clever invention, don't you think? And useful, too. It supposedly works on an unknown frequency. As it is, only one prototype of the machine exists, and your friends are in possession of it. In fact, they invented it. If I were you I would hurry and take my chances. Your friends can easily change their minds."

"They are not my friends." Jesse said crossly. He had to be careful. *This could be a trick.*

"You can trust me or not: that is entirely up to you," Barnward said frostily. He was raising his right hand, punctuating each word. "I assume there are many things you would want to share with your wife. Correct?" The Norwegian was quite insistent.

"Yes, of course. Let me think about your proposal."

"It would ease her mind. Mary—that is her name, is it not? She would be relieved to hear from you, don't you agree? In fact, she told me so personally. I once was married myself. I know how devastating separation can be. Believe me, if I tell you my story of how I lost my wife—I don't even want to think about it. I swore to myself that I would never work for those bastards again."

It looked as if this strong and distant man was near tears, notably when he mentioned his wife.

"Why can't I see Mary in person?" Jesse asked again.

"Are you kidding? They would never allow it."

"Who could stop me?"

"My dear man," the Norwegian said calmly, "I believe you do not quite understand your situation here. No, you are not a prisoner, but by all practical means you of course are. This is how the council operates. Believe me, I know from personal experience. I have worked here long enough to know. They could keep you locked up for years."

"I would most certainly protest," Jesse said, even though he knew well that any protest would ultimately be completely ineffective.

"You make me laugh. You Americans still think you are in control of the world. The world is a different place now. The Year of the Dog changed everything. Make up your mind. I am only trying to help you. There is no time to lose. She misses you. I could see it in her eyes."

"Why can't I use the device myself to communicate with my wife? Maybe—"

"I'm compromising my position for simply suggesting this whole thing. Now you either take it or leave it." Barnward was running out of patience.

"Let's assume I went along with it. How would it work?"

Barnward took a deep breath. "At four p.m., you will get a prompt on your monitor. Instead of answering it directly, you will leave the living room area and go into the bathroom, right about here." He pointed at the bathtub.

"You want me to take a bath?"

"That is up to you. Whatever relaxes you. What's important is that you get yourself into a relaxed position. You do have experience with meditating, don't you?"

"Just tell me what to do."

"So take a bath if you wish. Get settled in and then think of all the things you would like to share with your wife. It's that simple."

Barnward smiled knowingly. "You don't fight your thoughts, you let them come, acknowledge them, and then let them go. Between you and me, I used to be a yoga master myself. The difference here is that you invite thoughts rather than reject them."

"How do you know all these details about a device you knew nothing about only a couple of hours ago?"

Barnward again had a logical explanation: "Good question. I had a long conversation with Joe, the inventor. Quite a clever fellow, he is. He explained to me exactly how his gadget works. He even gave me a short demonstration. The way it actually works and why it works is a mystery. Joe seemed to have stumbled onto something here, a new field or something, and no one understands its real nature. It's like discovering electricity all over again. Except that this field is not an energy field of photons and electrons, but of something much more fundamental."

"A field that is the carrier of information or consciousness," Jesse continued the Norwegian's explanation, but he was speaking almost to himself. "When you tap into it you can connect with all the minds in the universe. The mysterious Akashic Field, dream of ancient sages." Jesse was in his element. This was the topic of his most recent work, but he had decided not to publish for fear it would fall into the wrong hands. Could it be possible that these two novices, two unaccomplished guys, simply by happenstance, had stumbled across this field and even developed a machine that tapped into the power of this mysterious energy?

"So it's a go then. We've lost precious time already."

"One last question. Why in the bathroom? Didn't you just tell me that the bathroom was magnetically protected from remote communication?"

"Good point. The bathroom is protected against conventional intrusions, such as wireless imaging, remote voice projection, radar, and the like. This device, however, seems to operate via a medium that, quite frankly, is unknown to current science. Nothing seems to stop it."

"Interesting, interesting. Now I understand."

The Scandinavian grew impatient. "We better get to work. Oh, by the way, your wife mentioned something about her dress. She wanted me to ask you if you noticed it."

"What? Her dress? Why? What was I supposed to notice about it?" Jesse was puzzled.

"Only you know your wife."

"I have no clue, honestly."

"That's all she said. Go figure out women. It's useless. Four o'clock then?"

"All right then, four o'clock it will be."

Jesse finally decided to go with it, wherever it would lead. He could not pass up the chance to provide some emotional relief for his poor wife. She must be worried to death. But equally important for him was his desire to learn more about this contraption.

Twenty Three

Dr. Wong was feverishly processing the events of the past day. The news from the High Council was foremost in her mind. Once again Carlisle and the hardliners had succeeded to push through their uncompromising agenda. Carlisle's last statement before the council still rang in her ears: "We have to make sure that the whole delicate process is executed with discretion. At this volatile point in history, the Science Council cannot afford negative publicity." She had to agree that Carlisle's argument was logical when he assured the council that "the lack of traceable data will actually work in our favor. Once they are incinerated, everything can be denied." *On the surface this sounds so convincing*, Dr. Wong argued in her own mind. But deep inside she was troubled. She asked herself again and again whether it really could be justified to sacrifice thousands for the benefit of the rest.

On the other hand, Dr. Wong was quite excited about Mind-link and its obvious potential. For a moment she smiled, remembering her own irritation when she discovered herself bare-naked in Blanchard's mind. The audacity of that Frenchman! She stepped in front of a full-length mirror and stretched her upper torso. With both hands she lifted her breasts and noticed their relative firmness with satisfaction. Her dark hair flowed freely over her slender body. With daily exercise and a balanced diet she was able to hide her age gracefully. Few people, observing her, would have guessed that she had passed midlife.

Just then her prompter activated, and she heard Carlisle's familiar voice requesting an urgent videoconference. For Carlisle, Dr. Wong was always available. It was expected. After a few static streams, Carlisle appeared in front of her, leaving Dr. Wong wondering where he really momentarily resided. The system just left her enough time to throw a flimsy gown over her nude body before her presence too would appear somewhere halfway around the world.

"What gives me the honor?" Dr. Wong asked. "I should be angry at you for leaving us so soon. I expected you to assist in the analysis of these events."

"I myself had hoped to spend some private time together with you. Forgive my emotions, my dear Ping."

Dr. Wong teasingly rebuffed her colleague's advance with a smile.

"Can we just stay professional, if you don't mind, please?"

"As always, the spoiler."

"In our position we can't afford to put private lives ahead of public service." She said.

"I know, I know. Well said." Carlisle conceded. "Now let me fill you in what happened here."

"Why? I believed the meeting was over when I signed off. Was it not?"

"The council is in upheaval, and that's putting it mildly."

"Tell me all about it. Here I thought everything was decided in near-unanimity. That's the impression I got when the meeting ended. I take it you are still at headquarters then? Your arguments were—what can I say?—convincing. To me it sounded like your point of view carried the day. Did I get that wrong? Sure, I did sense some disagreement toward the end, but—"

"Get this: the crucial exchange happened after the international monitors were turned off. This is why I felt a need to contact you right away."

"Are we on a secure line?"

"As secure as anything ever gets. At this point I don't really care."

"You sound angry." Dr. Wong said. Corlisle's emotional outburst took her by surprise.

"To tell you the truth, I am pissed." Carlisle continued.

"Why? What happened?"

"This whole project, it just has to succeed, Ping. Yes, it's radical, but it's the right thing. You do agree, don't you?"

"I said it sounds convincing."

"Sounds convincing? Come on. I don't get it. Once and for all we can get rid of a whole bunch of extremists in one swoop. Everybody always talks about attacking the root cause. Here is the chance. Religious intolerance breeds fanaticism. You know that. We must create a world without even the memory of any religious sentiment."

"Carlisle, stop it, please. Yes, yes, I agree. You are preaching to the choir. You don't have to convince me, remember."

"I am just venting my frustration."

"So tell me, what happened after the monitors were turned off?" Dr. Wong asked edgily.

"Viswamitra walked out. Can you believe it? After all the monitors were turned off, he simply announced that he wanted to voice his dissent and that he had to think more about this, and so on and so on...you can gather the rest."

"But the meeting was over. He should have voiced his dissent while the meeting was still in session and lines were open. Now it doesn't count. It's illegitimate. The meeting was over."

"Well, yes and no. It is under contention."

"What do you mean? It would be against all precedence and rules."

"Rules are just rules, obviously, even at the highest level." Carlisle sounded resigned.

"This is unheard of. Have the other members been informed? What are the implications? More importantly, what are his arguments?"

Carlisle looked as if he was carefully searching for words. "We have to hammer out a plan. I don't think all is lost. At least, I hope not."

"You had the majority, and most importantly, science is on your side. What if you proceed as if nothing had changed? The military has their marching orders. You just have to make sure that no part of the operation is recalled or changed."

"You are absolutely right. We must hurry before any of this spins out of control." Carlisle was satisfied that his friend supported him that strongly. "That sounds more like you. I have always known you as the pragmatist that you are."

"Just watch out. I sometimes have the feeling you take me for granted," Dr. Wong said.

Carlisle looked at her for a moment as if to say: *What are you talking about? Of course I do.* But he decided to ignore her remark and proceed with the task at hand: "Let's get to work. You get me the exact coordinates of the event. And from then on you can leave the rest to me."

"Since you left I have done a little research. Did you know that the area in question is known to the locals as the mountain of mystery?"

"The region around the Altai Mountains has always been trouble. Even the mighty Soviets could not convince those indigenous people that live there to give up their religious superstitions. So tell me, do you have a plan yet how to get the exact location of the meeting?"

"Yes, I do have a plan, and I think you'll like it. Yesterday, after you left, the GYs picked up a peculiar traveling trio. By sheer coincidence, our people came across their path—"

"Spare me the details," Carlisle interjected.

"You know already?"

"Of course, I do. What do you expect?"

"Barker's wife in pursuit of her daughter, who evidently had joined those Promise Keepers."

"The real question is, how did she slip away? After all, the girl was in our custody."

"This seems to verify those embarrassing rumors."

"Damn, yes, it does," Carlisle snapped back. "And I don't like it one bit. There has to be another explanation."

"Their physical bodies become invisible…to our technology."

"That's of course absolute nonsense. It will drive me insane until I figure this out."

"What about Barker's wife?" Dr. Wong asked.

"Leave that up to me. I already have a plan in motion." Carlisle said quickly.

"Will I get to question her?"

"You can question her as much as you like, but then release her, let her go."

"Let her go?" Dr. Wong was surprised.

"I said, I have made my plans. Expect my instructions for further details."

"One more thing, before you sign off."

"Who says I'm signing off any time soon. You know I enjoy your company. What's on your mind?"

"This mysterious machine, they call it mind-link. Or do you know about that as well?"

"Tell me. This mysterious machine? What is that all about?" Carlisle asked curiously.

"Fascinating invention. This machine evidently does not operate within the known spectrum of electromagnetic waves."

"How can you know this?" Carlisle asked skeptically.

"We've tested it. We received communication from inside an otherwise impenetrable location. No radio waves have ever been able to go through the protective cage surrounding the bathrooms in the Novotny compound. A few hours ago we set up an experiment. It worked. This invention quite possibly is able to penetrate the veil of clouds as well."

"Interesting idea."

"Barker's daughter supposedly is among those invisibles. She is on the track to the Altai. The two young men, the inventors of mind-link, who incidentally are here as well, followed her by tapping her mind."

"Fascinating—and strange. Perhaps a trick or outright fraud?"

"I myself tested it. I put on the gear and found myself in Blanchard's mind. That's all I can tell you." Dr. Wong felt a little embarrassed even talking about it.

"Now I understand what the Frenchman was talking about." Carlisle said.

"He told you? Should I be embarrassed?" Dr. Wong said. "No, honestly. I'm not saying that I was reading his thoughts. It was stranger than that. I had his thoughts. You probably think I'm crazy. Honestly, I felt his feelings. His mind was my mind. But at the same time we were still quite separate, two separate beings."

"Hold on, stop it, stop it. You're talking nonsense, scientific nonsense."

"Believe me I was as skeptical as you. But I have experienced what I have experienced. It was not a hallucination. This is obviously repeatable—this is testable."

"It doesn't fit with anything we know."

"It might engage you when I tell you what I found in the Frenchman's mind. In fact, this is almost funny. Or did he tell you that as well?"

"Now you're holding me in suspense?"

"I should try it with you some time before I give you the details," Dr. Wong snickered.

"Come on, tell me. What did you see?" Carlisle sounded like a curious teenager who felt that his friend was teasing him.

"As he was looking at me, while I was in his mind, he started, quite shamelessly, to undress me. And then he had the audacity to dryly say that a Frenchman thinks sixty sexual thoughts a minute."

"That's so typical."

"Don't tell me you are the same?"

"I am not a Frenchman. But…"

"Trivia aside. The phenomenon I witnessed was similar to the experience during the GeV 1000 experiment. We all had the same sensation of being in the minds of other people. Maybe we are really onto something."

"I promise you we will figure this out. Of hand, denying it is the safest strategy. But now I actually have to get going."

"Oh, do I get the honor?" Dr. Wong jumped up from her chair and moved toward Carlisle's image.

"Hold on, just a moment. Over our chat I almost forgot the most important reason for my visit," Carlisle said.

"And what would that be?" Dr. Wong sat back down.

"You are the last member of the council I must consult."

"Consult about what? Now you're holding me in suspense."

"We all have agreed to relieve Viswamitra from his duties as president, effective immediately. You must agree that his behavior at the last meeting was unacceptable. Everyone here agrees. Besides, our ways have quite obviously parted. What's your verdict?"

"Sounds like a full-fledged palace revolution."

"As I said, I have consulted everyone. Your consent is the last one needed. We have to act swiftly, before the news gets out. I don't know how much longer I can keep the lid on this."

"I must say I'm not completely surprised. What was his response?"

"Whose? Viswamitra? He doesn't know yet. We can't afford to inform him prematurely. He might rally his supporters. The facts must be accomplished before the world has an inkling of any dissent."

"Too bad we are meeting only virtually."

"Why is that? Are you afraid to talk?"

"Not at all, but if you were here I would propose a toast now. I have here a bottle of the best champagne the Crimea can offer. We could celebrate your promotion. Don't tell me I'm wrong."

"I am so glad you see it that way. That makes my job that much easier."

"I didn't say I agree with you, just that I'll drink with you."

"I'll take what I can get. Join me here just as soon as you can get away. Perhaps you can bring that bottle with you? But now I seriously have to sign off. Work is to be done. Goodbye, dear."

"No, wait, let me have the honor, Mr. President."

"Oh, sorry, I forgot. You like making me disappear."

For a scientist she sometimes acts like a child. That makes her so incredibly charming, Carlisle thought and smiled. *As long as she's on my side. Now I have to talk to the rest.*

Dr. Wong jumped up from her chair again and moved swiftly toward Carlisle who opened his arms for a passionate embrace. But Dr. Wong's advancing arm cut through his image more like a dagger than a lover's touch.

A virtual box lit up instantly pronouncing the obvious: IMAGE VIOLATION. TRANSMISSION STOPPED.

Part Two:
Entering the Field

Since there exists in this four-dimensional structure [space-time] no longer any sections which
represent "now" objectively, the concepts of
happening and becoming are indeed not completely suspended, but yet complicated. It appears
therefore more natural to think of physical reality as a four-dimensional existence, instead of,
as hitherto, the evolution of a three-dimensional
existence.

Albert Einstein

One

Mary stared at the empty walls that surrounded her and despaired. Tears rolled down her face. Within a few weeks her life had turned from happy to completely unraveled. She was worried about Jesse, whom she got to see for just a few minutes before the guards dragged her out of the interrogation room. She could only think that he was a prisoner just like her. Why wouldn't they let her talk to him face to face? They had offered her a conference with Jesse via Mind-link, but she declined. Her frustrating experience in trying to contact Melissa had only made her worries about her daughter worse. Even though during the periods she was connected she knew her daughter's every feeling, the fact that she was unable to intervene, powerless to change anything, and unable to follow her motherly instincts contributed immensely to her despair. Ultimately it did not bring her closer to her daughter at all. If there was such a thing as hell, Mary thought, this device would be it: silently observing everything, knowing the innermost pain of all people, seeing and knowing everything, but not being able to intervene.

Mary considered herself an activist. When she saw a problem, she immediately had to think of a way to fix it. When she saw someone who needed help, she thought of a way to provide it. This was one of the reasons why, after she gave up seeing patients, she had joined the Sisterhood of the Thousand Lights, a worldwide service organization. Here she met like-minded women who were not just talking but actively doing something about people's needs.

For the first time in her life, Mary did not have any idea what to do next. Being the practical person she was, whenever she lost focus on the here and now, the demands of the moment, which right now dictated devising a plan for how to get out of here, prompted her to think of a solution, but her mind drifted back to her little girl.

Where was she? What strange sickness engulfed her? Why did she go on this journey without telling her mother?

Initially Mary was convinced that the government had taken Melissa into custody. The same thing had happened to her a few months earlier, when government agents detained and questioned her about her association with the Sisterhood of the Thousand Lights. But she succeeded in convincing them that the Sisters were not involved in spiritual activities, but rather were mostly concerned with the material wellbeing of children. After a few hours they finally let her go, and Mary had hoped the episode was over.

On the morning of Melissa's disappearance Mary had expected her to show up again soon. Yet this whole ordeal had left Mary shaken and despondent. She had no idea that her daughter was involved in a worldwide rebellion against the Science Council. Mary now had to admit to herself that Melissa had grown distant from her. She was not a little girl anymore. When Mary looked back on the last year of their life together, she realized that she should have picked up on some of the clues that came from her daughter. As a trained psychologist herself, Mary blamed herself now for not seeing this coming.

Ever since Melissa had turned from a girl into a young woman, her interest in her tribal heritage became more and more obvious. Mary did not want to stifle that interest. After all, her daughter had a right to find out about the part of her life that came from the bloodline of her birth father.

As a young, aspiring professional herself, back in her student years, Mary had developed an interest in everything Native American. The gentle spirituality of the Hopi and Anasazi especially fascinated her. This, of course, was back in the times before the infamous Year of the Dog, before the Great War and before the Science Council fundamentally changed the way things were done.

During a field studies trip to a Hopi reservation in the mountains of southern Nevada, Mary, barely a woman herself, fell in love with a young Hopi man. After a few months of courting they were enga-ged. Soon after, she married Cha'risa Catori, a truck driver from the Hopi nation. But less than three years later, Mary was single again. Cha'risa had died in a car crash, leaving her with a two-year-old child, who from then on became the sole focus of Mary's life.

Mary wiped the tears from her eyes and took off the color-ful black and red dress she had been wearing when she saw Jesse some hours ago. It was the same dress she had given to herself as a birthday present from Jesse. Now she had a sad smile on her face as she carefully folded the dress and put it away in her traveling bag. Her mind went back to the last morning she said goodbye to her husband. She had gotten used to Jesse's ways of forgetting things. His work totally consumed him. Sometimes she even had to remind him to eat. When he was deeply involved in his work, he could for-get that the world existed. At times this was difficult to bear. On those occasions Mary felt that for Jesse she didn't even exist. She nevertheless loved him dearly. She knew his forgetfulness was not neglect, but absorption in his ideas.

Hoping that she could soon be on the road again, released from this strange situation, she put on a rustic khaki pants suit, which was her favorite outfit for traveling. From a side pocket of her bag, she took the little picture that Melissa had painted for her. Mary looked at the familiar face of her first husband for a long time. She remembered the morning, a couple of days after Melissa had disappeared. She had packed a travelling bag for the big journey and then took a last look around the house. Her eyes fell on the picture of Charisa Catori lying on her kitchen desk. Following a sudden impulse she picked up her daughter's gift and stuck it into the side pocket of her bag.

Again and again she looked at the picture and asked herself the same question: How could her daughter have been able to draw the image of her birth father with so much detail? Looking at the pain-ting now, Mary suddenly realized that her husband's Indian name,

Charisa Catori, was written in tiny, almost invisible script on the lower right side of the painting in the place where artists typically leave their signature.

Just then a knock at the door and a turning key brought Mary back to the reality of her imprisonment. She was surprised to see the Chinese woman they called Dr. Wong enter her room. Dr. Wong looked around.

"I am so sorry for keeping you in such abject circumstances, Mrs. Barker. I had no idea. I will initiate a transfer immediately. Or perhaps this might not even be necessary. I have a few questions for you, and if you answer them satisfactorily, you can be on your way home."

"I would like to see my husband, and I want to know about the whereabouts of my daughter if you have anything to do with her disappearance," Mary said. Her voice was trembling. She completely understood the powerlessness of her situation.

"I am sorry, Mrs. Barker, but I don't know the answer myself. I wish I did. As far as your husband is concerned, he left our facility, and he is on his way home. On the whereabouts of your daughter, we have no idea. I assure you our agency has nothing to do with her disappearance. This brings me to my question. What do you know about your husband's work?"

"Jesse never shares anything about his work with me. I am sure you have asked him yourself. Why do you need me?"

"Have you ever heard him talk about higher dimensions? Tell me anything you know."

Even if I knew, why should I share it with you? Mary thought. "I have absolutely no idea. Jesse never talks with me about his research. Sorry to disappoint you."

"What about interspecies communication? Have you ever seen your husband communicate with his cat?"

Mary looked at Dr. Wong, shaking her head in disbelief. "What do you think? If you people believe my husband is crazy, why would you be interested in his research?"

"No one thinks your husband is insane, Mrs. Barker. Quite to the contrary, your husband might be in the possession of knowledge we need. And he refuses to share it with us. I only thought you might want to help your husband in his situation."

"Didn't you just tell me that Jesse was on his way home?" Mary asked. Why, if his case was not closed, did they release Jesse?

"As a psychologist yourself, or should I say, a former psychologist, you should know that we have various means at our disposal. I am sure you understand."

Mary understood quite well. In a last attempt to comply, she said, "What do you want me to do? I will do everything you ask me if it can help my husband and my daughter. But I cannot tell you anything I don't know myself."

"Never mind." Dr. Wong suddenly was in hurry. Quite unexpectedly she stood up and opened the door. "By the way, you are free to go. I am sure the local chapter of your Sisters will be more than willing to assist."

This change of events took Mary by surprise, but the cynicism in the Chinese woman's last statement did not escape her. It sent shivers down her spine, knowing what these people were capable of doing.

Without further ado Dr. Wong was gone. Mary packed her few belongings hastily and left the building. No one on the way out made any attempt to stop her.

Two

At sixty thousand feet, the engines of the Stratojet were all but inaudible. Richard and Joe sat comfortably back in their first-class recliners. They toasted each other with the champagne that was provided gratis. The two entrepreneurs had good reason to celebrate. Their mind-link invention promised them a lifelong government stipend connected to an open account they could use for all their needs. This was actually much more than either of them had expected, even in their wildest dreams. What more could they want? To have reached financial independence and economic security at the young age of twenty-eight was more than anyone could hope for. And with the mighty Science Council as a guarantor, not much could go wrong.

True, in exchange for their award they practically had to sign their lives away. They had agreed to turn any future inventions over to the government, but that was no sweat, since they really considered themselves government property in the best meaning of the word. From now on their lives and the Science Council were linked together. There was no backing out. Though initially this arrangement had made them both a little uneasy, the offer was too good to reject. Once they understood that the government was offering them an open account for anything they would ever desire, it only took them minutes to come to an agreement. This type of award was generally only given to accomplished scientists, military leaders with long-standing careers, and public servants of the most impeccable kind.

"Did they make you turn over your access chips?" Richard wondered.

"No way, compadre!" Joe grinned and pulled a tiny chip out of his blazer pocket. "It's all in here: access to Melissa's brain. I taught them the technology. That's all they asked for. For the rest, they'll have to cut their own material."

Abruptly the jet lost speed. As they were rapidly declining the aircraft seemed to change course as well.

"What's going on?" Joe asked. He waved to an airhostess and inquired about the sudden loss in altitude. She said something about having to return to Moscow. Something had come up, but she had not received any updates. After a while the voice from the cockpit calmly announced to get ready for landing. Another few hours later they arrived back at the accelerator facility at Lake Baikal. Nobody had bothered to provide them with an explanation.

Three

"I hope you are having a splendid meal, Professor," Dr. Wong said as she arrived at the cafeteria where Jesse had just taken a seat. Jesse took notice of the dark blue, deep-cut dress uniform that Dr. Wong was wearing, which skillfully accentuated her slim and trim body. But his mind was not set on lighthearted conversation. A full day had passed since his virtual meeting with his wife, but Jesse had heard nothing from her since. He now was certain that the whole Mind-link operation was a setup to invade his mind. The only excuse he could find for his stupidity was his eagerness to learn more about the invention. But, alas, he had learned as good as nothing and the whole thing might as well never have happened. In his frustration and anger he could not even find anyone to file a formal complaint with. No one had contacted him or informed him about any further procedures. So Jesse was naturally anxious to meet with Dr. Wong to clarify his status and vent his anger.

"Finally someone I can relate to and get some answers from," Jesse grumbled. He could hardly conceal his frustration. "How long do you intend to keep me here, if I may ask? Am I a prisoner? It most certainly appears that way," he added.

"I hope you have not been mistreated, Professor. You are, of course, our guest, as always." Dr. Wong sounded relaxed, taking a seat next to Jesse.

"Strange concept of hospitality you people have indeed," Jesse replied sarcastically.

"These are strange times, Professor. May I remind you that we all serve a higher purpose."

"Please don't try to placate me with such nonsense. Where is my wife? I must know."

"This is precisely why I came. Your wife left the compound yesterday. We had no reason to keep her."

"And? Where did she go? Where is she?" Jesse probed.

"She left without saying."

"But you, of course, know exactly her whereabouts, don't you? I don't believe for a moment that you people just let her go without shadowing her! Where did she go in the middle of Russia? You must tell me! I need to find her, and I need to find my daughter. Enough is enough. What good is your so-called higher purpose if it effectively destroys lives?"

"You are right again, Professor. We did shadow her. I invite you to come with me. You must see for yourself."

Within half an hour Jesse and Dr. Wong had boarded a helicopter and were on their way straight across Lake Baikal, heading for the northern shore. Looking out the window, Jesse could see the mouth of a river emptying its brown water into the clear, blue sea. The aircraft followed the river bed for over an hour. Jesse could see a high mountain range appearing in the distance. Then suddenly the helicopter swooped down and landed in a little clearing. Dr. Wong indicated to the pilot to wait and jumped off, motioning Jesse to do the same. She quickly took his hand and dragged him away from the wind and noise of the still-rolling blades. Slowly the engine of the chopper died down, and they were surrounded by the silence of the taiga.

"Follow me!" Dr. Wong said. Jesse complied while trying to read Dr. Wong's face. He had the impression that Dr. Wong had suddenly become very somber. He wanted to ask her where they were going, but had an ominous feeling that soon he would find out. And indeed, the path followed a curved incline and quite unexpectedly opened up to a large meadow that stretched for several thousand meters before a different stand of trees indicated a more mountainous terrain.

What appeared before Jesse's eyes went far beyond any imagination. The view immediately churned Jesse's stomach and made him feel sick. The grassy ground of the meadow, as far as his eyes could see, was littered with human corpses, hundreds, perhaps thousands of them—bodies of men, woman, even children and whole families. They were lying everywhere like disjointed pieces of some strange puzzle. Jesse suddenly noticed an intense stillness. *The stillness of death*, Jesse thought, a *truly Stygian abyss.*

"What is this?" Jesse said, petrified. His voice cut through the silence like thunder. "Who did this to them?"

"No one did this to them, Professor." Dr. Wong replied. She gazed for a reaction in Jesse's face. "They did this to themselves."

"How? Why?" Jesse wanted to know.

"Religious fanaticism," Dr. Wong said wryly, "the sad doings of some religious cult. They chose death, expecting redemption in some other world. Come with me, Professor. I hope the stench does not bother you."

Dr. Wong pulled out a couple of facemasks and handed one to Jesse. "Come along, Professor. Take a good look at their faces. Look at their positions."

Dr. Wong moved on, navigating among the dead bodies. Jesse followed as if in a trance. Dr. Wong stopped at an assembly of four or five corpses embracing each other in death.

"Look at this group," she said. "They are holding each other's hands. Notice the frozen smiles in their dead faces?"

"Oh my god," Jesse kept repeating. "Oh my god."

"Collective death in the name of their god. That god, whoever he is, must be pleased with his creation indeed; don't you think so, Professor? But suspicion aside, what is it that drives the human animal to such horrific deeds?"

"Collective suicide has become more frequent among certain animal species such as lemmings and seals. It is even a common occurrence among certain domesticated insects. Over the past decades, domesticated bees have become virtually extinct. For no apparent reason they leave their hives and never return."

Even to himself Jesse sounded cold and scholarly. His detailed knowledge showed that as a scientist he was not only interested in dead little particles. "This phenomenon has also been found among dolphins and elephants."

"You seem to be well-informed," Dr. Wong said.

"As a scientist I have to be informed not only in my narrow field of expertise."

"And what is your conclusion as a scientist?" Dr. Wong inquired.

"My conclusion so far is this: these animals kill themselves out of hopelessness."

"Hopelessness?" Dr. Wong asked skeptically.'

"Animals have been able to sense environmental degradation," Jesse said. "Instead of bringing more of their own into this world, they collectively choose to die. We witness the undoing of evolution. Instead of a will to survive, a general will to die prevails. The disintegration of bee populations has been well documented. Scientists have called it colony collapse disorder. That type of disorder has become epidemic."

"But with human beings it is different. Wouldn't you say?"

"How so?" Jesse asked. "I am not entirely convinced."

"The cause is not hopelessness, but misguided hope." Dr. Wong bent over and took a little book out of the hand of an older man with a large gray beard that even in death commanded dignity. The old man's empty shell was lying in front of her on the ground. She handed the little book to Jesse. "Here, check this out. Therein is the difference."

Jesse looked at the book and read: "The Fourth Dimension— Gateway to Eternal Life."

Dr. Wong looked for an impact in Jesse's face before continuing: "This is by far not the first cult that constructed an escape into another world and made death an acceptable, even desirable solution to all our problems. Japanese warriors were known for their suicide missions in World War Two, Muslim jihadists largely contributed to the recent clash of civilizations that led up to World War Three. Christian martyrs preceded them all."

She took another look at the little book in Jesse's hand. "Are you familiar with this publication?" Dr. Wong asked. Before Jesse could answer, she added, "Of course you must be. You once wrote a paper yourself on the subject, did you not?"

"It was a scientific paper," Jesse protested. "You are not bringing this cult in connection with my publication, are you?"

"Everything has consequences, does it not? Your paper on the fourth dimension was the last scientific paper you ever published. Why did you stop publishing? Why did you give up a promising career?"

"Disappointment over popular imagination?"

"What do you mean?"

"Scientists are appalled when ordinary people take their ideas and make a cult from them."

"Is that what happened to your work on the fourth dimension?"

"My work had nothing to do with this cult, especially not with anything like this." Jesse felt utterly exhausted. How could anyone blame him for this insanity just because of some scientific discoveries he had made years ago?

"Let me show you something else, Professor." Dr. Wong started moving toward a small hill that was covered with corpses as well. She carefully avoided stepping on any bodies. As they came closer to the hill, Jesse froze. His eyes fell on a familiar piece of clothing. A shock charged through his whole system and nearly paralyzed him. He was looking at the corpse of his wife. Her lifeless body still wore the dress she donned when he last saw her, a dress that was supposed to remind him of something specific. He suddenly realized that it was the dress she wore on their last morning at home, the dress she had bought for herself as a birthday gift.

"You must have known, Professor, that your wife belonged to this cult?" The sharp voice of Dr. Wong pierced through Jesse's memory.

"What cult? The Sisters of the Thousand Lights? They were cleared by the government. My wife did not belong to any cult."

Jesse uttered these words in some secluded department of his mind, but they never left his frozen mouth.

"You knew about the Fourth Dimension?" Dr. Wong snapped.

"Mary had nothing to do with that." Jesse's words were barely audible.

Dr. Wong was ready to squeeze her victim and emotionally prepare him for complete collaboration, but she quickly realized that Jesse was so deep in shock that he could hardly respond to her investigative questions. For Jesse, Dr. Wong's voice might as well have come from another planet. His mind had escaped into a different world where his wife was alive and smiling. "*Take care of Melissa,*" Mary said. "*Take good care of Melissa.*"

When Jesse's mind returned he had only one thought: *Where is Melissa? She must be in grave danger. I must find her.*

Four

After their grisly discovery, Dr. Wong was waiting for the right moment to probe deeper into Jesse's psyche. She calculated that the loss of a loved one would soften his mind and make him more willing to cooperate. Jesse's immediate response to the tragedy was to refocus on finding and rescuing the only other person he really cared about, his daughter Melissa. Practically thinking, all he could do for his wife now was to insist on securing her body and giving her a proper burial. Realistically he knew that whatever they offered him, he had little choice but to accept and move on. His top priority now had to be locating his daughter and reunite with her.

Jesse tossed around in his bed trying to find rest. The dream in which he had seen his wife as a deer, killed by his own gun, kept haunting him. In quiet moments, it flashed before his mind and drove him to near insanity. His rational mind told him that dreams are just dreams and of no consequence, but in his current mental state images of the subconscious easily merged with a fragile sense of reality. Tears welled up when he thought of his wife. His mind went back again and again replaying the images of smiling frozen faces. A stinging pain in his forehead dragged him back into the present and prevented him from falling asleep.

After a while Jesse got back up and went into the bathroom. He soaked a towel in cold water, wiped off his burning eyes and then pressed the cooling wedge against his forehead. The thought that he was poulticing brought some momentary peace to his mind. It felt good to stand there in the dark with closed eyes. A small nightlight barely illuminated the full-length mirror before him.

A sudden noise right in front of him ripped through his brain. Opening his eyes he realized that the sound had come from inside the mirror. *Was this the timid meow of a cat?* He stared into the mirror. He rubbed his eyes and stared again until he realized he was looking into the eyes of Tiger, the cat he had left behind in his big and empty house on the other side of the world. *Heavens knows, I just hope he's safe, but I have enough here to worry about.* Jesse trembled and realized that the darkness around him was frightening. He moved swiftly through the flat and turned on every light source, until the whole place was lit up brightly. Then he pulled a blanket off his bed and curled up in the bathtub. He finally felt safe and fell asleep.

The next morning Dr. Wong announced an upcoming meeting and specifically requested that Jesse attended this session. During the meeting she explained a government plan to send an exploratory expedition to the Altai Mountains.

Afterward she took Jesse aside, put her arm around his shoulder, and said, "You look stressed, Professor. Again, I am deeply sorry about the loss of your wife. I am sure you must miss her terribly. Perhaps I can offer you some recreation. How about a swim in the pool?"

Jesse was taken by her compassionate, motherly tone, and accepted her invitation. A few minutes later, he took a refreshing dive into the blue water of the Olympic-sized pool. After a few laps he noticed that Dr. Wong had joined him, swimming laps in the next lane. For thirty minutes, there was only the sound of two pairs of arms beating the water and of swooshing bodies. Finally feeling refreshed and pleasantly tired, Jesse stopped at one end of the pool. On the next round Dr. Wong stopped as well. Lifting her limber, slender body out of the pool, she said, "How about a soak in the hot tub? I think our bodies will be grateful. It will also give us a chance to chat."

Soon the two adversaries were submersed in the steaming water and relaxed. After a while Dr. Wong broke the awkward silence:

"I have a proposition for you, Professor. You are aware how much we value your expertise?"

"Why don't you just tell me what you want me to do?" Jesse said frostily. Even half an hour of swimming could not dispel his displeasure with the whole situation. The loss of his wife weighed heavy on his mind.

"In 1995, you took part in an International Boy Scout Jamboree in this area?"

"I am aware of my past," Jesse snapped back. "What is it you want from me?"

Dr. Wong produced a rare smile. "Wouldn't you like to be reunited with your daughter?"

"And? Please come to the point." Jesse said impatiently.

"Does the name Zolotaya Baba mean anything to you?"

Jesse instantly recalled the time in his youth when he was fascinated with ancient mysteries. Zolotaya Baba, he remembered, was the local name for a mythical character known as the Golden Lady.

"The Golden Lady?" Jesse said. The name stirred up old memories. "Zolotaya Baba."

"It is the center piece of an old story?" Dr. Wong asked probingly.

Jesse recalled his obsessive interest in one of the oldest mysteries surrounding the area around the Altai Mountains, some thousand kilometers away from where they were now. The mystery of the Golden Lady had caught his attention when he visited here as a teenager. Fascinated by the ancient story, he had made it his Eagle Scout project to find out as much as possible.

But Jesse's mind simultaneously remembered the strange woman visiting him in his office who claimed she was bringing him a message from the Golden Lady. What was the mysterious message she was trying to give him? He had mulled her words over in his head, but could not come to a conclusion.

"Legend has it that Zolotaya Baba, the Golden Lady, can be found inside the mountain of mystery, the Altai Mountain." Dr. Wong continued, showing off her detailed knowledge. "The Vikings already made an expedition to find her. They believed it was a figure made entirely from gold. Hitler even showed interest. He sent an elite troop of soldiers to find the idol. The Fuehrer hoped that unraveling the story would aid the Aryan cause. On the other hand, it might have been the mere lure of gold that attracted those grave robbers. What is your professional opinion, Professor?"

"What else do you know about this Golden Lady?" Jesse asked in return.

"The legend goes back even before Aryan times. The locals here believe that an ancient people originated from the Altai Mountains. Still today they call it the cradle of civilization."

"Pardon the question, Dr. Wong." Jesse finally interrupted. "What does this ancient mystery have to do with anything here?"

"That I hope you will help us to find out. But now let's first clear up something else. You are aware of the government's position on, how shall I say, mystical events?"

She looked at him expectantly, but Jesse just shrugged his shoulders. "So what?"

Dr. Wong smiled engagingly. "Let me be straightforward. What you experienced during the experiment at 1000 GEV cannot be explained with current science. What has happened here, at this facility, when the accelerator reached the critical energy, is embarrassing, and that's putting it mildly. It flies in the face of scientific evidence. Do I need to say more? This so-called unitary crisis is not only absurd, it's potentially damaging, far more so than your speech back in Buenos Aires could have predicted."

Jesse remembered well the lecture he had presented to the Science Council many years ago about the possible dangers of reaching 1000 GEV.

"Back then it was only speculation." Dr. Wong said. "But now we know what happens. Or do we, Professor? Why do you still hesitate to share your experience with us?"

"Can you blame me?" Jesse made a last attempt to conceal his inner resistance to revealing the content of his experience and preserve his integrity. But ultimately he was now more concerned about the fate of his wife and his daughter.

"From one colleague to another: We at the Science Council firmly believe that eradicating mystical thoughts and aspirations from human minds will serve us all best in the long run. Now this—the unitary crisis, an embarrassment beyond belief! We need an explanation."

"You want an explanation so you can counteract the spread of the truth more efficiently. Right?" Jesse snapped back.

Jesse sensed immediately that what he just uttered in haste would come back to haunt him. For only a moment he had let down his guard.

"Truth? You call this truth?" Dr. Wong shot back. She was pale and irritated. "What is your truth, Professor? What secrets are you guarding?"

As if upset about her own emotions, Dr. Wong hurriedly stepped out of the tub and put on a bathrobe, wiping her face with a towel. "When you are ready you can join me over there for a coffee if you like."

"I am ready now," Jesse said. He too got out of the tub and wrapped himself in towels. When he finally took a seat again next to Dr. Wong, she had calmed down. "Jesse—as a colleague, may I call you by your first name?"

Jesse nodded agreement.

"I want to be totally open with you. What you don't know is that we all, every single person in attendance, had a similar experience. We are all in the same boat, so to say. The only question now is what we can make from this—in scientific terms, I mean. How can we tailor our experiences to fit the truth—the scientific truth?"

Jesse looked at her in disbelief. "You tell me, Doctor."

Twisting the truth is not what I call science. Can she really be serious?

Dr. Wong continued eagerly: "All right then, if I can't get you to speak, here is what I know. When the critical threshold was reached, all scientists present encountered some sort of out-of-body experience. Their minds left their physical bodies. But that, as you well know, is not possible. Mind cannot manifest itself outside of a body. Do you have an explanation? Or is what happened perhaps a—miracle? You see, I am laying the cards on the table. I only wish you would do the same and not hold back any longer."

After a long silence, Jesse finally conceded. "Yes, I had a similar out-of-body experience, a very powerful one." Jesse looked straight at his adversary. He suddenly felt utterly exhausted.

"Finally we are communicating. Now we need to know how this can be explained." Dr. Wong appeared relieved.

"There you go again. You are not at all interested in the truth, but only how to manipulate it. And for this you need me?" Jesse took a sip from his coffee and continued: "To manipulate your experience into something people can comprehend? Come on. Do you really need me for this?"

"So how do you explain it? Honestly. I am asking." Dr. Wong chose to overlook Jesse's aggressive tone. "We know about your interest in cross-species communication. You have done extensive research in paranormal phenomena and extra-dimensional realities, and we are aware that you yourself have voluntarily undergone psychoactive experiments. Just tell me how you see it. That's all."

"Perhaps it cannot be explained. Science has lived with contradictions before. Why not accept this as a simple anomaly and move on? It would not be the first time in history." All sort of thoughts went in quick succession through Jesse's mind. *These people have done their homework. Any one of these accusations could cost me my freedom.*

"Naturally we have already considered this option. You mean, of course, the famous Copenhagen Interpretation, which by the way, a scientist of the stature of Einstein never accepted."

"Yes, in 1936, most famous quantum physicists agreed that a logical solution to the problem posed by the dual character of quanta could never be found. The smallest particles known to man stubbornly defy rational understanding."

"The wave and particle duality remained one of the great unsolved mysteries of the twentieth century."

"And yet the theory that was built on it became one of the most successful theories of all times. Why not find a similar solution in this case?"

Dr. Wong was well aware of this possibility. "Here is the problem: when these scientific mysteries are translated into popular language, the way ordinary people speak, they often are misunderstood, misinterpreted, even abused."

"You are right," Jesse conceded. He thought of his own discoveries and why he had hesitated to publish them. "Quantum mechanics is an immensely difficult theory. But once common people got a hold of it, those so-called quantum mysteries quickly became the root cause for insecurity and pessimism. Simple quantum contradictions became universal mysteries. Scientific insufficiency took on metaphysical significance."

"We cannot allow this to happen again. You must agree, Jesse?" Dr. Wong asked. She was encouraged that Jesse perhaps finally could see her point.

"I do agree, and I don't. First of all we can't make a scientific theory responsible for world wars, mass extinction, ethnic cleansing on an unseen scale, and global terrorism. The problem is interpretation, not reality."

"But Jesse! Don't you see? Perception is everything. Long before scientists understand a new theory, people's imagination takes off with it. They jump to conclusions, mostly false or misleading. Poets, writers, philosophers, and even theologians get in on it. That's precisely the reason why we have made every effort to wipe out these dubious professions. Human life, we believe, will be the better for it."

"Then why not leave it with that? Why spread the questions? The unitary crisis does not exist, unless you allow it to exist. Why not stop the rumors right in their tracks? As of now, only a handful of scientists are aware of this truly strange phenomenon, this—mind explosion."

"Ah, that is exactly what it is, Professor. That's why we need your help. You put your finger on the depth of the problem. A mind explosion is exactly what happened here. Unfortunately, though, it might be too late to contain this thing."

"So the news of this experiment is already out? I thought I had followed every bulletin, yet until I came here, I knew nothing about it."

"On the way here, did you notice thousands of people moving in a trek?"

"You mean the characters I saw at the airport and along the road we crossed over en route to here? I'm sure it's nothing but a strange coincidence?" Professor Barker put on a light smile.

"Not a coincidence at all." Dr. Wong looked sincere. "We are talking perhaps millions of people, and they are coming from around the world, quite literally. Incidentally, we must assume that the group your wife belonged to was part of the same movement. All these people appear to be on their way to the Altai Mountain. That much we know for sure. Why the group of your wife's decided to go ahead and commit exodus early, we don't know. But we have indications that once at the Altai they all will stage a mass exodus, a collective suicide of a massive proportion. Compared to this impending holocaust the one we saw yesterday will be child's play. I hope you understand the magnitude of our problem. Our task is to reeducate the human animal and teach him again survival as the supreme good. We need your help, professor."

"I still don't understand how this is connected with what happened here at the accelerator? What do these gatherings have to do with the unitary crisis?"

"The unitary crisis appears to have caused not only a mind explosion for the attending scientists. It caused a global mind explosion, not more and not less. I cannot frame it in any other terms. From what we can gather—and it is not much at this point—at the moment when our accelerator produced 1000 GeV, for the first time and then again later, something like an inverse explosion, a consciousness meltdown of like-minded people around the globe, occurred. People in every continent and country connected and received a message to congregate in this area, in western Siberia, somewhere in the Altai Mountain chain. In one instant, all like-minded people around the world were mysteriously linked, if you can imagine. It goes beyond scientific know-how, and yet it happened."

"But my wife, Mary, had nothing to do with this. The Sisters were a simple service organization, nothing else." Jesse still tried to clear his wife's name.

"I honestly don't know." Dr. Wong said and appeared sincere. "Whether those people we saw yesterday were part of the sisterhood or some other group, I can't say. What is clear to me is that they had joined the trek, your wife included. Evidently they could not wait for the final goal. But regardless, we have brought you here, Jesse, because we hope that you will join our exploration and give us further understanding. And by the way, we know that your daughter is on her way to the Altai as well. Your daughter has joined the trek."

Jesse suddenly had to think back to the night when he felt that somebody was watching him in his sleep, the night he found his daughter sleepwalking on the balcony of his house. He wondered whether in that brief moment his mind had joined the collective mind of all scientists in the world, at least those who had some kind of sensitivity? Could these events be connected? Before he could think any further, Dr. Wong continued.

"These events are intricately connected with the disappearance of your daughter, Jesse. You must believe this."

"How so?" Jesse muttered. Of course he wanted to do everything he could to find his daughter. Dr. Wong had Jesse's full attention.

"Millions of other people around the world vanished at the same moment your daughter disappeared. And all these people had a predisposition for the occult, for mysticism."

Jesse wanted to make a last attempt to defend his daughter. But Dr. Wong interrupted him sharply:

"Hold it, Professor. Must I repeat again, this is not about accusations. This is all about investigating a truly peculiar phenomenon. So as I said, your daughter disappeared that very morning. We have reports of assemblies, forbidden assemblies of large amounts of these kinds of people. Some met in underground garages, malls, and in the open air in remote parks. In most cases we have only anecdotal evidence. But for you it may suffice that we know, and we have followed their movement."

"And?"

"They have all gone on an incredible journey. As we speak they are assembling somewhere nearby in Siberia, in the borderlands between Russia and Kazakhstan."

"And have you reacted, how shall I say, in the usual way? We all know that such assemblies are against the law."

"We did not and could not and indeed. Why? There is a simple answer. We didn't have a clue. Before we got news about any of these assemblies, they had moved on. Embarrassing, isn't it? For a large part, this tremendous and unprecedented movement of people remained undetected. Don't ask me how and why. Things are at play here that we cannot explain."

"Is that why your police did not interfere with the suicide we witnessed yesterday? Why didn't your almighty police force interfere?"

"Quite simply because we have not been able to track any of these movements by global surveillance? Only in hindsight do we know they took place."

Now it was Jesse's turn to be surprised. There was a little glee in his voice when he said, "The Science Council prides itself to have in place some of the most advanced surveillance equipment available anywhere. I thought you people monitor every inch of the globe."

"We do." Dr. Wong moved her chair closer and looked around to see if anyone else could overhear their conversation. Then she continued, "Let me be frank, Jesse. Those assemblies simply didn't show up on our monitors. It was as if they did not exist."

"What are you telling me? Are they like ghosts?"

"Perhaps worse than that. We know about them by hearsay only. What's most embarrassing is that they are visible to the human eye. When you actually see a group of them, as we did on the way here, they are real, but when you point a laser device or any other of our surveillance systems at them, they are like ghosts, for lack of a better word. There is literally no trace of them."

"Collective transfiguration?" Jesse asked.

"As with Jesus in the bible." Dr. Wong replied.

"As with John Doe in Star trek." Jesse replied with a smirk. "But how do you know they've all come here, to Siberia?"

"From verbal reports we received—from credible sources. You yourself have seen a small part of the evidence."

"You are telling me that there are a million people congregated right now somewhere in this area and your instruments cannot track them?"

"Several million people. Do you understand our urgency? We do not comprehend what's going on. Truly."

"And you want me to find out?"

"That's right. Of course, we hope this adventure will also reunite you with your daughter. We are ready to launch an expedition. Five vehicles are packed with every scientific instrument you could possibly need. It's a sophisticated lab you're taking with you."

"And where is this expedition headed for?"

"We have an idea of the general area, a mountain range in Siberia. But no one has observed them crossing the pass. Once in the mountains, they completely vanish. We have sent fighters across the area and surveillance aircraft of the most advanced kind. The reports we receive are negative."

"And all these millions of people disappear into thin air?"

"Yes, that is what we assume. Come with me for a moment. I will show you something."

They left the café with Dr. Wong leading the way. Walking through a maze of hallways they finally reached her spacious underground office suite.

Dr. Wong quickly activated some controls, and a large overhead screen appeared showing the aerial picture of a mountainous terrain. She pointed a laser at a green area that appeared to be a valley: "This is where they are congregating. It's been going on for weeks. When I zoom in, you see, there's nothing. We can go down to the level where we can detect a mouse. We know they walk through this valley, and then here is where we are told they all disappear. Now we cross the mountain and you see nothing but clouds. A permanent cloud cover obscures the vision. Not even our most advanced radar can penetrate it. What is hidden beneath these clouds? What kind of mysterious mist can obscure its content to our instruments? How can all these people become invisible? Unanswered questions. We hope you can offer some insights. Remember, the life of your daughter may be at stake."

"When is this expedition scheduled to leave?" Jesse appeared to have made up his mind.

"Everything is ready. You can leave in the morning," Dr. Wong said. "So I can count on you then.?"

"Can I ask you one more question?" Jesse said. "When exactly was 1000 GeV produced for the first time?"

"At 3:33 Universal time, on June 11. Why?"

Dr. Wong expected an explanation, but Jesse was less than forthcoming. In his mind's eye he recalled the eerie glare of his alarm clock back home. His scientific curiosity was aroused. He smiled thinly and said, "I accept the challenge, Dr. Wong. Things are getting interesting."

Five

A caravan of five Dirt Trackers made its way slowly along the dusty highway that stretched north of Lake Ezevoe in the borderland between Russia and Kazakhstan. As far as the eye could see, Siberian birch trees extended like a carpet over the earth. This late summer day showed the tundra in its most pristine character, a truly unspoiled landscape. Soon this whole area would be blanketed with a thick cover of snow, and it would stay that way for the larger part of the year. Roads would become all but invisible, and the only way to get from place to place would be on a sled of a local animal herder or by army helicopter.

By evening, the small caravan had reached the foothills of the mountains. As night set in, they pulled into a small mountain village where Johann Barnward, the Scandinavian manager of the expedition, announced they would stop for the night. Baggage carriers set up several comfortable tents, and a meal was prepared.

A group of children from the village hung around the small camp. They held their hands out, knowing well that strangers passing through often handed them candies, chewing gum, or other small items. What they really needed were pens, books, and a school in the village.

The native Ukra tribes had little chance to catch up with the rest of the civilized world. Under the Soviet regime they were persecuted and had almost become extinct. The Soviets had tried to reeducate them in Marxist atheism but failed. These indigenous tribes hung stubbornly on to their ancient beliefs.

After dinner Jesse broke away from the group and went for a stroll through the village. As he turned the first corner, he noticed a dark-eyed girl of about twelve motioning him to follow her. She wore a ragged dress and walked barefoot. As soon as the village girl had Jesse's attention, she swiftly walked up to him, took his hand, and dragged him along.

Jesse instinctively turned off his communicator, which he was ordered to wear at all times to stay in touch with base camp. Filled with curiosity, he followed the youngster. She took him through some dark alleyways and ended up in front of a sparsely lit store. A small gas lantern dimly illuminated the scene. Several native men with wind-beaten faces and bushy dark beards were bent over the barrier of what made the impression of being a little display of goods for sale.

The girl said a few words to the men and then quickly disappeared in the dark. Seconds later she was gone as if the night had swallowed her. The men now turned to Jesse and greeted him, extending their right hands toward him while tapping their chests with their left. One of them had a band with beads rolling through his fingers. Jesse wondered in which language they could possibly communicate, but before he could say anything, one of the men said in broken English:

"Welcome to my phratry. I invite you to be bear. You, come with us to bear festival. You understand festival? Phratry is great festival. You are on great journey. You need strength. You, come with."

As if drawn by a mysterious force, Jesse obliged. He had heard about the great bear rituals these native tribes occasionally performed. Could he be lucky enough to attend one?

"Phratry in next village, next valley. You know, official police not like this. We have to keep secret. Come with."

They took Jesse's arm and led him out of the village and along a small mountain path. For over an hour the men walked in silence. Jesse admired the brilliant stars above. No city lights were anywhere nearby to spoil the clear view of the northern night sky. After a while, he noticed an orange glare on the horizon. The moon would be coming up soon and brighten the path.

Finally Jesse could discern some buildings in the darkness. The men stopped in front of a giant wooden gate set into an ancient stone wall. The moon was shining brightly now, illuminating the doorway. One of them shouted a few words in a language Jesse could not understand. A voice answered from the inside. Suddenly the heavy wooden gate began to move. The view opened into a small yard in which several small and one larger tent became visible. Lanterns from inside the tents illuminated the scene, but still leaving the inside of the large tent in darkness. The floor was covered with thick carpets.

Only now did Jesse notice a group of men sitting in a side partition of the yard. They were holding drums between their legs. As Jesse followed the men's gesture to enter, they began tapping their instruments. Jesse was asked to take a seat on the carpet in the large tent. Another man entered with a platter of glasses, offering one to Jesse. He proceeded to pour a steaming liquid in Jesse's glass. Jesse's eyes got slowly accustomed to the darkness inside the tent. He noticed a person bent over in the center. The person wore an iridescent dress and a strange furry hat. He reminded Jesse of a shaman he had met when he had visited this area before.

After Jesse had taken a few sips of the steaming hot brew, the monotonous rhythm of the drumbeat intensified. The low thumps vibrated through his whole body while Jesse's mind told him: *160 beats a minute, correctly adjusted to induce a trance.* As he was thinking this, images already began emerging out of the dark. Jesse did not resist. The sweet liquid of the strange tea caused a burning sensation in his mouth and began to fill his stomach and then his entire insides. He felt his stomach grow larger and his extremities expanding while things around him appeared in a bright orange glow that slowly faded into a blue hue. A light smoke that rose from a fire burning somewhere outside permeated everything.

The drumbeat intensified, and Jesse noticed the person in the center getting up and swaying with the music. Someone stepped behind Jesse and put a mask over Jesse's face, covering it entirely. Even though he was in an utterly strange environment, Jesse did not feel any fear. Inside the darkness of the mask he felt a sensation of energy flowing through his entire body. A voice began chanting in a strange language.

Now he was alone with the drumming, the chanting voice, and the darkness. Out of the darkness, faces appeared before him.

His daughter Melissa came first. She stayed only for a brief moment, but Jesse noticed that she was smiling. He heard her say, "You are on the path. Don't be afraid."

Then her face faded and morphed into the face of a young bear. Another voice, which he recognized as the voice of the woman who had visited him in his office began speaking, but her face remained dark and empty. "I am Oxana. You have met me and know me. I will be your power animal. You will go where few humans have gone before. Follow the voice and follow your daughter. She knows the way."

Jesse sank into a deep sleep.

Six

Dr. Wong was awakened suddenly by a frantic tele-call. Barnward, the leader of the expedition, was transmitting an urgent message. Contact was lost with Professor Barker, the message said. After dinner, the professor had distanced himself from the convoy. He had disappeared somewhere in the mountainous area. The professor's communicator was inoperative. Barnward asked for further instructions from headquarters. When Dr. Wong replied, she sounded upset but confident.

"Naturally I should be angry with you for neglecting your duty, but there is no need to worry. We have him covered."

Filled with confidence, Dr. Wong got up from her bed and walked over to the communication complex where Joe and Richard were in charge of staying in contact with Jesse via Mind-link, only to find the two inventors deeply asleep. Not even her entrance disturbed their deep slumber. Both were slouched comfortably in their leather lounge chairs. Their eyes were shut, and Joe's mouth hung open. It made a whirling sound every time the air escaped from his lungs. Richard wore the headpiece, while Joe was in front of the computer controls. If they were supposed to monitor anyone in particular, they gave every indication that they had left their assignment.

"Gentlemen!" Dr. Wong's voice pierced the air. Both bodies jerked into an upright position so fast that Richard's headpiece came dangerously close to falling off. "Gentlemen, the government is not inclined to follow through with its generous offer if you are not holding up your end of the bargain."

"Whoa, whoa! Not so fast. We're up. We're awake," Joe mumbled.

Realizing the situation, Richard rushed to their defense. "We sold the gadget to you after you made us an offer. Remember?"

Joe wiped off the saliva that had slipped down his chin while he was sleeping. "Yeah! We held up our end of the bargain, but you changed your mind and called us back. Technically speaking, hum, we are on a new assignment, and we should be negotiating a new contract." Joe tried to be firm, given the fact that he had just been woken up. But in the large scheme of things his argument had little substance.

Dr. Wong indicated with a quick gesture that she was not at all interested in negotiating anything. "You knew what you agreed to when you accepted the contract. In all honesty, gentlemen, you signed yourself over to the government—for a decent price, may I add." She had a victorious grin on her face. "You are now government property, and we can assign you any duty we wish. Of course, given your expertise, we will always make sure you are assigned the appropriate task. Have I made myself understood?"

Both Joe and Richard nodded their heads sullenly like two schoolboys who had just been caught by the principal smoking in the bathroom.

"So then why are you not on duty? What can you report about the whereabouts of your subject?" Dr. Wong continued her interrogation.

"Our subject? Hum. He is asleep. Very deeply asleep," Richard muttered.

"And that bestows you the privilege to sleep as well?"

"Well?" Richard indicated that he saw nothing wrong in this logical sequence at all.

"Enough. Where is your charge? I have reports Professor Barker is missing."

"Responding to this is a somewhat difficult proposition." Joe made every effort to sound sophisticated. "We can only see what our subject sees, and we can only know what our subject knows."

"When our subject passes out, so do we," Richard said with a grin. "Literally. This is not a global positioning device."

"I understand that quite well. Tell me what you know!" Dr. Wong demanded impatiently.

"From what we can gather, he left his group and met up with some men who took him…somewhere. Then it went dark. After several hours of marching through complete darkness, they entered a yard through some big wooden gate. Oh, yes, he admired the stars, and the moon was just rising." Joe grinned broadly.

"Get to the point."

"Music started playing, drums, mostly. We drank something that put real fire into our belly. Then it got even darker, and our man got all woozy, if you know what I mean. That must have been some strong potion, that stuff. Then he fell asleep, and I fell asleep. Yes, and his mouth was burning, and his stomach was on fire."

"Where is he now?" Dr. Wong interrupted this lengthy explanation.

"Well, I will be happy to oblige and take a peek."

Richard arranged his helmet and closed his eyes.

"Sir!" Dr. Wong's voice came sharply.

"No, no, I'm not sleeping. I have to concentrate." He smiled thinly. After a few intense minutes Richard opened his eyes. "I don't seem to get a signal. Maybe we should reboot. What do you say, Joe?"

"Then reboot, by all means!" Dr. Wong shouted. "I should've known I am dealing with amateurs."

"Amateurs?" Joe raised his voice a little and grinned. "I take it you mean the term in its original meaning. We truly love what we are doing."

"No, I mean it in the most direct way. You two are imbeciles."

"I don't even see, why we should tell you what we observed, when we kept an eye on the professor's wife, precisely as you requested. Isn't it so, Richard?"

"I request a full report." Dr. Wong left no doubt that she was in charge. "What is it you observed after she left here?"

"What was strange was this. When she left here she wore a khaki pantsuit. Then we lost her and then, when we got contact again she was lifeless. We have absolutely no clue what happened in between. By the way, do you have any idea how weird it is to see the world through the eyes of a dead person? Wasn't it weird, Richard?"

"Shouldn't you also report that one thing was different."

"Right. Mindlink works differently inside a dead person."

"And how is that?" Dr. Wong asked. Joe's remark had raised her curiosity.

"You sort of hover over the dead body. That's what's weird." Richard said.

"And that fact enables you to see yourself from the outside." Joe added.

"Come to the point, please. I don't have all day. What is it you observed."

"She was lifeless." Richard repeated.

"No Richard, we have established that already." Joe corrected his friend. "What was different is that her dead body was dressed in a different outfit. When she left she wore the khaki outfit, but now she wore the same dress she had on when she first came here. You can decide for yourself if this is important."

"Yes, you decide." Richard agreed. He couldn't tell whether this information meant anything at all. Dr. Wong seemed unimpressed.

"Let's get on then. There is work to be done. I will be back in half an hour and expect a complete report about the missing subject."

With that, Dr. Wong left the communication center. Richard and Joe hurried to reboot the computer.

Back in her office, Dr. Wong placed an urged call to Carlisle. When he did not answer his communicator she left him this message. "I need to talk to you right away. It's about Barker's wife, Mary. I don't appreciate anyone meddling with my projects."

Seven

In his new state Jesse suddenly saw his whole life before him as if painted in an album. He marveled over his new ability to perceive many things simultaneously. A fantastic sense of infinite possibilities and limitlessness overcame him. He had left the confines of one particular perspective behind and could perceive things from many perspectives. He could exist on many levels as if a mysterious field connected everything. One and many were no longer a contradiction. He could be one and many, traveling seamlessly between different perspectives.

In Jesse's last paper on the fourth dimension he had speculated that beyond our reality there must be a higher dimensional world of pure consciousness. Ancient Hindu sages had named it the Akashic Field. Even in his new state, the thought that he had existentially entered the A-Field made him tremble with excitement.

Jesse looked back at his life. The album of his life was only a memory, but it was real at the same time. He realized that this review had been his last memory before he slipped over into the other reality at some point in the midst of the drumming during the night. Now it was before him like a frozen chain of images. Solid as if in a block-universe, he saw everything but he could not change anything. His life book was laid out for him, but it was too late to make any changes.

Jesse saw Oxana as a young girl, in her native village in the Russian taiga. He saw her brother Alexei playing soccer with other boys in the dusty streets of the village. Oxana was looking out of the door of her parents' house, waving her hand. Jesse realized that she was waving to him. He was playing soccer with the other boys.

After the jamboree at Lake Baikal, Jesse had been invited by Alexei to come with him to his village. They had traveled a full day, by railway first, then on a cart pulled by a horse until they reached

Alexei's village. He was to spend four weeks during that late summer in the Russian taiga with Alexei's tribal family. It turned into four months.

Jesse had quickly made friends with Alexei's beautiful sister, and by the end of the summer he had fallen in love with her. Everything Jesse ever knew about love, life, and how to connect with nature he had learned from Oxana during those few short weeks. His relationship with Oxana had grown strong, especially since she made it a point to introduce the eager young man to the ways her people had lived and communicated with nature for thousands of years.

One day in early fall, Oxana took Jesse on a long walk across the river that separated her village from that of the Targa people. In the other village they were greeted by elders with courtesy, invited into their tents, and offered goat milk to drink. On the way back it began to snow, at first only lightly, but soon the sparkling flakes covered everything, and the world turned into a glistening white. Wherever Jesse looked everything was white. The powder came down so swiftly that it was impossible to discern any objects. Jesse began to worry how they would find their way back home. He kept saying to himself that he should trust his new friend. Oxana did not seem to be concerned in the slightest. On several occasions, she scraped away the snow from the ground, and by reading the frozen plants she seemed to recognize their location.

After walking for a long time, a large gray animal suddenly appeared out of nowhere. Perhaps a wolf? The animal circled them and then closed in. Jesse's heart froze in fear. He pulled a knife he carried inside his garb and made a launch. The wild creature rose up as Jesse's knife ripped deep into his shoulder. Before Jesse could resist further, the animal had pinned him down to the ground and stood over him growling fiercely, fletching his teeth. Jesse thought that death would come instantly. Just then Oxana called something out in her native language. The wild animal let go of

Jesse immediately, winced, and went down to the ground. Jesse got up slowly still weary of the angry beast.

"What are you doing?" Oxana shouted. Jesse had never seen her so angry before. "He could have killed you."

"I know," Jesse said, trembling while still holding the bloody knife.

As Jesse looked back from his present state to that scene in the frozen taiga, he saw not only himself holding the bloody knife, but he also saw the bleeding animal through the eyes of Oxana. He felt her care for the animal and the compassion with which she treated him. Then he was aware of himself again, looking on with amazement, as Oxana kneeled down next to the animal and comforted him. She rubbed his wound, sucked out the dirt with her mouth, and put some snow on it. Then she looked up to Jesse.

Still with anger in her face, she said, "You must never do this again. They are our brothers and sisters. How could you treat him that way? Luckily his wound will heal soon. Let's go now. The wolf will show us the way. He will lead us home," Oxana said with confidence. The gray wolf jumped up on his feet and guided them back to the village. Just when they recognized the first houses the animal disappeared in the white blowout.

Another time, Oxana took Jesse to the home of the village shaman. He lived in a small hut buried half underground outside the settlement.

"That's where his father lived, and his father before him," Oxana said. "We consider it the shaman's home. He speaks with the winds and the water. In dreams he communes with dead people. The doors to the other world are not closed for him, as they are for us ordinary people. We bring him food, secretly."

"Why secretly?" Jesse asked.

"The government does not want us to go to the shaman. They send their doctors, but they come only once a month or even less often. When someone falls ill, our people prefer the power of the shaman. He knows the herbs and the mushrooms, and he knows the spirits. The government wants us to mistrust him. The government teaches us to mistrust him."

They walked on in silence until they stood in front of the ramshackle home. Before they entered, Oxana said something in her native language. Jesse heard a rusty voice coming from the inside. It sounded like the voice of a woman.

"My uncle says you are not Mlecha—he does not want to see you."

"Is it bad not to be Mlecha?" Jesse asked his friend. He had no idea what she meant.

"No, it is quite the opposite. My uncle believes that a Mlecha is not worthy to meet a non-Mlecha."

"Can you explain?" Jesse asked.

"I don't think it can be explained in your language," Oxana said and smiled. "It is part of an ancient curse our people believe in. There is only one non-Mlecha he would ever feel worthy to meet."

Almost jokingly, Jesse said, "How does he know I am not the one non-Mlecha he is waiting for?"

Oxana gave Jesse a strange look. Her dark eyes were full of wonder. Then she smiled again and said, "I will ask him this question."

She and her uncle exchanged some words and suddenly the old wooden door shrieked open. Warm air flowed out from the inside. It was filled with a strange aroma of burning wood and herbs. They had to climb down a small incline since half the dwelling was underground. Jesse's eyes slowly adjusted to the darkness inside the cave. It vaguely reminded him of the inside of some animal's den. Everything, even the ceiling, was covered with fur. As his eyes adjusted, he saw a frail body lying on a thick bed of furs. The shaman stretched out his hand and motioned him to come closer. He took Jesse's hand and held it for a long time with closed eyes. Jesse felt the soft hands of a woman. When the strange appearance finally opened his eyes, he seemed to radiate peace and contentment. Jesse stared curiously back at him. But the shaman's gaze seemed to look right through him into another world.

The shaman suddenly pulled Jesse closer. He put his other hand on his head and uttered some words that Jesse could not understand. Then he let go of him. Without interpretation, Oxana took Jesse's hand and pulled him out of the den into the open air. It was dark now, and the sky was covered with millions of brilliant little stars.

"What did your uncle say?" Jesse asked. "Was it bad?"

"No, not at all. He gave you his blessings," Oxana said. Then they walked back in silence.

Jesse became slowly accustomed to his new power. As Oxana walked next to him in silence, he could fully experience the world through Oxana's eyes. Looking back, he felt her warm feeling toward him, and he understood what the shaman had said in her native language. He realized now that the old shaman was actually already in contact with the A-Field. Being inhabited by two spirits, male and female, opened the gateway. This peculiar man could see everything from two perspectives. While this was still far from the powers of the real field, it was high above the singular processing power of ordinary people.

After a while Jesse broke the silence. "Why are you so quiet?" he asked, taking Oxana's hand, which was covered in a thick, furry glove.

"I am sad you are leaving," Oxana said.

They had reached the farmhouse. Until now Jesse had been sleeping on a bed in the men's quarters with the other men. The women's quarters were above the animals, which kept the rooms warm and cozy.

"Come with me," Oxana said and pulled Jesse up the wooden staircase toward the women's quarters. When they had reached the entrance to her room Oxana stopped.

"Wait here," Oxana said and disappeared into her room. She returned with a golden ribbon and hung it over her door.

"In our tradition this is the sign for a lover to know that he is welcome," she murmured into Jesse's ear and then disappeared quickly behind the door.

Jesse had learned much about the customs of these people. It was always left up to the woman to let a man know that he is welcome to share a night with her. The man never stayed with the woman. He had to return to his mother's house, where he lived for the rest of his life. These people did not know about marriage.

Jesse stood there for a long time, tempted to follow the invitation. But as the chill of the night crept into his body and his confusion grew he returned to his own bedroom. For hours he lay awake, contemplating whether he had made the right decision. He finally fell into a light sleep, but it did not bring relief. In his mind's eye he saw her voluptuous body as naked as nature had made her. The vision of her soft breasts stirred his glowing passion.

When finally the first rays of the new day touched the tops of the high trees, he rose up from his bed. With sleepwalking accuracy his body navigated its way to the bridal chamber. The golden ribbon, lovingly placed on the upper trim of the door, invited him to enter. The inside of the room was still soaked in darkness, but a body in love does not need lanterns. He found his way to her side and embraced her in passion. With his youthful fingers he caressed her soft breasts until they responded.

The next morning Jesse departed. His heart was broken. He was lamenting the separation from his first love; but even years later, after that pain had long subsided, he sometimes still wondered what secrets the old shaman had revealed to his friend and lover.

These events were clear in Jesse's mind now, and he began to understand many perspectives. As he walked next to Oxana along a stony path in the mountains, he realized that he would have to learn a lot as he entered this new and wondrous four-dimensional world of unlimited perspectives. Just as in the past world, learning would continue. Looking back at his life he could feel again the fire of his first love in his loins, but it was more like a feeling he observed from a distance than a feeling he actually had.

Just then a donkey came running toward them and abruptly stopped in front of Jesse.

Oxana pointed at the donkey. "You have a choice now. Our people believe that every person has two souls. One is your animal soul that stays behind, the other one is the spirit soul that continues on. Now you can choose where you want your animal soul to be at home."

As if her thoughts were his, Jesse understood the meaning of her words. He took a look at the donkey before him and then glanced at Oxana. He saw her smile and saw her nod of approval. The gray-haired donkey pointed his ears upright, as if listening intently and then let out a long howl that sounded nothing like the sound of any other donkey. But Jesse understood its meaning and without great effort his animal soul slipped into the skin of the donkey. The animal instantly turned around and ran away in the opposite direction along a narrow path. As Jesse looked through the eyes of the donkey, he held on for his life. Never before had he run this fast. There was joy in this new world that he had not felt before; indeed, Jesse experienced an unknown bliss of being inside an animal in an animal's world.

Eight

"I have contact!" Salty drops of sweat dripped down from Richard's forehead and into his eyes. He had been trying to get a reading on Jesse Barker for hours now. They were flying in a government helicopter low over the foothills of the Altai region, searching for any sign of the professor. After they had lost contact with his brain, partially because the professor seemed to have slipped into a deep sleep, Richard had not been able to reconnect. Since the main expedition also had lost connection, Dr. Wong quickly organized a helicopter to rush to the area to see if they could reestablish contact on closer range and find Jesse. Dr. Wong mercilessly kept up the heat, inquiring every few minutes and requesting progress. She had just returned from a short break and asked for a report, visibly relieved that progress might be imminent.

"Where is he?" she demanded.

"Just a minute, just one more minute. I have a strong signal now. I will give a complete report in a minute. It's him, it's definitely him. But I can tell you only what I see. What he sees, what he feels, and what he says is what I see and know. If he were in possession of a GPS and activated it, then I could tell you exactly where he is, because the coordinates would register in his brain. Understand? But he is not carrying such a device."

"Spare me speculations," Dr. Wong snapped back. "What do you make out?"

"Right now, he's eating. He must be very hungry. I see a field of corn, ripe ears of corn. He's devouring whole stalks. There is a voice in the distance. It's the voice of a young boy, but I don't understand what he's saying. It's a language I don't understand. The voice is coming closer. He seems to be calling a name."

"What name?"

"I don't understand. Now we're running. The boy's coming closer, and he's beating on my back. He's holding me by the neck. I feel a strong pull on my neck. He's still hitting me. It's a stick; he is striking me with a stick."

"The professor must be riding a horse," Joe asserted.

"Are we coming any closer to the source?" Dr. Wong said, ignoring Joe's comment.

"The signal's getting stronger. I think we should go down now. I think we're real close. Down there, yes, it's coming from that direction, from that little forest over there. Let's land in the meadow. That's a perfect place. He's somewhere in this forest."

Just as the helicopter came to a stop, a small boy came running out of the woods chasing a donkey.

"That's him, that's him!" Richard screamed excitedly.

"That's a boy chasing a donkey," Dr. Wong said sarcastically.

Joe, who was sitting next to his friend, pulled the head gear off Richard, trying to get a better reading. He saw his government pension slipping away in clouds as thick as the ones he had been watching covering the Altai Mountains in the distance.

Richard's face went pale as a bleached towel. Dr. Wong screeched at him, demanding explanations.

"I've no idea what's happening, Doc. The signal is definitely coming from the beast. Professor Barker wouldn't fill his stomach with raw corn, would he?"

"Don't try to be smart, young man," Dr. Wong snapped back. "Why's your machine connecting us with an animal?"

"I've no idea. I'm so sorry, but I have no explanation."

Joe took off the head gear. He looked as pale as his friend. "I've no explanation either," Joe stuttered. "I think we're missing some crucial detail here. Perhaps we should take the machine back to the drawing board."

Nine

The next morning Dr. Wong was on her way to India to attend an urgent meeting of the Science Council. On approach to Chhatrapati Shivaji National Airport of Mumbai, the government-issued jet was diverted to a military airfield nearby. As soon as she got off the plane, a messenger from the Science Council headquarters met Dr. Wong on the runway and directed her to a waiting helicopter.

"Sorry for the inconvenience," the Indian man shouted over the noise of the jet. "I have orders to bring you immediately to headquarters."

"Why did we not land at Chhatrapati?" Dr. Wong asked.

"Terrorists have taken over the airport, we hope only temporarily. Religio-fascists. The meeting is in less than an hour. You will have barely time to catch your breath."

After a short flight they arrived on the landing pad on top of the central command headquarters. As soon as Dr. Wong got out of the chopper, Carlisle came up to her and seized her arm.

"You must come with me. I was waiting for you. We have good news and bad news. Bad news first. Let's go."

Before she even could properly greet her friend, the two members of the council found themselves in a wing of the building that was often used for interrogations. Carlisle asked her to wait. He pushed a few buttons on his communicator. In front of them on the teleport appeared a contraption that looked like a sophisticated hospital bed. The cramped surroundings suggested that the whole scene was located inside an aircraft. The steady humming of jet engines confirmed the location. On the bed in front of them was an unconscious body, hooked up to wires and tubes. The person appeared to be in a deep coma. Just then a doctor in a white hospital gown entered the cabin.

"I assume you recognize the patient?" Carlisle asked his friend. Only then Dr. Wong looked closer and indeed recognized Professor Barker.

"Barker?" Dr. Wong was utterly surprised and her voice expressed disbelief. "How did you find him?"

"Never mind how we found him. The point is *your* people lost track of him, as you well know. So we had to do something."

"You shadowed my operation again?" Dr. Wong was taken by surprise.

"The good news is we found him," Carlisle said, ignoring Dr. Wong's question. "Now I must ask you, what were you thinking? This man is far too important for us to send him on a no-return mission. Sending him on the Altai expedition was a mistake, especially when considering the possible finality of the outcome. But, alas, I should have briefed you earlier."

Without waiting for an answer from his surprised friend, Carlisle continued, "The attending physician is Dr. Eisenstadt." Raising his voice, Carlisle addressed the projected doctor who presently was busy reading the vital signs of his patient. "Can you hear us, doctor?" Again he turned to Dr. Wong. "Dr. Eisenstadt is a specialist in rare brain conditions and neurological disorders, which is a perfect sequel to the bad news."

Dr. Wong felt she had been chastised for something she had done without full knowledge of the circumstances. She was clearly upset and dismayed over the fact that Carlisle's people had evidently apprehended Barker's wife and possibly even liquidated her, and then made it appear like suicide. Now it appeared that Carlisle also had interfered with Professor Barker's expedition. This was an operation, which Dr. Wong herself had carefully strategized. Now she found that Carlisle had simply ignored her. *It's high time for me to level with him, just not now. I have to wait for the right occasion.*

Carlisle had already turned his attention back to Eisenstadt, who had just finished monitoring the instruments. "Please, Doctor

Eisenstadt. Tell us what you have found. What is the diagnosis? Have you come to a conclusion? When will we be able to interview Professor Barker? We at the council are eagerly waiting for your report."

Dr. Eisenstadt set his glasses a little higher up on his nose. "As you know, the comatose body of the patient was flown to Moscow, where I was consulted. The team of physicians investigating the case initially could not agree on a diagnosis so they called me. My preliminary findings are this: Professor Barker is suffering from a severe case of Klein-Levin syndrome, a quite rare disease. It only affects about two dozen people at any given time around the world. In fact, no case of this sickness has been reported for the past ten years."

"And what can you tell me about this disease, Doctor? What is the prognosis?"

Klein-Levin syndrome belongs to the recurrent hypersomniac group. It is a rare and generally benign disease, occurring usually only in young men ten to twenty-five years of age. Since our professor is well out of this age range, we must keep an open mind as to finding a completely different diagnosis. Until then we must go with what we know.

"The diagnosis of Klein-Levin is first of all clinical. The hypersomniac episodes, joined to psychiatric symptoms, are irregularly recurrent, and extend quite possibly for years. Diagnosis is uneasy during the first episode and in the attenuated forms. Since this illness has been first recognized, a total of not more than five hundred cases have been described all around the world, but it's highly likely that many patients have not been registered.

"This syndrome is what we generally call a primary pathological hypersomnia. From a clinical point of view, the cardinal and constant symptom is an inability to stay awake. From a therapeutic point of view, prescription of psycho stimulant drugs is recommended, and some treatments are used in a preventive way such as Lithium and Carbamazepine. But I must add with caution that in the present case several of these general indications do not apply. Professor Barker's case is, in other words, highly unusual."

"I am much obliged for your exhaustive and, I must say, somewhat inconclusive diagnosis, Doctor," Carlisle said sarcastically.

"I wish I could give you a better prognosis."

"Have you begun administering any drugs?" Carlisle asked.

"We started an intravenous regimen of Lithium and Carbamazepine a few hours ago."

"Dr. Eisenstadt, can I ask you a question? I am of course not a physician, and I'm sure you know what you're doing. I am just curious," Dr. Wong asked.

"Dr. Wong, as I indicated, these drugs are used more as a preventative measure. There is no known cure for the disease. And in our case, the patient seems to be non-responsive."

"So are you telling me that Professor Barker is not available, not even for a brief interview? He does wake up at times, does he not?"

"It is too early to tell. If the patient behaves in accordance with the known history of similar cases, the answer is yes. But as of now we have not found any brain activity while our instruments simultaneously tell us that the brain is not dead. His physical body only appears active."

"Keep us informed of any changes in the condition. And, please, call us immediately should Professor Barker regain consciousness. We will talk to you soon, Doctor. And I am requesting you stay with the body until it is safely turned over into our custody here in Mumbai." With that, Carlisle cut off the communication and turned to his bewildered friend.

"There are a number of things I am not in agreement with. We need to talk. But aren't we supposed to meet with the council this very minute?" Dr. Wong asked.

"First things first. I know you are upset. But please, let me fill you in. There are some details you need to know," Carlisle said.

"Look at you, you're exhausted. By god, I haven't even had the chance to welcome you properly."

"Forget the niceties."

"You need to understand the big picture, so please, bear with me. Once I have filled you in, I promise I will let you talk. But now, you must listen."

Dr. Wong knew that it was better to listen. If there were questions in her mind they would have to be dealt with later. Carlisle continued: "I have canceled the meeting. There was no longer any need. Everything has been worked out as planned. That is the other piece of good news. I hope you brought that bottle of Crimean champagne."

"I am not in the mood for celebration."

"Then I will drink it alone. Indeed. Meet the new head of the Science Council. President Dean Carlisle has been confirmed. How is that for a surprise?"

"Well, congratulations—my sincerest congratulations to you! You have indeed reached the top," Dr. Wong gasped. Even though she was taken by surprise over the speed of Carlisle's advance she had seen it coming and quickly decided that the best strategy was to play along.

"You are very welcome, dear Ping. I assume you have decided to accept my proposition and become my vice-president."

"I truly appreciate your trust." Dr. Wong almost gagged as she said this. "I hope this can be arranged without having the appearance of—"

"Don't you worry a bit. Everything is under control. I canceled the meeting because everything is fine. I will brief you later about the details. But first I must ask you for another favor."

"I hope I'll be able to comply. Frankly, I expected some praise for putting this operation to the Altai together. By the way, whatever problems you had with me sending Barker, I could not foresee them. He seemed an ideal candidate. Perhaps you need to brief me better."

"I'm so sorry. I promise for the next mission you will be fully briefed."

"It's time to let out the details."

"This time I need you to...It's about Viswamitra, the former president."

"What about him?"

"There is a little problem: he does not know."

"You must be kidding. You're not telling me he still believes he is the president?"

"Technically, yes."

"What do you mean? He was not informed right away? What else did I miss? If you want me to effectively work for you I must know everything. Is that understood?"

"Of course, of course. Viswamitra is in his residence, but we control all his communications. So for the time being he is safe."

"You mean you are safe. And he doesn't know."

"That's where you come in." Carlisle looked at her expectantly.

"Me?"

"Yes, you will tell him. We have made an appointment for you with him in his palace. He's expecting you. You will, how shall I say, gently inform him and if necessary..."

"You do the slaughtering, but when it comes to delicate diplomacy you choose a woman—the only woman on board. I understand."

"Oh, you are so astute. I personally convinced all the other members. The top prize I left for you. The helicopter is waiting. Perhaps we need more than diplomacy from you if you know what I mean. Viswamitra is not exactly predictable. I have a bad feeling about him. Find out what he's up to. Use your best skills, Ping."

"Before I go on this mission, you must brief me fully."

Carlisle looked surprised. "I thought I just did." He noticed Dr. Wong's reaction and quickly added: "Of course, dear, what would you like to know?"

"Forget the dear. I want to know everything," Dr. Wong said. "If you want my cooperation, I want to know everything about Dr. Barker's work. Why is he so extraordinarily important that you scolded me for sending him on one of the most sensitive missions facing us today? What could be more important than getting the coordinates of the assembly in the Altai Mountains? What do you know about his research? You must tell me before I go on this mission. I need to know!"

Ten

"Here is what we know: Barker appears to have found proof for the existence of a new dimension, a field of mind or consciousness," Carlisle explained while Dr. Wong listened intently. "This unknown consciousness field could hold the key to the understanding of the human mind. Needless to say, it could also explain recent events. You can imagine the tremendous importance of this discovery. If his formula is correct, Barker's name will be up there with those of Newton, Maxwell, and Einstein. Speculating that such a field exists is one thing, having the mathematical proof, quite another. I can't even imagine what kind of technological breakthroughs could come from this. The age of intelligent machines,—and the human being?— A mere link in the chain."

Dr. Wong nodded as if in total agreement. "I see what you mean. Just like Newton's discoveries unlocked gravity, Maxwell's equations harnessed electricity, and Einstein's formula proved the existence of curved space and the absolute speed of light, so Barker's equations could provide technological access to this mysterious Akashic Field. The architecture of consciousness finally revealed." Dr. Wong fully understood the impact of this discovery. Deep inside she shuttered when she contemplated what a man like Carlisle would do with this power. But she decided not to let her guards down. This was not the right time to confront Carlisle.

"That's it. I knew you of all people would understand the importance of this knowledge right away." Carlisle took her silence for agreement. "Now you know everything we know, and I hope I can count on your full support." Carlisle sent Dr. Wong on her way convinced that he was sending a friend and supporter.

A short time later, Dr. Wong boarded a helicopter. After several hours in the air, the chopper dropped down in the midst of a maze of lush green, manicured gardens surrounded by falling waters and toppled with native flowering bushes. This secluded island was the preferred presidential residence.

As the chopper descended, Dr. Wong recognized, beneath the dark blue waters of Lake Pichola and in the middle of the lake, the L-shaped residence of the president. The sparkling white marble buildings surrounded by spectacular, multicolored gardens had in the past served as a luxury hotel and before that as the residence of powerful Indian nobility. More recently, it had been converted again into the residence of the world leader and head of the Science Council.

"Ah, welcome, welcome!" President San Viswamitra greeted his guest with open arms as Dr. Wong swiftly moved away from the churning blades of the chopper. "We've been expecting you." The aging president tossed a piece of meat to his two Labrador dogs playing near him. "These animals love eating meat. It is their nature, of course. We humans have a choice. Wouldn't you agree, my dear doctor?"

"Of course, Mister President, how could I disagree? So you've been expecting me?"

Secretly Dr. Wong was hoping that Viswamitra had figured out for himself what was going on, which would make her job so much easier.

"Your arrival was announced to me, of course. But no one told me your mission. That, I believe, was left up for me to figure out."

"And? Did you? I mean, could you guess the purpose of my coming?" Though Dr. Wong tried to be diplomatic about this, she had the immediate feeling that this would not be easy. Viswamitra let out a little laugh and threw another piece of meat to the dogs, which they devoured eagerly.

"In the English language, the word dog backwards spells G-O-D. It seems for Anglos these two creatures are closely related. What do you think? It's just a matter of direction: read it from the left you get a vicious beast, take it from the right you face the most powerful being in the universe, uncontested as it is, not like in the ancient religions where gods, just like dogs, had to struggle for survival. Everything in nature has two faces. I myself prefer Shiva. I saw the writing on the wall, as they say. As everyone near me knows, my interest is not at all in power. I once believed that through my involvement with the council I could truly benefit humankind. But that seems a difficult task indeed. At times it seems hopeless."

Briefly Dr. Wong had the impression that the old man looked sad, even discouraged. "I am sorry to be the messenger of bad news then."

"Oh, my dear doctor, don't be sorry. Not at all indeed. It has nothing to do with you. The messenger of bad news is quite often the unsuspecting victim. Let's not invoke pity either. We are both in the same boat. And you have now the more difficult task. When I was at the rudder I was often bogged down by the weight of responsibility. Now it is your turn. You must make difficult decisions. I am an old man. According to the customs of my people, it would be the right time for me to relinquish my past. You will understand what I mean."

"They made a decision to go ahead with the plan even without your input."

Now that Dr. Wong knew that the president was informed about the council's decision, she tried to bring the conversation on a more urgent path. She sensed that Viswamitra understood the full purpose of her visit, and there was no need to be cautious. On the other hand, the aging diplomat could be playing an elaborate game.

"They did?" The president sounded almost casual. "I am not surprised. Were you?"

The chopper had already taken off again, and the noise of the blades disappeared in the distance. The lavish gardens surrounding them made an organic statement of silence. Only the murmuring of running water, splashing from one bowl down to the next, gave a background of peace and tranquility. Under the gray water in a nearby pond swarms of gigantic coy swam about in their silent ways.

This bucolic picture was enhanced by the president's appearance. In his white tunic that left his right shoulder exposed, he gave the impression of a sage. A white beard flowed freely from his face. A string of expensive pearls was slung around his otherwise bare neck, and another string of beads flowed through his fingers as he talked, carefully choosing each word. This man whom Dr. Wong only knew from official meetings and government functions to which he always came dressed in impeccable Western-style suits now appeared rather more like an ancient Hindu holy man.

"No," Dr. Wong said. "I was not surprised. Even though initially I was skeptical, as you well know, you must admit, it is a unique chance."

"What horrific times we live in, when the killing of millions of innocent people is considered a unique chance. Please forgive my emotions. At what time is the eradication supposed to take place?" President Viswamitra asked. He appeared collected again and carefully choosing each word.

"The other council members wanted to go ahead immediately."

"But I objected."

"Since you objected, they called another meeting and—"

"—decided to go ahead without my consent. I know. Tell them I offer my resignation. I will not cause them any difficulties. This is not why I took on the job. Now I know my direction. Tell them they have my deep gratitude."

"Well, sir, I am deeply grateful that you are taking the news so graciously. I suppose there is no longer any need to take more of your precious time. I will relay your wishes and be on my way. I am only sorry my transportation has already left. Perhaps I can recall it since there is no longer need for me here." Dr. Wong saw an opportunity for a fast retreat, feeling that her mission was accomplished.

"Quite to the contrary, I invite your extended presence. I trust you are not in any hurry, my dear doctor? Now that the thorny part of your mission is over, don't you think it would be splendid to spend some social time together? I'd like to chat with you, for a while at least, totally inconsequential of course, as one private person to another. I might now be on the other side of power, but I am still interested in world affairs, you see."

"I am flattered you think of me as one who can entertain your vast knowledge," Dr. Wong answered diplomatically and with caution.

"Please, please. I know well what an outstanding scientist you are. Your fame travels ahead of your presence like a shining arc. Tell me about the collision experiment."

"I would be obliged to. What would you like to know?"

"You supervised the collision in the Lake Baikal Accelerator Station? Honor me with your report. And keep in mind you are speaking to a non-physicist. But please speak frankly, I insist."

They sat down at a small table in a garden pavilion surrounded by lush ivy.

"But you have been briefed on everything," Dr. Wong protested. She tried to avoid a lengthy involvement.

"Please, please, I'd like to hear your perspective," Viswamitra insisted. "I have been waiting for the chance to have some private time with such an eminent scientist. You must accept my invitation to stay a day or two. You can take the English room in the west wing. Consider it yours. It has a lovely little balcony overlooking the gardens. I hope you accept."

"How can I refuse such a gracious invitation?" Dr. Wong said, wondering how much choice she really had in the matter, given the fact that she was on an island completely cut off from the outside world.

"But now your report, I am looking forward to your insights. Truly remarkable things have happened, have they not? Or do I sense you are tired? Perhaps we can continue our conversation tomorrow morning over breakfast. My servant will show you to your room."

"That is most kind of you. I will do my best to give you a full report in the morning. I am indeed quite exhausted and will enjoy the rest."

A servant had quietly been waiting in the distance. Now he approached them after Viswamitra had given him a wink. The servant politely accompanied Dr. Wong to her room in the west wing. When entering the luxurious suite, she noticed that her luggage had already been placed inside. It crossed her mind that this must have been executed before she had given her consent to stay for the night, even before they had addressed the topic of her staying at all, reaffirming her earlier thoughts. Immediately she checked out the plasma to see if she could get any news. A prompt asked her to enter her personal identification. News programs were tailored to personal interests and needs. Everyone's preferences were conveniently stored in a central computer. This of course also allowed government agencies to pipe in only the news that someone was meant to receive.

Dr. Wong put her hand on the device for identity recognition. After a short moment she was connected. The broadcast by the Central Science News team brought the most recent events from Mumbai airport. The radical religio-fascist takeover had ended in their defeat by government troops. Then the news was interrupted by an urgent bulletin. The speaker announced that President Viswamitra had given his resignation and stepped down. In a related report, the news bureau announced that a government airplane scheduled to land at a military field had been diverted by insurgents to an unknown location. Abruptly the broadcast stopped and the screen fell silent, leaving Dr. Wong with a new set of questions.

Momentarily she checked her whole body for a listening device. Since the invention of microscopically small nano-transmitters, it had become nearly impossible to avoid surveillance. She could easily have ingested such a device with her meal. It would reside in her body for at least twenty-four hours and transmit everything she said to whoever listened. From her purse she retrieved an antidote, which, when ingested, within minutes would purge her body of such devices.

Then she tried to use her specially secured communicator, but repeated attempts to make a connection with Carlisle failed. She realized that she was completely isolated from the outside world.

While this situation was strange, Dr. Wong was in no way unaccustomed to it. Never married, she had been pursuing a career as an intelligence agent from an early age. For many years she had worked as a secret agent before dedicating her life to science. As an agent she had found herself many times in similar situations. Disconnected from her support, she had to learn quickly to rely solely on her own instincts and skills, qualities she would have hardly acquired in the world of politics. Now her senses were acute, and like an animal in danger she noticed every slightest movement— every new sound. Even while sleeping she stayed alert. Her life could depend on this.

Before retiring for the night, she stepped out on the balcony to enjoy the evening. It was indeed a most gorgeous sight. In the setting sun, she had a beautiful view over the lake, while right in front of her were the pristinely manicured gardens of the palace estate. A sense of peace and calm radiated from everywhere, betraying the explosive nature of the current situation.

In the middle of the night, not long after retiring, Dr. Wong was awoken by a familiar vibrating sound. The thumping blades of a chopper increased in volume by the minute. She rose immediately and was fully alert instantaneously. After throwing on a dark outfit over her white nightgown she stepped out onto the balcony. Standing outside in the chilly night air, she saw the lights of the chopper approaching the island. Shortly before descending for landing the lights were turned off, and the sound of the blades became almost inaudible. Then the aircraft landed, and the tropical night fell completely silent again. From where she was she could not see what was going on at the landing pad beyond the garden.

Dr. Wong slipped back into her room and out into the hallway. There she took a place at a window opening onto the yard that was surrounded by the main buildings of the palace. From here she could overlook the whole inner yard. Everything lay in silence, and she almost wanted to leave her post to look for another place from where she was better able to observe. Her instincts told her that something important was going to happen. Just as she started to move away from the window, the gate opposite her building opened up. A group of dark figures, she counted at least four, carried a heavy freight right across the yard before they disappeared in the south wing of the palace. It looked like the body of a person on a stretcher. A few minutes later a light turned on in one of the rooms on the upper floor of the south wing. The lights flicked before it was dark again and everything lay in silence.

Back in her room she tried again to contact Carlisle, without success. Unsure of what to do next, she stretched out on her comfortable bed to get some sleep before morning. But her mind did not let her rest. She needed to know what freight had been delivered here in the middle of the night. Approaching the other building through the yard would be too risky because of the dogs. The only possible access to the room in the south wing would be over the roof. Even moving along the roof it was possible that the dogs could sense her presence. She knew that she had to be extremely careful.

In the evening she had observed that the various buildings of the palace were interconnected and that the roofs between them had only a moderate incline. She was confident that she could reach the other wing with ease. Dr. Wong slipped out on the balcony and surveyed the access to the roof above. She swung her slender body up to the rim of the roof and slid up the gentle incline, carefully avoiding making any noise. The moon had come up and illuminated the wooden shingles.

Soon Dr. Wong reached the south part of the palace and looked for a way to access the rooms below. Looking over the side of the roof she quickly spotted a veranda and lowered herself down. The glass door leading into a dark room was unlocked. She was ready to enter the room when she heard steps and then voices. She recognized the voice of the president. The other voice had a strong foreign accent. She was certain that she had heard it before. What were these people up to? She listened intently, hardly allowing herself to breathe. The voices came nearer and stopped in front of the room where Dr. Wong was hiding. She could now clearly hear the president's voice.

"I am grateful, my dear doctor, for trusting us with your precious cargo. I can't tell you how much this means to us. With the help of the Almighty we will get the information we need. Needless to say, of course, all depends on the patient's condition. In his present state he will bring us little benefit. I know your diagnosis is hopeful. Please, Doctor, do your best. We need him alive. I must speak to him. In the meantime, I will find out exactly how much my Chinese visitor knows. She is our best bet right now to continue our efforts. Much is at stake. I have a guard placed in the room so when he wakes up we will be notified immediately. In the meantime I wish you a good night. You deserve some rest."

The door opened, and the president entered the room followed by the person he had called doctor. Dr. Wong quickly swung herself up to the roof and began her climb back to her room. For now she had all the information necessary to plan her next move, though questions abounded. She quickly put the newscast together with the body delivered here to the compound and concluded that it was no other than Jesse Barker who had been kidnapped, and the strange voice of the other person belonged to none other than the doctor she had met in cyberspace a few hours earlier.

So the trusted Dr. Eisenstadt turned out to be a traitor. It also was clear to her why these people had an interest in interrogating Jesse. After the briefing by Carlisle about Barker's research, she completely understood the importance of this precious cargo.

Although in general terms Jesse's discoveries were well known, the underlying mathematics and the exact nature of his theory could change the course of history. Being familiar with the general ideas of the theory was one thing; being able to use the equations and develop new technologies could promise nearly unlimited power over the human mind. Every party involved raced to be first. Each wanted to beat the enemy and get hold of the secret to power and control. Dr. Wong tossed and turned using all her mental powers to find rest. Finally she fell into a light but relaxing sleep.

Eleven

Ever since Melissa Barker had left her home that fateful morning, she thought of her journey to the East as an extended vision quest. Her arrest and detention, the interrogation that followed, and her escape from the SuperMaxRobomate—in her mind this was all part of a larger plan. Confinement in the SuperMaxRobomate was often used for corrective education. A few weeks in robotic confinement without any human contact would convince the most hardened ideologue to return to the accepted path. But in Melissa's case, the fact that a giant electronic super brain operated the whole prison had played out in her favor. On the morning she escaped, she simply walked out of the prison, in spite of its multiple security gates. It was as if the robotic eyes had been unable to detect and the robotic arms incapable of apprehending her.

The crime she was charged with was her participation in tribal ceremonies and her involvement with Native American spiritual practices. In those secret meetings leading up to this day she had learned the ways of her ancestors. Going on a sacred quest was something her Hopi people, the ancestors of her birth father, had been undertaking since the dawn of time. As much as she appreciated her Western upbringing, she had become increasingly more involved in her native heritage.

While growing up, her mother had never told her much about her father. All she knew was that her bio-dad had died in a car crash when she was only two. Therefore Melissa had grown up knowing little about her father's native tribe. But as she grew into adulthood, she became more and more interested in her heritage, and the more she read and learned the more her fascination grew. She had joined a secretive support group of native people, even though in her area few natives had survived and even fewer were inclined to preserve the tribal ways. Ancestral customs, she found, had been exceedingly spiritual. Unfortunately the new Scientific Purity laws had outlawed even these time-honored expressions of ancient wisdom.

Once out of prison Melissa had found her way to the familiar underground assembly underneath the Great Mall where she met up with thousands of like-minded people. Soon she had followed the march of people moving eastward. They mostly used land transportation, trains, buses, and often they walked on foot. After several months of trekking, during which time they had joined up with more and more people, they finally had made it to the Siberian tundra. In the distance they could see the snow-covered peaks of the Altai Mountains coming closer. A cool wind blew from the west and became stronger as they moved on. With every passing hour, the crowd of about a thousand people became more excited.

Melissa spotted a young man among the people walking a little ahead of her. He had thinly braided blond hair floating down his shoulders. Even from the back she recognized him. His name was Frederik, a Caucasian chap in his early twenties. She had briefly met him a few days earlier when passing through Moscow. After their short encounter, Melissa knew that the two of them could easily become friends and hoped to meet him again soon. Frederik was an upbeat fellow, but he did not appear shallow. Melissa was eager to catch up with him after they had lost sight of each other in the crowds. But her feet were hurting badly from all the walking.

"Frederik!" Melissa shouted. "Wait up for me."

The young man turned around and recognized his friend. He slowed down his pace and waited for Melissa. When she caught up with him, he said, "Hello there, tired? Of course you are. Exciting, though, isn't it?"

Melissa was happy to see him. "My feet hurt quite a bit today. It's been weeks of walking."

"Soon we will be there, and we all can rest."

"I know," Melissa said, smiling. "Everyone is so full of optimism, but really, no one knows. Don't you think this whole thing is a little weird?"

"You can't have doubt in your heart, you know. The prophecy may not come true," Frederik said with a strange smirk on his face. Melissa was not sure whether he tried to make a joke or whether he was serious.

"You really mean that?" she asked, probing his face for a sign of cynicism.

"Maybe you do need rest," Frederik continued without engaging her doubt. "Over there, there's a little shed. Let's go there, out of the wind, and rest for a while. I'm sure we'll be able to catch up in the morning. And if not, it seems this trek of people never ends. We'll just pick up the next group tomorrow and follow them."

Melissa did not object to a little rest. They left the caravan and found a dry place, sheltered from the cold wind, inside a hut that was erected by some native farmer. The hut was only half filled with dry hay. Melissa immediately threw off her shoulder sack and stretched out on the hay.

When Frederik hesitated, she pulled him down playfully and said, "Come on, carpe diem. Let's enjoy this moment." He was taken by surprise, lost his balance, and stumbled on top of his new friend.

Quickly pulling back Frederik said shyly, "Stop it. We barely know each other."

Melissa laughed and said, "Sorry for moving in on you too fast."

"You Americans are so direct." Frederik took a seat next to her in the hay. His face even seemed to blush.

"Forget your Scandinavian shyness," Melissa laughed. "That's where you're from, isn't it? Originally? I can detect an accent."

"Actually I'm German. But these days that does not make much difference. The world has come so close together."

"Do you speak German?"

"In my family, we do. But our school instruction was all in English. It's the law. That's another one of those stupid ideas, don't you think?"

Melissa agreed.

"They try to wipe out all differences. We all speak the same. We all buy the same stuff. We even are supposed to dress the same and look the same."

"I like your dreadlocks." Playfully Melissa touched a strand of his hair and felt its texture. When she saw Frederik's uneasiness, she laughed again in her innocent way and said, "That's funny. Does that make you feel uncomfortable? Okay, let's change subjects. Do you still go to school? How did you get involved with this?"

"I don't even know where you are from." Frederik was curious.

'Me? I'm from Frankfort."

"Frankfurt? No way. That's where I'm from. Don't say you're German too."

Melissa laughed again. "Now that's real funny. Frankfort, not Frankfurt." She strained to pronounce the second Frankfurt in German. "Frankfort is a small town in Illinois, right outside of Chicago. It's a real small town. A few years back they built a university nearby, so I guess now it's not so small anymore. How large a town is your Frankfurt? I know it's pretty big."

"Frankfurt is big, all right, but much of it is in ruins once again. But what about you? Do you still go to school?" Frederik asked.

"Yes, I'm a student. What do you do?"

"This may sound funny. I'm a cyber-athlete."

"Oh, one of those?" Melissa said.

"So you know?"

"Yes, of course. They are quite popular in my country. Do you do world competitions?"

"I have, but not anymore. I actually quit since I had an experience."

"An experience? What kind of experience?" Melissa asked curiously.

"Back home it's not really cool to talk about it, you know."

"I know what you mean. It's not cool to talk about certain things in my country either. But I mostly ignore it. You have to know who you are sharing your ideas with."

"That's just it. You never know. Everybody can be a spy, at least that's how it is in Germany, or what's left of it. Everything seems to come from the top down. The Greens are everywhere."

"Same here. We call them the GYs. But here we are among us, don't you think? I don't believe the guards have infiltrated this trek. This is different. People say that they can't even see us on their satellites."

"Rumors."

"You don't believe it?"

"Who knows? You just never know these days. Everybody is suspicious of everybody. I have learned to live with it."

"That's pretty sad. So why did you bring it up?"

"What? Oh, that with the experience?"

"Yes, and by the way, I had an experience too—several experiences. If you tell me yours, I'll tell you mine. You can trust me. I wouldn't be here if I wanted to turn you in. Honestly."

"Never mind. Of course I trust you."

"So then go ahead. Tell me." Melissa poked her new friend.

"When I look back, it's really not all that much. Perhaps it meant nothing. I actually never talked about it with anyone. Maybe my mind was just playing tricks on me. That's how they explain everything, right? That's how you can explain everything—even the weirdest things."

"Give me a try. I understand weird, believe me. And no, I don't believe that you can understand everything that way. Some things are different. Come on. Give me a try," Melissa insisted, but when she noticed that her newfound friend still hesitated, she quickly said, "Okay, then I'll go first. Here is my story. As a child I must have been very fragile. I had many fevers and no doctor could give any good reason. It was something I just learned to live with. During several of those episodes, I had visitors. They came to me and talked to me. It was very real. Often they were Native Americans, Indians, as people call them. As a child I did not know that my real father was a Hopi. That is one of the most spiritual Indian tribes. Do you know them?"

"I've heard about them," Frederik replied.

"My father died when I was very young, so I don't remember him. But in my encounters I met him—several times. I can still see him and hear him speak to me. One time I must have talked in my fever and mentioned a name, Cha'risa Catori. When I finally came out of the fever my mother asked me what I meant when I kept saying Cha'risa Catori. First I was surprised. How did she know? But then she explained to me that I had said these words in my fever. I told her that it was the name of a man I had met in my dream and that was what he called himself.

"She looked at me strangely, but then she held me really tight. I must have been about four years old then. She probably thought that I was still too little to tell me the truth. Only in my dreams things were right." Melissa stopped for a while reminiscing about her childhood.

Frederik, suddenly gaining confidence, said, "I don't think I ever dream; that is, I never dreamed when I was younger. But why don't you go on. I really want to hear about your experiences."

"A few years later, I was walking through a forest behind our house. We lived in a small settlement then. My mother was quite poor. That was before she met my new father, my stepfather, I mean. She married my stepfather when I was about seven. He is a professor at the new university they built in Frankfort. He was always very good to me and showed me many things. The last time I saw my other father, my Hopi father, was a few days before my mother introduced me to my stepfather. I played often in the woods and was never afraid. My mother always was so worried. He came from behind a tree. I recognized him. He said that I was on my path and that I should trust my new father. I didn't even know that my mom was seeing anyone. My father hugged me and said that I will learn great things and that my mission was to reconcile the wisdom of the elders with the white man's knowledge. That's what he said. And that I should not be afraid of anything, whatever happened. He would be looking out for me. Then he disappeared, and I never saw him again."

"How strange. Was it true? Did you get a new father?" Frederik asked when Melissa paused.

"When I came home that day, my mother was waiting for me," Melissa said and paused again as if lost in the past.

"Sorry for interrupting," Frederik said. "Why don't you go on?"

"Immediately when I entered the house she called for me and said that she wanted me to meet someone. It was Jesse. That's my father now, my stepfather. She said that he would be looking out for us now, and that he and she had decided to get married. Within a few weeks we moved to his house in Frankfort. I always wished for my birth father to come back, though I had nothing to complain about with my stepfather. He has always been good to me. Do you understand what I mean?"

Frederik just nodded. Melissa noticed sadness in his face. Perhaps he was thinking of his own family.

"Go on, please," he said.

"I hope I'm not boring you."

"No, no, quite to the contrary," Frederik said. "It's interesting. I like to know about your past."

"It's getting late and morning will come soon. Perhaps we should get some sleep."

"No, no, quite the opposite. I couldn't sleep now anyhow. Please go on," Frederik insisted. "As long as you're not too tired we can continue. This interests me very much."

"I have a bit of an ache in my throat," Melissa said. "Maybe I'm getting a cold."

Frederik searched through his bag and pulled out a root. "Here, chew on this. This will give you strength."

"What is it?" Melissa asked curiously.

"It's something I learned in the Amazon. An herbal remedy the native people use."

"Thanks." Melissa began chewing on the root.

"Do you find this all very strange?" she asked after a while.

"Not at all." Frederik's answer came back slowly and after a pause. Melissa noticed that he was yawning.

"You are tired," she said. "We should try to get some sleep. We have a hard day of walking ahead of us. They say it's still about a day's walk to the entrance."

Melissa continued chewing on the stick. When she looked again at Frederik he was already asleep. She watched his strange and yet familiar face for a long time. His deep blue eyes were now shut, and she saw a pair of soft brunette eyelashes covering them. His hair was bright blond, almost yellow, and he had freckles on his face. Frederik was a tall young man, thin and sporty looking. He wore a soft fiber suit made from nano-material that kept the body warm or cool, depending on the outside temperature. The material self-adjusted to the needs of the body.

Many people had switched to this kind of body cover. You could not argue with the extreme usefulness of such a fabric. At night, it doubled as a comfortable sleeping bag, never being too hot or too cold. Frederik's suit had an added advantage of providing a shimmer of light in the dark, so a flashlight was rarely needed. Melissa knew these types of suits well but had never owned one herself. She liked the fact that she could recognize her surroundings in the glimmer of light coming from his suit. Flooded in an incandescent blue glare, Frederik appeared to Melissa like an alien being.

Melissa looked up and around and could see the outlines of the old barn. A gaping hole in the roof let a beam of moonlight pour into the dark interior. There was hay in the corner where they were both stretched out now. Suddenly she became aware that someone else was in the shed. She strained her eyes to see but could not detect anything. Large parts of the small building remained in the dark.

"Anyone there?" she asked, raising her voice. The sound of her voice made Frederik stir. She calmed herself thinking that it was probably just her imagination and her restless mind. Moving a little closer to Frederik, she closed her eyes, and after a while she too fell into a light sleep.

In her sleep, she noticed a small snake crawling up her leg. She was not afraid. She actually dreamed of snakes often and considered them her friends. She held out her hand, and the snake crawled up on it and wound itself around her arm. The snake was bright green. As she looked closer, the snake dissolved and disappeared in the darkness.

Twelve

In the morning, Dr. Wong was awakened by a knock at her door. A servant delivered a little card on a silver tablet with the message: "Dear Dr. Wong. You are invited to the Garden Pavilion for breakfast." Next to the card on the tablet was a freshly cut orchid.

How attentive of the old guru, Dr. Wong thought while getting ready for the meeting. With the events of the previous night vividly in her mind, she descended the stairs and was greeted by Viswamitra again with open arms.

"Welcome, my dear doctor. I trust you had a pleasant rest. I have breakfast prepared in the pavilion. You are not frightened of my dogs, are you? Once they have taken your scent they will know you forever." He threw a few pieces of meat to the dogs, which followed him playfully.

After they sat down, Viswamitra said, "You must continue with your report, now that you are rested. I am curious to hear your take on the events of the last few weeks, especially the events at the Baikal Accelerator."

"I will be happy to comply."

"You must tell me every little detail."

"All right then, where should I begin? I guess, since you know the official report, I will give you my own interpretation." Dr. Wong smiled charmingly. She wanted to make the president feel safe and confident in her collaboration with whatever his plans might be. She realized her situation and was aware of her isolation. She had to depend on her own wits to construct a way out while getting as much information as possible about the ex-president's plans.

"That is the spirit, go on, please." The president evidently took the bait.

Dr. Wong began telling the history of GeV1000 the way she had arranged the facts in her own mind. She explained how physicists all over the world had rushed to reach this unimaginably high energy.

She ended by saying, "I must confess the reality of the event left all speculations behind."

"Wasn't Professor Barker at one point one of the leading physicists in that field? Whatever happened to him?" Viswamitra asked casually. *What a pretender to ask such a question*, Dr. Wong thought, *while the poor professor's body is resting unconscious in the south wing of the compound.*

At that moment, another man approached the pavilion. Dr. Wong recognized him immediately. It was Dr. Eisenstadt.

Spotting the doctor, Viswamitra got up and welcomed him: "Ah, Doctor. I am so glad you can join us. Let me introduce you two. I want you to meet my dear friend, the eminent physicist Dr. Wong. Dr. Wong is an honored member of the Science Council and has just recently returned from Lake Baikal, where, as you perhaps know, she took part in an astounding experiment. In fact, we have just been reminiscing, and Dr. Wong began giving me a detailed report. I am sure it will interest you as well, Doctor. And my dear Dr. Wong, this gentleman joining us here is none other than the world famous neurologist, brain specialist, et cetera et cetera, my dear friend, Dr. Eisenstadt. I can't even tell you how happy and honored I am to be in the presence of two such esteemed scientists. But please, do sit down. Let us continue with our report."

Wearing green-checkered knickerbockers, matching green socks, and a khaki army shirt, his head covered with a Tyrolean hat complete with a feather, Dr. Eisenstadt fit the image of a European explorer. In his right hand he swung a delicately carved wooden walking cane. A well-trimmed brown beard almost totally obscured his thin lips.

Viswamitra turned to Dr. Eisenstadt and explained, "Let me fill you in, my dear doctor, as much as I understand from a lay person's perspective. Dr. Wong will be kind enough to correct me if I misrepresent any crucial part. Scientists call it the unitary crisis. You might not know this, but among physicists this unitary crisis has been a matter of much speculation for decades. For years, this event was strictly theoretical. Now it has happened, deep under the icy waters of Lake Baikal."

Turning to Dr. Wong he continued, "But please, Dr. Wong, go on with your eyewitness report. And be assured, Dr. Eisenstadt has my complete confidence. He is privileged to all we know. He is, should I say, as close as anyone could be to the heartbeat of power, if you will forgive my metaphor." Moving to Eisenstadt, he said, "This of course is quite classified information, as you may expect."

Dr. Wong wondered momentarily why Dr. Eisenstadt should be privileged, but then decided to continue. "Physical events can be described in mathematical language. This had been the great accomplishment of Isaac Newton, whose laws of motion once were called eternal laws of nature."

"Ah, the eternal laws of nature?" Viswamitra interrupted. "What a magnificent concept of the Western mind. In reality, everything is in constant flux. Only Brahman is eternal, and yet it is incomprehensible. What a pity." As deeply as the president seemed engaged in abstract thoughts in one moment, in the next he seemed to immerse himself in aesthetic sensuality. Turning to Dr. Eisenstadt, Viswamitra said, "Isn't she a charm, introducing us two lay persons to the intricacies of physical law? What a splendid lecture."

"I am sorry, I didn't mean to…" Dr. Wong felt a little uneasy.

"No, no, to the contrary," the president replied. "I am quite curious to see how you will make the connection to our current state of affairs."

"There seem to be no physical explanation to the present conundrum, as much as I have been wracking my mind. What happened to all attending scientists when finally that ultimate energy was reached cannot be explained in conventional terms. Recent events seem to burst open the limits of materialist science. At least, that's how it appeared initially."

"That is what I have heard. Fascinating. Please carry on. I have a feeling you see a way out, some scientific explanation perhaps that will save the day." Before giving Dr. Wong a chance to answer, Viswamitra turned to Dr. Eisenstadt.

"You see, my dear Dr. Eisenstadt, what happened during the experiment is astounding—outright unscientific. Would you believe that all the attending scientists experienced an old fashioned out-of-body experience, hahaha? Isn't that hilarious?"

"Perhaps only a freak psychotic fluke caused by the stress of the experiment," Dr. Eisenstadt speculated.

"Not at all, dear doctor," Viswamitra interrupted. "Tell him, Dr. Wong. Tell him. You see, what at first appeared to be only an isolated psychotic episode turned out to be shared by every single person present. Not true, Dr. Wong?"

"We all encountered something that could only be characterized as a classical out-of-body experience," Dr. Wong confirmed. She tried to figure out whether the old sage's cynicism was real or whether he actually was mocking their dilemma.

"Astounding!" Viswamitra shouted in glee. "Of course, we all know that such a thing is not supposed to exist. Scientifically, consciousness is considered to be an epiphenomenon, solidly linked to material presence and not capable of existing on its own, independent from the material world. Am I not correct?" Viswamitra looked around almost triumphantly. *What was he trying to prove?*

"What happened here is the stuff of outdated mysteries and erroneous beliefs," Viswamitra exclaimed.

"Have you considered a case of collective psychosis?" Dr. Eisenstadt evidently was missing the tension between Viswamitra and Dr. Wong.

"Of course we considered this," Dr. Wong continued, a little irritated by Viswamitra's arrogance. "Collective psychosis was quite improbable as well."

"And needless to say," Viswamitra finished her sentence, "this would be not any more scientifically acceptable than individual psychosis. Our brave scientists saw no honorable way out. Am I not correct, Dr. Wong?"

Before she could answer, Viswamitra continued, "And then all those people disappearing around the world. Millions of people just vanished. Can you imagine—reports started coming in from around the world of thousands of people simply gone."

Seeing Dr. Wong hesitate, he quickly continued, "Remarkably, those cases reported missing were all identified as, how should I say, spiritual practitioners, believers of some kind, quacks, lunatics, poets, even philosophers. Rumors had it that they were on the way to Siberia, millions of people, but our sophisticated radar was unable to spot them. Gone, disappeared. Had they all become ghosts? I can fully understand the council's frustration. Then when I offered them an explanation, they, in turn, relieved me of my duty."

"You what?" Dr. Wong asked. "An explanation for what?"

"My dear doctor, there are many things in this universe science does not understand and perhaps never will."

"But that does not mean we need to give up trying. Are you saying that you have a logical, a scientific, explanation for the events in the Baikal station?"

"That's precisely what I'm saying. I don't say that I can understand everything, but the parts I cannot explain theoretically I understand by filing the blanks with my personal experiences. I know from experience that higher dimensions exist. I know that consciousness is more than a simple electrical brain function. I know from personal experience that the universe is alive. And on and on."

"You offered that to the council and in return they ousted you?"

"Precisely."

So that's what happened at the council meeting behind closed doors, Dr. Wong thought. *Carlisle obviously didn't tell me the full story.*

"But that is not all yet," Viswamitra continued. "I had already challenged the council during a prior meeting to provide proof.

It was at that point that the council decided to involve that nuclear specialist, an expert in dimensionality, was he not? What was his name again?" Viswamitra asked even though he had mentioned Barker's name a few minutes earlier.

"That is when the council requested Professor Barker to assist us in our analysis." Dr. Wong decided to play along.

"Now rumor has it," Viswamitra speculated, "that the professor succeeded in making some important discoveries about the nature of the fourth dimension. This of course could explain the whole dilemma. And, as everyone is convinced, he has scientific proof, but the professor is unwilling to speak. What a pity. The professor is not in the mood to share his findings with the world. Am I not correct, Dr. Wong?"

Dr. Wong nodded. She tried desperately to keep her composure. Viswamitra continued, "To be perfectly honest, his findings about the fourth dimension are old news to us. Indian philosophers had this knowledge many thousand years ago. I personally would be more interested in his discoveries in cross-species communication. I only wish I could speak with my labs. Perhaps the good professor could help us solve the whole problem of reincarnation."

Viswamitra did not appear to be joking.

"Tell us, Dr. Wong, what became of his visit? You must tell us everything you know about this man, especially what you know about his new theory. Does it indeed contradict the great Einstein? Very remarkable."

Just as Dr. Wong was searching for an answer, a servant approached the group. He whispered something into Viswamitra's ear, which made him get up immediately. Viswamitra excused himself without much formality and rushed off. When he was a few hundred yards away he turned around and shouted back: "Ah, Dr. Eisenstadt, your help is urgently needed. You better come with us. You, Dr. Wong, in the meantime may enjoy the gardens."

Dr. Eisenstadt quickly caught up with the president, and they both disappeared. Dr. Wong instantly went up to her room, contemplating what chance she would have to get off this island. She stepped out onto the balcony when suddenly she heard the sound of a helicopter engine revving up. She grabbed a few of her belongings and ran back down. Carefully avoiding being detected, she crossed through the garden in the direction of the sound. Perhaps this was her ticket out of this prison.

She noticed with satisfaction that a row of dense bushes went right up to the place the helicopter was waiting. Hidden behind a bush as close as possible to the waiting helicopter she heard approaching footsteps. It was Viswamitra and Dr. Eisenstadt.

"Appears we missed our chance," she heard Viswamitra say. "According to the servant, Barker woke up, asked for food, and after drinking some nourishing yogurt, fell immediately back into oblivion. I have never heard of anything like this. We need to catch him awake to find out where he's hiding his secrets. This is our best chance, Doctor. We can't afford another missed opportunity. You will stay with him while I see after things in the camp. I was just informed of trouble in the ranks, so I must have a quick visit on the mainland to see after things. My transportation is waiting."

Thirteen

If it wasn't so awfully windy, I'd be able to enjoy the view, Dr. Wong said to herself. She even managed to put a smile on her face. Suspended in the fuselage of the helicopter, flying at several thousand feet height over Lake Pichole, she saw the northern shore quickly approach. Dr. Wong had managed just in time to find a secure place underneath the helicopter—holding onto the fuselage before Viswamitra boarded—and then the aircraft took off. Now they were descending into a wooded area near the shore. Underneath, she could see a settlement that vaguely looked like an army camp. Hundreds of blockhouses were arranged in neat formation. In a large square, she saw a crowd of several thousand people assembled around a colorfully decorated podium.

The helicopter landed on a small strip away from the crowd. Dr. Wong remained motionless underneath the craft until the blades were turned off, and Viswamitra stepped out. She spotted his feet less than five yards away from her. Two men immediately approached him.

"We are so happy you came right away, Guru. They are expecting clarity from you. Rumors have been coming in all day. Most of all they want to know why they are not the chosen ones. Is it true that the chosen people all were called to the Altai? You must tell us the truth. Unrest is possible."

The group was swiftly moving away from the aircraft and the voices disappeared in the distance. Dr. Wong slipped out from underneath the fuselage, dashed unnoticed across the landing pad, and quickly hid beneath the nearby underbrush. Just then an explosion rocked the air, and she could hear screaming people in the distance. Dr. Wong worked her way carefully through the brushes to get nearer to the source of the commotion. In a clearing, she spotted a group of children around ten to twelve years of age. About forty of them appeared to be engaged in paramilitary exercises. The children were crawling along the ground and combating each other in groups of two. At one point, they all lined up and their youthful commander, not more than eighteen years old, asked them to recite the pledge. With one voice, the youngsters recited:

"We will stand in unity and defend righteousness. Vishnu, Abraham, Jesus, Mohammed, and all messengers of truth, help us overcome conflict and disunity. Long live our prophet."

The children raised their left arms over their heads and made a fist as a sign of solidarity. Under the cover of bushes and trees Dr. Wong quickly moved on to further explore the camp. Soon some barracks appeared in front of her. She observed them for a while and then slipped into the building through an open window. Inside, she landed in a bedroom where a number of uniform-like overcoats were hanging in a closet. This would offer her an ideal disguise. In a few seconds, she walked out into the open, appearing to be one of the camp's supervising staff.

Moving around more freely now, Dr. Wong almost casually strolled along the camp road. Suddenly she spotted a small crowd of people surrounding Viswamitra. With his long white beard and his white flowing outfit he looked like a prophet. Several woman were following, one was bending down kissing his garment. Another woman holding a baby rushed up to Viswamitra and held her baby in front of him to receive his blessing.

"Please, Guru, give him your blessing!" the woman pleaded.

"Woman, do you promise to bring this child up as a peaceful warrior for the cause of goodness to all living things? To be a steward to all life and hurt none? Will you promise this?" Viswamitra asked solemnly. The woman nodded and raised her child a little higher.

"Are you a Muslim then, woman, and is Mohammed your prophet?" Viswamitra asked.

"Yes, Guru, blessed be his name."

"Indeed, blessed be his name and blessed be the child. May your son grow up respecting all religions and all life."

Viswamitra blessed the child. Several other women holding children up to him surrounded the former president but a man approached the group.

"Guru," he said, bowing his head in reverence, "it's good you were able to come. Everything is prepared and the people are waiting."

Viswamitra was guided away to where a large crowd of people was waiting while Dr. Wong followed them cautiously from a distance. She soon mingled in with the crowds when Viswamitra arrived at the podium, which was richly decorated with thousands of exotic flowers. The crowd was nearly hysterical as their prophet approached the stage. Calls of "Father, Guru, Master, Savior, Prophet!" in many different languages filled the air.

"My dear brothers and sisters," Viswamitra began, calming the applause of the crowds. "I know these have been trying days for you. I am so happy that I am able to spend time with you and console you. You are asking me, many of you, whether the end times are truly near. Are the forces of good and evil engulfed in the final battle? I hear you asking these questions. Are we then the holy warriors preparing for the final fight?"

"Yes, tell us, is Armageddon near?" someone shouted.

The crowd was silent now and everyone was intently listening to the master's words.

"My answer might surprise you. I say no. Those who feed you this nonsense are poison mixers, false prophets. They spread those lies in order to instill fear in your hearts and for no other reason."

Another voice was heard shouting from amidst the crowd. "Then why are we not among the saved ones, Guru? Why are we here like lost souls?" the heckler shouted.

"We have done all the right things, have we not?" another one said. A murmur of approval went through the crowd.

"Dear brothers and sisters, I will address all these questions in due time. I know there have been rumors that millions of people have assembled in Siberia. It is true that these things have occurred."

"But why are we not among the saved?" The voice was heard again. "Why are we not among the blessed ones who will ascend to heaven?"

"My dear, faithful brothers and sisters," Viswamitra continued. "You are all assembled here to hear a message of great importance. You are the holy avatar, you are the light in the dark. The world government is on the wrong path. I have relinquished my position as the president of the Science government in protest so I can serve you better. I neither agree with their tactics nor do I approve any longer of their goals. We must start over again. Listen to me carefully. Reason must prevail. But reason is embedded in community. Reason is the voice of our ancestors. We are only as strong as our communities. This is what our ancestors have taught us. We cannot only be concerned about saving ourselves. In isolation we are nothing. We are creatures of this earth. She is our mother. As humanity we have forsaken her for too long. We must start over again, give humanity one final chance to live in peace with all the other creatures that populate this beautiful planet—or the earth will dispose of us like an ugly cancer."

Dr. Wong was taken aback by so much compassion in the old man's voice. It brought up memories of her childhood. In her mind's eye, she saw herself sitting as a little girl on the lap of her grandmother in a tiny village in the mountains near the flower city of Kunming in Southern China. Her grandmother was singing a love song of her native Bai people that now came to her mind. The village people called her grandmother Bimo, someone who communicates with the gods through dancing and singing. During her teen years, young Ping had been selected to attend a boarding school for the advancement of minorities. Later she was privileged to be educated as a scientist and for several years attended Harvard

University. Here she was introduced to the physics of the universe and the intricacies of the Western mind. But she had never completely forgotten how different the standard Western scientific theory of the universe was from the mystical stories told by her ancestors in the little mountain village. Lost in memories, she stood next to Viswamitra who continued with his inspiring speech:

"I once was full of hope," Viswamitra said. "I was full of hope that the universal belief in science would lead humanity away from the throngs of tyranny and war and unite the world. Our dreams were lofty. Through science we believed we could once and for all overcome fear and the senseless division of the universe into heaven and hell. Now I know that this was the right goal, but we chose the wrong path. Fanaticism is rearing its ugly head once more, even in our own ranks."

Suddenly there was a commotion again in the middle of the crowd. A man jumped up onto the podium and shouted: "We have a right to be fanatic! They have taken our faith from us! I was born a Muslim, I will always be a Muslim!"

"And I am Jew!" a young woman screamed. "My ancestors were Jews. You can't take that away from me." Many people in the crowd cheered and applauded.

But Viswamitra calmly explained. "Religions are the manmade spokes of the sacred wheel. Its hub must remain empty so that the holy can manifest itself. In order to reintegrate humanity into the natural order of things, we all must return to some simple values, taught to us by Mother Nature. Those values are not competition and survival of the fittest, but cooperation and community. True science will teach us this as factual. Cooperative communities are the fundamental building blocks of the universe."

Viswamitra looked straight at Dr. Wong as if he was addressing her personally. She wanted to sink into the ground when she saw him extend his hand in her direction and heard him declare, "My friends, I am happy to announce that another member of the council has joined our cause. Dr. Wong is an eminent scientist from the great country of China." All eyes turned toward her. "Dr. Wong! Please, join us up here on stage. Please, my friends, let her pass."

A movement went through the crowd and then there was silence. The people between her and the podium had parted like the waters of the Red Sea. Dr. Wong was facing Viswamitra who waved her to join him on stage. As if drawn by a magical power she followed his invitation. When Dr. Wong finally appeared up on stage, applause rang out from all sides, while Viswamitra embraced her like an old friend.

As he kissed her on both cheeks, he whispered in her ear, "You and I have much to talk about." Then, without losing a beat, he turned back to the audience, calming the applause.

"Talk to us about death, Master! What is death?" someone shouted from down below. "Don't we have to fear death?"

"Death is the moment of birth into a higher existence, as ancient sages have told us repeatedly. Ancient Hindu philosophers talked about the existence of a uniting field in which everything is connected and everything is spirit. This is an energy our current materialistic science knows nothing about. The ancient people called this the Akashic Field. This mysterious field was believed to be the primordial ocean from which everything is born, a purely spiritual field of connected potentiality. Once we understand the full truth, this will become scientific. We all yearn for the time to know the full truth. But one thing is already clear today. Living here on earth our main concern must be life, because we share this precious gift with many other creatures. Their pain will forever be ours, as their joy will survive with us into the next life and beyond.

"Our faith must above all be free of violence. We must abstain from violence in all forms, especially when it comes cloaked in religious garb. We must accept and celebrate differences. I see the day come, and it is not so far away, when Christians, Jews, Hindus, Muslims, Buddhists, Zoroastrians, Jains, Sikhs, Bahais, and all the hundreds of other religions that make our world a colorful place, can walk hand in hand. What a wonderful dream it is. This was the dream of our great prophet, Mahatma Gandhi. It was also the dream of Mohammed and the dream of Jesus."

Minutes later, while the crowds still applauded, Dr. Wong was ushered to a backstage hospitality room. The speech of the former president still reverberating in her mind, she struggled to overcome her apprehension. *Is Viswamitra perhaps a type of Bimo, who interprets the messages of the gods for the rest of us?*

She remembered her last visit to the small mountain village. Her grandfather was the only one still alive from her immediate family. Grandmother had passed away almost ten years ago and her parents had perished in an earthquake when Ping still was a child. Now all the villagers came out to greet her. Her grandfather had decorated the small dirt path leading up to his farmhouse with greens and wild flowers. Her grandfather was an English teacher at the college in Dali, but when he retired he moved back to his village, to finish his life near where his ancestors lived. A saying of her grandfather's came to her mind: "All beings strive for a reason. Earth is the body of the Creator. When I embrace the land I awake to the words of the ancestors."

Dr. Wong felt as if her ancestors had gently touched her soul through the words of the old Indian sage. Even though she had not cried for many years, tears flowed down her face freely.

Fourteen

Light poured through the cracks of the old shack and a hole in its roof when Melissa woke up the next morning. The place next to her was empty. Her companion must have gotten up early and left while she was still asleep. She looked around and noticed something else. There was a donkey standing in a corner of the barn. *That must have been the presence I felt last night,* Melissa thought to herself. She got up, rubbed her sleepy eyes, and found the gate that opened up to the outside world. There was dew over everything. The sun was just getting ready to break through the morning mist. In the distance she could see the snow-covered mountains. She pulled her shawl tightly around her body.

Melissa was looking straight at the fiery circle of the rising sun when she saw Frederik, who came running across a small hill toward her.

"Hello!" she shouted. "I am up now."

As he came closer, Melissa noticed that his face was pale. At first she thought it was just from the cold, but then she realized that terror was written all over him. Something horrifying must have happened.

"Cyber-athletes can't be afraid," she said jokingly, but immediately she realized that joking was inappropriate.

"Come with me!" Frederik said and took her arm. She felt his arm quivering. His hand was like ice. They walked for a while in silence. But then Melissa could not contain her curiosity and asked, "What is it?"

"You have to see for yourself," Frederik said and walked on in silence. It was clear that he was not willing to give any further explanation. They walked up a small incline. When they came to the top of the hill a valley opened up in front of them. Melissa immediately recognized the source of Frederik's horror. The valley before them was completely covered with dead bodies. Countless corpses were littered everywhere—bodies of men, women, and children.

"Mass suicide," Frederik said. His voice lacked any emotion.

"Suicide or murder?" Melissa asked. "What makes you sure it was suicide?"

"Take a look at the smiles on their faces. Many are clutching a little book in their hands." Melissa now noticed that Frederik held one of the little books in his hand, offering it to her.

"Here, take a look. See the title? It's called *Escape to the Fourth Dimension*. Subtitle: *A Manual for Salvation*. I think that answers your question."

Melissa stood for a while in silence. *Escape to the Fourth Dimension?* Something gagged in her throat and made her feel like throwing up. She was all too familiar with her father's paper on the fourth dimension, but her mind struggled against making a connection.

The sickening smell of death filled the cool morning air.

"It always ends this way, doesn't it?" Frederik said almost matter-of-factly. "Maybe they're right. Religions are a curse, the source of all evil."

"Do you call this religion?"

"They called themselves a church, a religion. Look here, it says so right in their book: The Church of the Higher Dimension." Frederik pointed to a page in the little book in his hand.

"My father talked often about higher dimensions. He said it's scientific. There are more dimensions than we can see."

"So what? Does that mean we can trash this place, because we can escape somewhere else? Does this mean we can just give up and move on?" Frederik was agitated.

"Let's go back," Melissa said, trying desperately to take control over her emotions. "There's nothing for us to do here. I feel sick. Besides my feet hurt, and we have a long walk ahead of us. Let's just focus on the positive."

"I feel we should do something."

"About what?" Melissa just thought of her aching feet. "There is nothing we can do."

Melissa had already started walking back. All she could think about was to get away from this horrible scene.

Frederik caught up with her. "Would you have preferred I—?"

"No, it's okay!" Melissa said. "Let's just get on."

They had reached the top of the hill when they spotted a donkey.

"Look at that! A donkey! I wonder where he came from."

The animal came trotting up the hill toward them.

"Look at that," Melissa said. "I think he misses us. He stayed with us in the shed last night."

The donkey stopped right next to Melissa.

"He's offering you a ride," Frederik said. The odd behavior of the animal made them forget the horror around them, at least for the moment.

"I've only ridden a donkey once in my life at a petting zoo. But I suppose it wouldn't hurt to give it a try. My feet would appreciate it." With Frederik's help, Melissa climbed up on the back of the donkey. "Now what? Where's the start button?"

"You have to tell him what to do." Frederik mustered a thin laugh. "When I was in the Amazon, I rode many donkeys. It's the main mode of transportation there."

Seeing that Melissa had no clue, Frederik took the donkey by a rope that was slung around his neck and started pulling him in the direction of the shed. But at that moment, the donkey wasn't so compliant.

"Hold on!" Frederik shouted as the donkey started running away in the opposite direction. He ran up the hill and back into the killing field maneuvering skillfully between the dead bodies. Frederik ran after them but was unable to catch up. Melissa had no control over the animal.

Then, suddenly, the donkey stopped abruptly. Startled by the sudden stop, Melissa tumbled off the donkey's back and landed on the ground directly in front of a dead body. She stared into the face of a woman. Looking closer, she gasped in horror and disbelief. Her mind blanked out momentarily, and she fainted. When she woke up, she looked into the worried face of Frederik, who was holding her head and gently stroking her hair.

"I will bring you back. I should never have brought you here. I am so sorry," Frederik said.

"No, no. It's…" Melissa tried to raise her head, slowly regaining the memory of what she had seen before she fainted. She opened her eyes and again stared into the dead face. Her body began shaking violently.

"What's wrong? Let's get out of here." Frederik tried to calm her although he was gasping for air himself.

Melissa nodded her head in between the tremors. She tried to say something but she was unable to utter a word. Suddenly she started scratching the frozen ground with her bare hands until blood came out of her nails.

"Stop this! Melissa, don't you see, it's insane. Tell me what's wrong?" Frederik held her tied for a moment, but she broke loose again and continued scratching.

"Let's go now. There is nothing we can do!" Frederik shouted in desperation. He grabbed his friend and pulled her away from the horrible scene. "We have to get on our way."

"No, no. Leave me alone. I must stay here. Don't you see?" Melissa threw herself on top of the dead body and clung to it. Exhausted, Frederik sat down on the ground next to his friend. He was at a loss of what to do. He was afraid that his friend was losing her mind. He took her hand and gently stroked it. Then he pulled her close to him and gently held her until she calmed down.

After a long silence, Melissa finally rose slowly and pointed at the body in front of her. She was trembling and choking, and tears now poured freely down her cheeks.

"This is my mother," Melissa whispered.

Fifteen

"Would you like some hot tea?" Frederik was sitting by a small fire, holding a pot over it with one hand and stroking Melissa's hair with the other. "It's almost ready."

Melissa was sitting on a large rock next to him soaking up the sun's warm rays. Her ice-cold body was still in shock over the terrifying experience, and her mind was numb.

"I am so sorry." Frederik looked at her, wishing he could help.

"Thanks for being here," Melissa whispered, struggling for words. "I just don't understand. I can't see how my mother could've gotten involved with such a horrible cult."

"Unfortunately it's pretty common." Frederik said. "Once people believe that death is only a passageway to a better world, well…"

"But—this is my mother. Don't you think we would've had some clue?"

"Have a cup of tea." he said, handing her the steaming cup.

Melissa sipped some tea.

"You'll have to go on without me. I have to stay here with her. I can't just leave. It wouldn't be right."

"If you stay, I'll stay."

For a long time they just sat in silence. Melissa moved closer to the fire and warmed her hands on the cup. The donkey walked over, joining them at the fire, almost as if to indicate he was part of them. Melissa gave him a few good scratches underneath the neck, which the animal seemed to enjoy.

"Now I have lost both of my parents," she said sadly. "What about your parents? Do you miss them?"

Frederik looked up. "I never had much of a relationship with them to speak of. My father worked for the military. We moved around a lot."

From where they were sitting they could see the track continuing toward the mountains in the distance. The small shack obscured the view to the other side. Suddenly they heard a trumpet playing and the noise of many people. Soon a group of about fifty appeared, walking north toward the distant goal.

The donkey, who had been lying down next to them, jumped up and nudged Melissa with his muzzle.

"I think he wants us to join this group. What do you think?" Frederik looked at Melissa.

"Okay," Melissa finally said. "I just hope my feet can make it."

"What about the donkey?" Frederik was already packing up their few belongings.

"Oh, no! You want me to trust him?"

"Don't be afraid. I won't let go of him again."

"But we can't just take him."

The donkey watched them walking away. As if making up his mind, he started running after them and quickly caught up.

"See," Frederik said, "he is following us. Let's try it once more."

While Frederik held onto the rope that was hanging from the donkey's neck, Melissa climbed up on his back using a large rock as a platform. Soon they had caught up. The man with the trumpet introduced himself and welcomed them to travel with them.

With every step the donkey took, Melissa's mind became a little clearer. The upbeat spirit of the group was contagious.

After a long time walking in silence, Frederik cleared his throat. "What do you think about coincidences?"

"What do you mean?"

"Do they have any meaning?"

"That's a big question. Are you always this deep?"

Frederik did not respond. After a while Melissa said, "I didn't mean that in a bad way. Like a put down or anything. I've thought about that myself."

"And?"

"Like the fact that you and I met...I have wondered if that means anything?"

"Funny, I was just thinking the same thing."

Melissa held her hand out to meet Frederik's hand. They looked at each other for a moment, gazing into each other's eyes.

"Cyber-athlete!" Melissa said teasingly.

"So? Something wrong with that?"

"No, not at all. I just think it's funny. Tell me all about it."

Frederik was happy to help his friend forget the horrible impressions of the morning. "They called me the Snake."

"What?" Melissa's mouth hung open. Her dream from last night was vividly in her mind.

"What...what's the matter?" Frederik saw a look of disbelief on Melissa's face. "Is that so hard to believe for some reason? It's not so different. We all had game names. The Snake was my name as a cyber-athlete."

"Sure. Of course. It just reminded me of something. That's all. Go on, please. Talk about coincidence."

"What? Now you made me curious."

"In my dream last night, I saw a snake crawling up on me, that's all."

"Are you afraid of snakes? Many people are."

"No, no. Not at all. It's just a weird coincidence. I can remember asking my teacher once about coincidences."

"And? What did he say?"

"I got the official response."

"Not scientific, or something along those lines. I know that's what my teacher would have said."

"Exactly. So they called you the Snake, why?"

"Have you ever seen a real cyber game?" Frederik asked.

"What do you think, I was born yesterday? Of course I've seen games."

"I played from the time I was four, maybe even earlier. At four, I won my first trophy. From then on I took part in regional events—every year at least once. And nearly every time I won. When new games were developed I was often the first to try them out. For a while, I worked for a big company as a game tester. By the time I was ten, I was known all over the world. That is when they started calling me the Snake. The company I was working for developed a game just for me. A snake was the central character. And the game became a hit around the globe. That's when I lost interest."

"What happened?"

"One day the snake spoke to me."

"The snake spoke to you?"

"Right, I was the snake—within the virtual games we played. The snake was my avatar. One day, in the middle of a game, the snake turned around and refused my command. The snake started talking back—stuff I had no clue where it came from. At first, I thought this was some kind of feature they had installed without telling me. Sometimes they do this kind of thing, if you know what I mean, just to throw you off. But this was different. The snake had taken on his own identity and started to argue with me. He told me to sign out of the game, or I would lose the round, which I couldn't afford. So I signed out. But when I signed back in, it was just the snake and me. No more game, just that snake and me. I gave it the three-finger salute, just to get rid of it, but it wouldn't go away."

"What happened?"

"I finally pulled the juice. I was a total 404, like being in a black hole or something. I needed to get some distance so I pulled the plug and didn't check back for a couple of days."

"And then?"

"I didn't want to face the reality. A severe case of Gray Bear Land. It's like a mental illness but the source of it is virtual—your brain is affected. But when I eventually logged on again, I got into the game, but I no longer existed. They had moved on, the other players, I mean, without me. When I tried to communicate with one of my opponents, he was an Australian with the screen name Vampire. He said he had no clue who I was and what I was talking about. A snake had never been in the game, he said. I asked a few of the other players, all had the same answer.

"I had seen this kind of thing happening before that someone would steal your identity. But I couldn't even see anyone else posting as Snake. So if they had taken on my identity, they were deep in hiding. My properties were all gone. My shopping basket was empty. I was virtually wiped out. It was like I had committed suicide, no, even worse, as if I had never existed—ever. Now I had heard of parallel universes that you can reach through a wormhole. I came to the conclusion that this is what must have happened here. Maybe I still happily existed in some other universe but I simply couldn't get there. And why not? It was a total mystery. I'm boring you, right?"

"No, no, keep going. I like the way you tell stories. What did you do?"

"So I figured my identity was compromised, and I could no longer compete. I'd basically have had to start from scratch. Can you imagine? Years of your life just wiped out. But then something even weirder happened. I ran into a guy, it was in some arcade in Frankfurt, he said he was going to some cool assembly, a drumming circle. He said he was meeting up with a shaman. This is of course all highly illegal in our country as it is in yours, I imagine. But I was ready to get into something new and exciting, so I thought it couldn't hurt. I went with him and that is where it really got strange."

"This is so cool."

"We met in this small underground basement room. There were about fifteen of us. The shaman was already there. She had a single drum in front of her and a clay statue. The statue was a bent-over figure of some ancient god, about eighty centimeters high, so not quite life-size. Since the room was only dimly lit, I couldn't make out the face, just the position of the body. She asked us to take a long look at the statue and then slowly take on that position—imitate that same position with our bodies, sort of slip into that position, which I did. Then she asked us to close our eyes and remain like that while she started drumming.

"During the drumming, her voice produced a strange sound that enhanced the experience of trance. This is where I met the snake again. This time it became clear to me that this was not a simple hallucination. This snake was real. He was different from the snake I incorporated in the game, but still there was a resemblance. The snake communicated to me, that from now on I was in his power. He would give me all the energy I needed, and I would be sent on an exploratory mission in a far-away country, where there were people who needed me more than here. Everything would be arranged for me. I just had to trust my intuition and follow the stars."

"Trust in coincidence."

"Ever since, I believe things happen for a purpose."

Sixteen

Toward evening, they reached a little village at the end of the road. Right behind the small settlement a mountain soared high up into the sky. Thick clouds covered the peak. All one could see were rocky cliffs towering high up. No path leading up into the mountain was visible anywhere, nor did it appear that anyone other than an experienced mountain climber could master these cliffs.

As they came closer to the village gate, they noticed a post with a couple of green-and-yellow-uniformed guards which they recognized immediately by their clothes as being from the Ministry of Science. This was not a good sign. They hadn't seen any GYs since they had left Moscow. What were they doing here? There was a green and yellow helicopter parked in a field next to the improvised post. To their surprise the people from the ministry just waved them on. No controls?

Once they entered the village gate, they were immediately surrounded by a group of children. Three youngsters were carrying little bundles of flowers and bouquets, and they shouted something in a language neither one of the travelers could understand.

"Zolotaya Baba! Zolotaya Baba!" They said these two words over and over again. As they were singing a little song, the children were decorating the donkey on which Melissa was still riding by putting flowers and greens all over his head and saddle. One of the children handed a beautiful crystal to Melissa and a multi-colored seashell to Frederik.

Frederik and Melissa wondered what they had done to deserve this welcome. They could feel a strong draft coming from the direction of the mountain blowing through the one street in between the little houses and pushing away the slightly musty air that had been with them since they had left the tundra. The air coming from the mountain was fresh and clean and felt like a messenger of new vistas and of freedom.

The city they entered superficially looked like an average tourist town one would expect to find somewhere in America. Melissa remembered having traveled once with her mother to a place outside of Smoky Mountain National Park. This place looked a little like that. There was even a casino along the strip of shops, restaurants, and little hotels.

As they moved farther into the village, an old woman approached them, chasing away the children. The leathery skin on her face had many wrinkles and was burned from the sun. She greeted them with an opened mouth, showing her one tooth proudly. She took the bridle of the donkey and waved them to follow.

"Animal stay here. Get bath over there. You take bath for protection," the woman said with a screechy voice in broken English.

"Protection against what?" Frederik asked. Turning to Melissa he whispered, "Sure hope this isn't some kind of scam."

"No, no! No problem," the woman said, laughing. "You see. Come, young man." Frederik hesitated at first.

"Let's trust the moment," Melissa said, nudging her friend.

Frederik finally gave in, and they followed the woman into a large house in the center of town. Once inside, the woman indicated that the left door was for men and the right door for women.

"We will meet after whatever they decide to do to us. All right? Looks to me like some kind of Turkish bath."

"Yes, Turkish bath," the woman laughed. "Bath against magical power in cave. No enter without bath. Bath protect. Without bath, you dead. Magic in cave kills. After bath, you okay."

The woman threw up her arms and made a sign of no worry. When Melissa entered the steam-filled room, she noticed other native women lingering around. They immediately stopped whatever they were doing and came closer to Melissa, surrounding her in a circle. She heard them say the same words again over and over. "Zolotaya Baba, Zolotaya Baba!" A young woman indicated to Melissa to take her clothes off and then asked her to submerse in a bathtub that seemed specially prepared for her. Melissa enjoyed the unusual attention that was given to her body by these women. First she lay down on a heated stone table and the women poured warm water all over her. Then they placed steaming cloths on her while singing a haunting song in a foreign language. After about an hour of scrubbing and cleaning, Melissa emerged like a new person, clean, fresh, and smelling of a scent that she had never smelled before, which the local women had rubbed all over her body. The women dressed her in a red tunic that matched her dark black hair well.

More than an hour had passed when Melissa stepped back out into the hall. Frederik was already waiting for her.

"You look great!" Frederik cheered. "You look great!"

"So do you. You sure clean up nicely!" Melissa stroked Frederik's clean-shaven chin. The women were watching them and talking with each other. Then one of them motioned Frederik to go closer to Melissa.

"I think she wants me to give you a hug," Frederik said.

"Go right ahead!" Melissa opened her arms to embrace her friend.

The women clapped their hands and started singing. A few of them took the couple's hands and led them out of the building.

As they stepped outside they noticed that the children were gone and the streets were empty with no one in sight except a bulky man in front of the building that looked like a casino, which was perched on the mountainside. The women, still holding their hands, guided them toward the casino. The large guy was standing in front of a heavy wooden door. He wore a uniform like a guard you would expect to see in an old Austrian castle from the period of the last king. As the singing and dancing group came closer, the man smiled a big smile and invited them graciously to step inside.

"Welcome! Welcome to both!"

They entered a big hall, which was festively decorated. The whole community of men, women, and children seemed gathered here. As soon as Melissa and Frederik appeared, a group of musicians began playing their strange-sounding instruments.

"Looks almost like they were waiting for us," Melissa whispered to Frederik. "You have any idea what's going on?"

Frederik whispered back, "Off hand, it looks like we're invited to a local wedding. Should be interesting."

"Where are the groom and the bride?" Melissa asked, looking expectantly around the hall. In the meantime, the group of woman had ushered the two all the way up to the front.

"Maybe we are it. Maybe you and I are getting married," Frederik said. He was obviously joking.

Melissa gave her friend a big punch with her elbow. "You are kidding me, aren't you?"

Just then, they approached a place underneath lines of flowers that were skillfully braided to form an arch over the pair. A man dressed in a white tunic stepped out from behind a curtain. He had a flowing white beard and a helmet donned by two snakes intertwining their bodies so they appeared like one snake with two heads. The man, who appeared to be some kind of pagan priest, said something in a strange, ancient language.

The music stopped playing and the whole assembly fell silent.

"What's going on? I have a weird feeling," Melissa whispered.

"I think they're pretty serious," Frederik replied.

"Serious about what? I think I'm going insane."

"Me too. I have no clue what's going on."

Suddenly the man raised his voice to a chanting song. Then he laced Frederik and Melissa's hands into each other's. A young girl with beautiful blonde locks came from the right side. She was holding a red pillow in her outstretched arms, on which Melissa saw two golden rings. The priest took them and put them on Melissa and Frederik's ring fingers. Then he smiled over his whole face and said something else, which both of them understood as meaning that they could kiss each other.

"Should we?" Frederik asked.

Instead of answering, Melissa flung toward him and they exchanged a long kiss. The whole assembly applauded and broke out into another song. Then the small band started playing again, and people mingled with each other in celebration.

"I guess we're husband and wife now," Frederik said after he had caught his breath. Melissa's mind was still numb. Too much had happened in the course of less than twenty-four hours.

"I don't know anymore what to think," Melissa screamed over the noise of the dancing and singing people. A young man took Melissa's hand and dragged her center stage when suddenly an enormous vibration shook the building. It first sounded like the rumbling of a major earthquake, but then Frederik thought it was as if a giant airship was landing on top of the hall. Suddenly the door flung open and a man barged inside. He spoke in a foreign language, but Melissa could see that he was terribly agitated. Everyone in the hall suddenly seemed quiet, and fear was in their faces. The only words Melissa could understand were: "GY! GY!"

At that moment a slender young man grabbed their arms and shouted over the commotion, "Come with me, quickly. We must leave immediately."

"What is going on?" Melissa asked.

"Police! GY soldiers coming to city. Many, many GY soldiers. You not safe."

Melissa and Frederik followed the young man to the end of the hall. It was almost completely dark now, and people had quieted down. Suddenly the back wall of the hall opened up silently. Behind it the gaping mouth of a cave appeared. A strong draft of cold air blew toward them and extinguished several of the lit torches. The young man momentarily pulled them inside the cave. As soon as they entered, the wall behind them closed. For a while they stood there in complete darkness. The young man finally lit a match. He quickly set fire to several torches spread out along the wall of the cave. In the dim light, Melissa recognized a familiar creature. Against the wall was her donkey, the donkey that had been with them for the last day. The animal seemed ready again to carry Melissa's tired body. He was standing against the wall peacefully chewing some hay and corn stalks.

The man pointed to the donkey and motioned to Melissa that she could mount him.

"We have long walk. We must go. I am much honored to be guide," he said.

"What is your name? What should we call you?"

"I am Sergej."

"Sergej, good, finally someone I can speak to. Can you explain to me what this was all about just now?"

"GYs were coming to town. You not safe. We have to move."

"No, I got that part. What was going on before? It felt like it was a wedding."

"Wedding? Yes, you married. Zolotaya Baba and Snake married now. Many good things will come from this." He had a smile on his face.

"Just like that? Don't you think we should know about this, this getting married thing? Don't you think someone should have asked us?" Melissa was upset.

"Know about it? What you mean? I don't understand." Sergej looked truly clueless.

"Oh, never mind. I guess we are married now. Now what?"

Frederik looked quite amused. Melissa noticed his smirk and said, "And you, what are you snickering about? Does this make any sense to you? Any sense at all?"

"As much as anything makes any sense. I would never have gotten married any other way. I swore I would never marry. This worked out quite well. And by the way, this is how my life has been turning out for several years now, ever since my avatar turned against me and took control of my life. It's like I'm on auto-pilot. And now you're a part of this…cosmic plan or whatever it is. I like it." Frederik had a broad smile on his face.

"And here I thought you were shy," Melissa said and gave her new husband a punch in the side.

Sergej now pulled Frederik's arm and said, "We must go. We have to walk one hour to cave dwelling."

Sergej took one of the lit torches and started pulling the donkey's bridle. The small group began their long walk through the mountain along a path that in prehistoric times must have been carved out by a river. Water was dripping from the ceiling and at times the path was wet and quite treacherous.

After what seemed an eternity of walking through the dark and musty cavern, they reached a dome-like arena. The echo of their footsteps seemed almost lost in the vastness of the dark cave. The flickering light of Sergej's torch tried unsuccessfully to cut a hole into the darkness above them. Tired as they were, they appreciated the resting place that Sergej offered the young couple. Mattresses and blankets on the floor indicated the welcome presence of earlier pilgrims who had used this place for a rest.

Melissa and Frederik snuggled up to each other and offered each other the warmth of their young bodies. At some point, in the depth of the night, in the belly of the primordial cave, the honey bee and the snake found themselves in a loving embrace, and a new life was created.

Seventeen

After a few hours of rest, Sergej awoke Frederik and Melissa.

"Come with me," Sergej said. "Now we will visit Hall of Light. It is only five hundred meters, but you will see. It is very sacred place. When sun first rises, it is more beautiful. You will see. I myself see Hall of Light only one time. Priest give permission. You Zolotaya Baba. Very special. You will see."

They walked along the dark path holding each other's hands. It was even darker than before. The guide had let his torch burn out, but Sergej seemed to know the way. Suddenly a ghostly green radiance surrounded them, which grew in intensity.

Illuminated by this mysterious light Frederik suddenly stopped. He pointed at what looked like a large painting on the wall. "This is unbelievable. These drawings could be ancient, perhaps thousands of years old," he said. The anthropological instincts he had acquired while living in the Amazons were stirred up.

"This drawings made by Ob Ugrians," Sergej explained. "Eighty thousand years old. No, older. Innovative people. You understand innovative? Good technology. Understand physics like scientists today. Better."

"What do you mean?" Frederik asked.

"People live here many thousand years earlier and used cave for sacrifice. Do you understand sacrifice?"

"Yes, of course. They performed rituals here, I presume. Right?"

"Are there other remnants of these people?" Melissa asked. "If they were so highly developed, there should be buildings, ruins, artifacts, something."

Sergej said, "Yes, remnants. Ruins. Find in the right places. Live in harmony with nature, understand? No waste. Everything earth friendly. How do you say? Biodegradable."

"Hmm, interesting. But if this is so old, and they left no written documents or anything, how do you know all that?" Melissa inquired.

Frederik in the meantime had walked on. The green light grew more intense with every step. Now it revealed a series of detailed paintings that depicted the daily life of those ancient people.

"Over here, check this out, Melissa. Looks like a city. Check out this painting."

Melissa joined her newlywed husband. She leaned her body against his and felt comforted by his warmth. "Those dwellings look similar to the pueblos of Native Americans back home."

"Cities built with nature material," Sergej explained. "Look here. They had space traveling machines, spaceships without motors. Anti-gravitation, maybe. We still not know."

"Look here." Frederik pointed, calling their attention to a smaller painting. "You see this?"

"Two intertwined snakes, just like the ones on the hat of the priest last night. What does it mean?" Melissa asked.

"I have seen many similar paintings in the Amazon. Shamans there painted them after they had seen the inner composition of nature during their ecstatic journeys. Some say they represent the code of life."

"Look at that!" Melissa's face lit up. "It's the double helix. These ancient people knew about the secrets of life."

"Of course they knew, maybe everything," Sergej smiled. "Let me now bring you into Hall of Light."

The space suddenly opened up. Everything around them was filled with a myriad of colors. Beams of light cascaded like a waterfall from the height of the cave and revealed a spectacular world of towering crystals as high as the eye could see, a translucent dome of gypsum, forming a natural cathedral.

"When sun rises in outside world, many thousand meter above us…" Sergej struggled for words. Frederik continued, "…the light of the sun is carried by these natural conductors deep into the earth where we are. A natural wonder."

"Here is where the ancient worshipped. Come with me. I show you their God." Sergej led them around a bend, and suddenly in front of them appeared an oversized sculpture, the figure of a man more than twenty meters high. The whole figure was bathed in light giving it a lifelike appearance.

Melissa suddenly let out a shriek. Her hand clasped Frederik's hand tightly.

"What is it?" Frederik said.

Melissa stared into the face of this strange statue. Her mind reeled. Her face was pale as ash. She clasped Frederik's hand even tighter and whispered repeatedly, "Cha-risa Catori. Cha-risa Catori."

"What is it?" Frederik asked. "Tell me."

"This is my father. Cha-risa Catori."

"You told me he died in a car crash," Frederik said.

"I know, he is dead, but he visited me many times."

"This is statue of ancient god," Sergej continued, now almost sounding like a tour guide. "Some people believe it was last descendant of visitors from space who came to this earth and left again. Touching his feet will bring you good luck." Sergej walked up to the statue and touched the feet. Then he ceremonially wiped his hands over his face as if washing himself with invisible water. Then he invited Frederik and Melissa to do the same.

Melissa was totally immersed in the ancient statue as if trying to wring away its secret. But suddenly, like an invisible dark hand, the light disappeared, leaving them perplexed and a little frightened. Out of the dark came Sergej's familiar voice reminding them that they still had a long road ahead. He lit another torch and said,

"Mountain eight kilometers wide. After, five kilometers descending into valley. Then join with other people. Many hundred thousand people down there now. Perhaps million."

"And they all came along this path?" Melissa asked, picking up her belongings, as they got ready to continue their journey.

"Many weeks we guide people through mountain into Valley of Golden Lady, Valley of the Clouds. Valley invisible from outside. Big cloud cover. On ground temperature twenty-eight degrees— eternal spring time. Bananas grow and oranges."

As they silently walked along the dark and wet path, Melissa was overcome by the feeling that this cave was like a birth canal through which life had to travel in order to be reborn on the other side—in the Promised Land.

Eighteen

On the morning of September 20, the news traveled around the world that a coup had rocked the High Council of the Ministry of Science. The headlines in the papers spoke of a hard-line group having taken over the council, ousting the moderate former president. At the moment, the whereabouts of President Viswamitra remained unclear. Rumors quickly spread around the globe about the real reasons for this coup. There was widespread speculation that a new era of even more draconian policies would soon be announced. In spite of some severe measures that were introduced under the stewardship of President San Viswamitra, he was generally believed to have exerted a moderating influence on the council's decisions. Even a certain quality of wisdom was attributed to him. Many times when his colleagues at the Science Council wanted to push further advances in the eradication of all faith-based initiatives, President San Viswamitra had been pleading for calm and proportionate action. With his disappearance, there was no guarantee what the next phase of global history would bring.

Many people secretly talked about whether the end times were near. Millions of people had gathered somewhere in Siberia expecting imminent rapture. Other rumors spread about an impending large-scale pogrom against all believers and mystics everywhere in the world. No one knew exactly when and how this would be executed, but everyone was afraid to express an opinion on the matter, much less to voice dissent. In spite of all the chaos, the Science Council still appeared to be in firm control. Its powerful arm spread to the governance down to the lowest level. Other unverified reports had it that in various parts of the world secret meetings had been called and that voices of opposition, in spite of the enormous risks, could no longer be silenced.

On September 21, early in the morning, a body was delivered to the Suspended Animation Facility in Soldier City, Nevada. The sealed shipping box was only identified by a tag with a twenty-six-digit serial number and an encoded UPC tag. A helicopter from nearby Nellis Air Force Base delivered the shipment at 6:34 UT. The box was immediately transferred to the VIP storage room in the basement of the facility where an examiner opened the transport case to get the body ready for long-term storage.

A body was put into a state of hibernation by depriving its cells of oxygen. This treatment had become common practice for celebrities and important figures. Even some politicians who perhaps secretly hoped that in a later era they would have a better chance often consented to this ordeal. Wealthy people with incurable diseases frequently went into voluntary hibernation in the hope that when a cure had been found they could be reanimated for a new lease on life.

The supervising officer examined the body thoroughly, then turned to the delivery team and asked for the paperwork. The delivery person shook his head. "Nope! That's it! Classified case."

"That's it? All we have is this number? Not much to go by."

"That's all I got, sir. I thought there would be more documentation inside, sir."

"Well, that's not much. Okay, so what do we have? One Caucasian male between the age of fifty and sixty. Let's see, any identifying marks? No sign of external trauma. Cause of sickness unknown. Other diseases, unknown." He typed the information in a handheld device as he said almost to himself, "I guess we store him away until his number comes up again. Just as long as the cash is right."

With that, he began preparing the body for storage after he wiped a slight grin from his face.

By 8:30 a.m. on September 21, the newly constituted assembly at the Ministry of Science had convened in the Meeting Hall of the People in Mumbai. At that moment, the newly appointed president of the Science Council entered and immediately went up to the podium.

"Gentlemen," Carlisle said, "a new era is about to begin. Science will finally rule supreme. The operation is in process as we speak. We have prevailed."

"Not so fast, Carlisle," Dr. Wong, who just entered the room, raised her voice. She was the only woman present. Looking around she recognized some familiar faces. Now all eyes were on her.

"I see you returned from your delicate mission, Dr. Wong. I had reports that you wouldn't return at all, that you—how shall I say—had a conversion of sorts. What changed your mind again?"

"I have a request."

"I am not at all sure you are in the position to set conditions."

All eyes of the other council members were now fixed on the two high-ranking members in the middle of a face off.

"Hear me out first. I have a deal to offer," Dr. Wong came back.

"And what might that be?"

"You stop this insane extermination, and I will deliver you Barker's secret."

"...whose body has been stolen—and now I know who was behind it." Carlisle was enraged. "This is the worst kind of back-stabbing. I will have you arrested at once. I will not tolerate such dissent. Guards, take this traitor away!"

Nineteen

By morning, Melissa, carried by the donkey, and her two male companions had reached the end of the tunnel. They were ready to finally exit into the Promised Land, the mysterious Valley of the Golden Lady. The animal had not once expressed unwillingness to carry her. For the last half hour, they had felt a breeze of fresh air blowing toward them. The donkey too seemed to sense the end of the journey and accelerated his pace. Then they saw the first glimpse of light coming toward them. When they exited into the open air, it took a while for their eyes to adjust.

They found themselves standing on a small ridge high up above the valley floor. The small group stopped for a while to take in the view. Beneath them, down in the valley, they discovered a strange sight. What first appeared like an unimaginably huge field of strange flowering plants turned out to be hundreds of thousands if not millions of people, people as far as their eyes could see. In the middle of this seething ocean of people they recognized a pyramidal structure. The whole building emanated a strange luminescence.

"The Temple of the Ancient," Sergej said. "Built hundreds of thousands of years ago. Spirits still live in there."

Melissa noticed a strange luminosity hovering over the whole valley. Gazing upward she saw that a thin layer of mist covered everything.

"We must go," Sergej said. "Descent into valley hard."

With that, they started down a steep path that snaked downward in multiple switchbacks.

After walking only a few minutes they reached the first turn around, when suddenly the donkey refused to move. As if sensing imminent danger, something terrible that was about to happen, his body started to tremble, then he let out an almost human howl, made a sudden hundred and eighty-degree turn, and ran full speed back up the incline and disappeared into the open mouth of the mountain.

"Wait, wait, where are you going? Stop! Melissa, stop him!" Frederik hollered after her.

"This animal is going crazy," she screamed back before descending into the safety of the cave. When Frederik realized that the donkey was not about to stop, he too started running. He had just reached the entrance of the cave when a terrifying flash of lightning flared up behind him, covering the whole valley. Frederik flew into the opening of the cave and broke down in exhaustion.

When he woke up again momentarily, he was surrounded by the stench of burning flesh and hot air that blew up from the valley into the cave. Half crawling, half limping, he dragged himself deeper into the cave, trying to escape the explosion that had eradicated the ancient site. Then everything around him went silent.

Something strange happened on the floor of the valley. Those thousands of people, gathered there to receive a message, felt the impact of the laser fire instantaneously. The fire caused their bodies to incinerate, but their souls were set free. Liberated from the physical boundaries of their bodies, they remained grounded in the physical reality, but their minds had gained a new dimension. One mind became many minds and many minds become one. They were able to move about freely, inhabit atoms and molecules, or plants, animals, and even other people. With their newly found perspectives, they were able to provide guidance and help. The ancient field had finally reached a critical mass and now millions of bodhisattvas were on their journey back into the world to spread enlightenment.

And as if awakening from a dream, each one suddenly realized the meaning of the message that was given to them: Knowing Yourself is sacred, Designing Yourself is sacred, Living in Community is sacred.

Part Three:
The University of Self-Design

"No one has written your destiny for you. Your destiny is in your hands …"

President Barack Obama

One

Nearly two years had passed. Melissa sat motionless high up on the ledge of a cliff overlooking the vast expanse of the plains below. She had been sitting there for hours. Time seemed to stand still. For one week she had been fasting and cleansing her body in preparation for an important event that was to occur the following night. She was going to take a sweat lodge, which her mentor, the medicine man, had prepared. Now her mind meditated over the plains below, soaring through the air like a bald eagle.

When Melissa had first come to live here with her native tribe in southern Arizona, she had discovered this solitary place and immediately fell in love with it. Sitting up here, overlooking the land below her, the world seemed almost whole again. She felt removed from the incredible devastation that human beings had brought to their earthly habitat by incessant warfare, self-righteousness, and greed.

Melissa gazed up into the sky. On this late day in fall it was filled with beautiful dark cloud formations. She wondered if those formations could contain some message for her. As a child her mother had read her the story of Littlefoot, an orphaned Apatosaurus, who spent his life in search of the Great Valley where dinosaurs were able to live in peace. Deeply despaired and unable to find the way to the Great Valley, Littlefoot heard his mother's voice speaking to him through the clouds, pointing him in the right direction.

This story was in Melissa's mind now as she looked up trying to read the clouds. She was wishing those clouds could give her direction—a sign from her mother who had died among the suicide cult somewhere in the steppes of Siberia. Or perhaps a sign from Jesse, the only father she had ever known in person. But most of all she wished for a sign from Cha'risa Catori, her Hopi father. Now that she lived with his people, she felt closer to him than ever before. Yet Cha'risa Catori had not spoken to her since her early childhood.

Seeing Cha'risa's face hewn in stone in the Hall of Light deep inside the mountain had left a lasting impression on her mind. She often thought about this strange coincidence, but could not make any sense of it. Their Russian guide had said that the ancients revered the statue as a god. How was she supposed to understand this? If he was still somewhere, why wasn't he sending a signal instead of remaining silent?

Among the Hopi they called her Bahana. Bahana was a powerful name. The first day she arrived at the village, the medicine man looked at her with surprise and then he called her Bahana.

"Why are you calling her by that name, Grandfather?" the people asked.

"My name is Melissa. I have come to live with you. The world is an unsafe place for a woman in my condition." She pointed at her stomach.

"We will call you Bahana because you are Bahana," the medicine man said with conviction.

"Then tell me what it means, Grandfather," Melissa said.

"When the first Hopi man ascended from the underworld through the hole of emergence, he brought with him a sister. Her skin was white like the morning dew. Old stories tell us that she departed from the people and went into the world. But it also says that someday she will return. She will carry with her the sacred tablet containing the remnants of creation. You are Bahana. I welcome you to our homes."

Melissa was bewildered at first. But soon she learned to gratefully accept the generous hospitality of the Hopi people who welcomed her like one of their own. It took her a long time to get used to her new name. She especially wanted to know the meaning of the sacred tablet. Once the old medicine man had become her spiritual mentor, she gave up anxiously waiting for answers.

"The answers will come to you when they are ready," the old man repeatedly told her. "Relax your mind, be open, but don't anxiously wait. Spirits have their own schedule. Just like the flute is not creating the song, so we are not making meaning. We are only the medium through which wisdom is spread."

This was a hard message for Melissa to learn. Her mind was trained in analytical thinking. She had learned to use deductive reasoning to find answers. Now she learned that emptying her mind was a good start for the new beginning. Sitting up on the ledge overlooking the plains was a good practice. At first, it was hard for her to let go of anxiety. Like a novice magician, she wanted to conjure up voices. But voices were not heard anymore as easily as they were once in the *Land Before Time*. She now was looking forward to the sweat lodge, which she hoped would break open this curtain of silence.

"If you are ready, the voices of your ancestors will speak to you through the glowing stones. May your heart be open!" She heard the reassuring voice of her mentor making this promise.

Sitting there motionless, Melissa imagined herself a mere link in a long line of her people who must have sat up here, generation after generation, watching the brilliant sunsets of the American Southwest, observing the thunderstorms gathering strength and then unloading their power over the plains as they had done since the dawn of time and before.

Melissa too had once heard voices. They now seemed to have disappeared in the mist of the past. Even though she tried to strain her memory, she could not recall much anymore from those days when she was privileged to meet her Hopi father Cha'risa Catori in lifelike dreams. Today these events seemed to her like echoes of a distant time, perhaps even reminders of an existence in a mysterious land before time.

From her Hopi mentor she had learned that the past and the present are one, not separated as they were in her mind, which had been formed by the science of the dominant culture she had grown up in. Now she struggled with these concepts. To her the past appeared to be lost in the past, not present at all, and in some ways she liked that. All the horrible things she had seen, the incredible waste of human life that had accompanied her journey after she left the Valley of the Clouds, even the loss of her beloved husband Frederik, whom she had only been with for such a short while, now burdened her restless mind. She wanted these things to be in the past. How could one bear the presence of all these events? Her Hopi teacher observed her struggle and repeatedly told her to let go. In time, he said, the things of the past will become the things of the present, but only after they have been purified by the gold of the spirit and the knowledge of the heart.

Sitting up here, Melissa wanted to cry out for help. Deep inside she wanted to believe that help was not in the concrete answers of the Western intellect but in the silence of the living presence. But her rational, logical mind was unable to find reconciliation.

A child's crying voice interrupted her meditation. Melissa's mind quickly returned. Below the ledge of rock she was sitting on, tucked in a simple wicker cradle, a baby, less than a year old, started to stir. She hurriedly descended and picked up the child. Cuddling him in her arms she hummed her favorite lullaby, an old German song she had learned traveling with Frederik in the Russian taiga.

> *Slumber sweetly my dear — for the angels are near —*
> *To watch over you — the silent night through —*
> *And to bear you above — to the dream land of love.*

For a short moment, little Frederik opened his eyes, but quickly the child fell asleep again in his mother's arms. Melissa looked at his face inquisitively as she had often done to see if she could detect any features reminding her of her husband. When she first saw the four tiny freckles on his forehead she was ecstatic and cried. Every evening she placed a little kiss on them sending her love to Frederik.

Gazing out over the plains, she saw a dust cloud appear at the end of the road that led up to her village. A car was approaching, perhaps the mail or some government inspector. She followed the sight of the vehicle until it disappeared as it entered the small road leading up to the Hopi village that ancestors had built into the mountain hundreds of years ago. Government inspectors were never a welcome sight among her people. Since ancient times they preferred to be left alone and live the way of the ancestors whose customs and life she was here to learn and make her own.

But as much as Melissa tried, her mind was continuously troubled by the loss she had experienced. First it was the loss of her biological father who had endowed her with a mysterious heritage she so desperately tried to get in touch with. Later she had stumbled upon the dead body of her mother somewhere in the Siberian taiga. Then her adoptive father, Jesse, had disappeared as well. Called on the long journey to the east, she had lost track of him. All she knew is that he had been ordered on some secret government mission and never returned from it.

Perhaps most deeply Melissa mourned the loss of her only lover, Frederik, who had perished as a result of the great fire that had rained down from the sky in the Valley of the Clouds and killed thousands.

Mourning the loss of her husband, Melissa had first returned to Frankfort, Illinois, but when she saw the political upheaval erupting around her, she quickly decided to contact her native people and ask them for asylum. Having no one left in her hometown, she began to look for a safe place for herself and the child she expected. Some native friends transported her on an underground railroad in the middle of the Arizona desert, a safe haven from chaos. Here she had been living ever since. Disconnected from the great upheavals that shook the rest of the world she birthed her child, a healthy boy whom she named Frederik in honor of his father.

Now she descended from her mountain lookout carrying little Frederik in her arms. She calmed her mind and was filled with expectation of the things to come. This was to be an important sweat lodge for her, a vision quest that would finally give her full access to the spiritual heritage of her tribe.

Reaching the village, she had all but forgotten about the approaching visitor. When she came closer to the village, she saw a jeep parked near the entrance. No cars could actually enter the confines of the village since most of the houses were carved into steep rock and could only be reached by a narrow path and by climbing on rope ladders. A group of people were waiting for Melissa. They motioned for her and started moving toward her.

A young girl named Chumana, which in Hopi language means Slow Running River, who had taken a liking to Melissa, came running ahead of the group and shouted, "You have visitors waiting for you, Aunt Bahana. But don't forget about your sweat lodge. It's almost ready for you. These men came to see you." With that Chumana took little Frederik out of Melissa's arms and walked away with him. Frederik seemed quite used to her, as if she were his older sister.

Melissa wondered who would come here just to see her. As far as she knew no one in the outside world was aware of her whereabouts. Curiously she walked up to the group. From a distance she spotted two Caucasian men in their thirties among the villagers. Both wore khaki outfits as if ready for safari.

As Melissa came closer, one of them nudged the other and gave an indication of recognizing Melissa. He went up to her and held out his hand for welcome. "Melissa, hi! Remember me? I still remember you."

Melissa looked bewildered. She could not remember ever having met any of them.

"And how would I know you? Have we met?" she asked.

"Oh, yes, you wouldn't remember, actually. It's a long story. Isn't it, Richard?" His friend nodded. "This is Richard, and I'm Joe.

We met you a long time ago, but you wouldn't remember. We met, like, in cyberspace."

"We met you in a hot tub?" Richard said, grinning broadly. His friend nudged him again and said, "By the way, I'm Joe and he's Richard, or did I mention that already?"

"So tell me, how did you find me here? I thought pretty much no one knew where I was. And what is it you want?"

Joe grinned confidently. "Let's just say we have our way of finding people. How do we know you? For one thing, we were friends with your mom."

"Friends?" the other guy called Richard said, as if questioning his partner's choice of words.

"Well, no," Joe said. "We weren't really friends, more like business partners."

Richard nodded approvingly. "Yes, business partners."

"Business partners? With my mother?" Melissa asked.

"Well, kind of. When you disappeared we made a deal with her to help her find you."

"How did you know where I was? Are you from the Greens? Are you detectives?"

"Oh no, not at all. We are no police. We are businessmen, but we do detect things. Don't we, Joe?" Richard said, and his friend nodded again approvingly.

"So what is it you want?"

"Can we go somewhere where we can talk?" Joe asked.

"In private," Richard added.

"It would help if I knew what this is about before I invite you in. Generally we…" Melissa wanted to explain that outsiders were welcome, but not if they were government agents or other useless folk who just wanted to come in and snoop around.

But Joe interrupted her, "What about if we can bring you to your father? We could do just that."

"We also know things about your mother. Don't we, Joe?"

"You what?" Melissa was taken by surprise. "We could go to my place. But I have to tell you that this, unfortunately, is not a good time. I must prepare myself for an important ceremony."

"That's no problem," Joe said quickly. "Right, Richard? We can wait in the car, if you don't mind?"

"That wouldn't be very comfortable. The ceremony will take a few hours, and by the time it's over it will be night time. Maybe you could come back some other time?" she asked.

"No, no. We don't mind waiting, even if it takes all night, now that we have contact. Right, Joe?"

Seeing that they could not be persuaded to return some other time, Melissa decided to invite them into her dwelling, which was a cave carved into the side of the mountain about twenty feet above the ground. They reached the opening by climbing a wooden ladder leaning against the rock. Once inside, Richard and Joe were surprised by the comfort this simple nature dwelling actually offered. There were several chairs covered with fur, a writing desk, and a communication console, all illuminated by a light source fed by the energy of the sun.

Melissa noticed her guests' surprised looks and said, "This might be more primitive than you're used to, but we are quite comfortable here. Sit down, please. I can offer you a cold drink before I go. I'm afraid water is the drink of the day." She quickly poured three glasses of cold water. "Now I'll have to get ready for the ceremony. If you, gentlemen, will excuse me, as much as I would like to hear what you know about my father, I must leave you for now. Incidentally, I'm also curious to hear what you know about my mother. But that too will have to wait. Make yourselves comfortable."

Melissa had served the drinks, and leaving her drink on the table, she disappeared into the back of the cave behind a partition where she changed into her ceremonial white dress.

"We heard your father was a great scientist?" Joe said casually as he eyed her walking away. He motioned to his friend and pointed to Melissa's glass.

"Put it in," he whispered.

Richard produced a tiny chip from his pocket, which he proceeded to drop into Melissa's glass. When Melissa returned, Joe politely offered her the glass and said, "Here, this is yours. You may want a drink before you leave. It's still pretty muggy outside. You know, dry desert air."

"Thanks," Melissa said and took a drink from her glass. "You're so right. With this dry air here in the desert, you can't drink enough."

Richard and Joe raised their glasses, and Richard said, "To your health. Have a good... What is it you're going to? Did you say birthday party?"

"No, no. It's a sweat lodge ceremony." Melissa smiled a little. "Now you must excuse me. We'll talk later. You're of course welcome to spend the night in our guest house. I'll see you in a few hours."

Melissa took a final drink, leaving Richard and Joe to themselves. Minutes later, she made her way to the other side of the village, where on a small platform the medicine man had prepared a wooden structure for the impending ceremony. With every step Melissa tried to empty her mind, but the arrival of those two men still echoed within her. *Perhaps this is the way my father will speak to me*, Melissa thought. *Perhaps they are part of the plan.*

Joe observed Melissa as she disappeared down the path through the village. Then he turned to his friend, who was already snooping through the few things in the cave. "Don't touch anything, Richard. Especially stay away from her communicator. So far everything runs perfectly. We can't make her suspicious," Joe hissed.

"It is?" Richard asked. "We haven't gotten anything out of her yet, have we."

"Not yet. Don't be impatient. You have to give it some time. Just wait." Joe opened a traveling bag and retrieved a small communicator. After punching in a code, he heard a crackling sound and then the voice of a woman.

"Joe, is that you? How did the operation go?" the voice said.

"Couldn't be better. We're not quite there yet, but so far she trusts us completely. She even asked us to stay with her. Well, not really. We sort of squeezed our way in. But that is still good news. Don't worry, things will work out just fine. I was even able to slip a sensor into her drink. Now she's wired for two-way intercept. And guess what, she's at a sweat lodge as we speak. You know what that means?"

"A sweat lodge? That should make things easy. What an exquisite place to establish contact. You don't even have to pretend. In her mind it will be the voice of a spirit. You can tell her anything."

"You are so right. But now I need to get ready. I'll contact you again after the mission is over."

"Success at last."

Two

"Ladies and gentlemen, honorable guests, my dear friends and supporters. My gratitude and my joy are beyond expectation." President Viswamitra gazed with a satisfied smile over the festive crowd gathered on the ancient grounds. "I am so proud and happy to preside over this truly groundbreaking celebration, the inauguration of the first Akashic University, the first University of Self-Design. As you all know, the movement of self-design has swept the globe. From its first grassroots beginnings that started with a divine message in the Valley of the Clouds, a truly remarkable revolution took place that quickly inspired the minds of millions, and I am proud to be part of it."

Thunderous applause filled the auditorium of the newly constructed university in the heart of Cairo, less than a mile away from the ancient pyramids. The statue of the Sphinx, which presided over the entrance of the new campus, looked on in silence. Perhaps the goddess even smirked a little and approved of this evolutionary step humanity was about to take. Ancient Egyptian wisdom, preserved in the writings of the Book of the Dead, knew that first there was Chaos that created order out of the primordial nothingness. Now the Goddess wondered whether the birth pains finally would subside and give way to permanent order, or whether the eternal dance of Shiva would continue.

After it had become widely known that the destruction in the Valley of the Clouds had been engineered and executed by government forces, the reaction around the globe was swift. It took less than a month to topple the Science Council. A transitional government was established, which to no one's surprise was headed by formerly ousted President Viswamitra. But in stark contrast to earlier political takeovers, the current government came to power on a wave of popular support. Carried by a new message of self-empowerment and self-design, grassroots groups everywhere seemed inspired to renew the spirit of humanity on Earth. Rumors were chasing each other that the new movement had actually originated in the Valley of the Clouds. People said that a prophecy had been revealed. Some said that those present had not actually died but had all returned to spread the new gospel among the living. Though nobody had actually seen or met a survivor, those stories would not be silenced.

In the auditorium the applause subsided, and Viswamitra continued his inspirational speech: "Today, my friends, we are gathered to lay the cornerstone for a new era, the foundation of a new world. Perhaps we can auspiciously name it the Age of Peace."

Renewed applause interrupted him.

"Yes, my friends, a new age of peace is at hand. Let me recall the stepping stones on the way to Enlightenment. The first sacred step on the path to fulfillment is community. We human beings share a yearning for community with each other and with all of nature. The last two thousand years of human history were a movement away from this sacred obligation. Why is community so important? Because only in community with others will we advance to the next level and enter the sacred Akashic Field, which we now know is the fourth dimension. During and after the happenings in the Valley of the Clouds, humanity has been able to tap the resources of this powerful field of which the ancient sages dreamed. It has been revealed to us that we can reach this field through the power of community. This is a truth the ancient philosophers knew, but humanity turned a blind eye."

Again and again his speech was interrupted by applause. The enthusiasm of the privileged thousands who were gathered here on ancient grounds quickly spread to the billions who were following the ceremony from every corner of the globe.

"My friends, you may ask: but haven't we been disappointed by communities again and again, disillusioned, exploited, marginalized, even exterminated? This is true, my friends, in past centuries many communal powers have been used against you, not in your best interest, but in the interest of those who dominated. This is the reason why community alone is not enough. Community must be balanced by another value, a value that is particular to humankind.

"It was written in bold letters above the entrance of the Delphian Oracle. It was contained in the wisdom of the Greek philosophers. *Gnoti S'auton*, they said. *Know thyself*. A detailed knowledge of the natural world will bring us community, and the knowledge of ourselves in turn will reveal the pitfalls of power. The false usurpation of power has led to the decline of communal commitment everywhere. A false understanding of human nature has lead to domination, exploitation, and fascism. In short, a false understanding of the Self has eroded our communities and the trust in their power. A proper understanding of human nature will lead to a reacceptance.

"Recent events, and above all the so-called Valley of the Clouds prophecy, have revealed another core value embedded in nature, a value most prominently suitable for the human animal. We call it the value of self-organization. Self-organization, just like community, is one of those constants that drive evolution. From the smallest quanta to the largest galaxies, self-organization drives the collaborative process, creates communities, and yields progress. What scientists call self-organization we call self-design. The Akashic Field teaches us that self-design is a sacred principle. Far too long human beings have lived a life designed by others. Before you began to think, your life was already laid out, by parents, by friends, by culture, or even by nature herself. Through education, people were forced into their roles; they were manipulated to fulfill the dreams and aspiration of others. This must and will change.

"From now on, my friends, education will no longer create dependency, but empowerment. Education will finally fulfill the promise of the enlightenment, the promise of full emancipation of the human being. From early on, children will be asked to design their own lives, not according to the standards of others, but according to their own standards. How will those standards develop? Where will they come from, you may ask? They will grow from within, from your own nature. Let your own innate wisdom, your curiosity, be the guide. Listen to your own voice and it will tell you in which direction you want to go. Those around you will be there as your guardians and guides, but not as your rulers and manipulators. When you encounter problems along the way, they will offer you techniques to solve them. Some are ancient ones like meditation and yoga; others are new discoveries like neuro-linguistic programming, visualization, and memorization modules. These tools will help you overcome those problems.

"Much still has to be learned, and this brings us to the purpose of this new institution. Here at this very university, research will be conducted to facilitate the process of self-design. Here we will develop strategies that lead to a life filled with passion, a life of fulfillment. Empowered people will make empowered decisions. This will lead humanity to a new age of prosperity and peace. We will live in harmony with our earthly environment once more and draw energy from the newly discovered field. Like a magnet draws power from the magnetic field so the human mind draws power from the Akashic Field. The Age of the Fourth Dimension is here." The audience applauded wildly, echoing the excitement of the people and their agreement with this new message of hope.

As one could expect, not everyone was in agreement or happy with this new direction; people had acquired skills in hiding their real emotions. Everyone was aware that cameras were set up here and in most public places around the world scanning all faces. Everyone was identified and their emotions were instantly analyzed. Dissent and discontent were recorded and stored for later use. This had been standard procedure for many years.

Dr. Eisenstadt sat in the back of the spacious hall. He stared intently down at his writing pad in his lap, desperately trying to conceal his grim face. Dr. Eisenstadt found Viswamitra's popular message annoying and disturbingly democratic. With trembling fingers he punched a quick message into his Blackberry: "Must ride the wave, but contain his power. Get the formula then meet at my estate. Must design effective control device. Signed: Dr. Eisenstadt." He clicked on Dr. Wong's web address and sent the encrypted message on its way.

Three

Building a sweat lodge is an all-day affair. Many of the young men from the village take part in it. Supervised by the medicine man, they collect suitable wooden sticks of birch, tamarack, or willow. Because of the scarcity of wood in this area of the Southwest, the Hopis often use the same sticks over again. In the morning the men come together and carry the sticks to the site where the lodge is to be built. The men thank the woods for bringing their healing power into the lodge and then erect a dome of eight poles. Four more sticks are wound horizontally around the dome to give it stability. During all this, ceremonial tobacco is smoked to invite and please the spirits.

Shortly before sunset, the participants of the lodge arrive. They are dressed in traditional garbs, prepared for the demands of a sweat lodge. Women wear white cotton gowns that flow loosely around their bodies.

Melissa entered the twilight of the lodge and found herself surrounded by silence. The opening through which she entered faced east because east is the bringer of the new light. In the middle of the lodge, she noticed a circle of sticks driven into the ground. Within the circle there were several large rocks, which radiated pleasant warmth. These rocks represented the spirits of the grandfathers just as everything else in the lodge had ceremonial significance, a meaning that came down through the ages from distant ancestors and would continue on for generations to come. Melissa sat on the ground and opened her mind to receive as she had learned.

In certain intervals the medicine man entered quietly and brought more glowing rocks, skillfully balancing them on the tines of a long fork. He carefully placed the glowing rocks into the center and murmured some words. Then he left just as silently, disappearing like a shadow in the night. His white hair flowed as he moved about.

The sun descended below the fading horizon, and Melissa was surrounded by complete darkness. In front of her, she could see the glowing outlines of the hot rocks. Listening to the voices of the night she again tried to calm her mind.

For a long time there were only the sounds of crickets and an occasional howl of a distant coyote. Suddenly a voice came out of the dark as if it was riding on the wind.

"Do you know where your stepfather Jesse is now?" the voice asked. For a moment Melissa was startled. Was this the voice of the grandfather rocks speaking to her?

"I have no idea," Melissa whispered. Her voice was barely audible. "My father vanished."

"He wants to talk to you," the voice said.

"Then my father is alive?" Melissa asked with hope in her voice.

"Your father is dead and your father is alive."

"I don't understand what that means," Melissa said with anguish.

Just as suddenly as it had come the voice disappeared. For a long time Melissa only heard the sound of the evening wind. *Did my father send me this message? Is this the message of the grandfather stones? Are there any more messages in the sound of the wind?*

Melissa lost track of time. Hours later she found herself on the way back to her dwelling. The grandfather stones had not talked to her again. Eventually her mentor entered and said, "May you walk this Earth in peace, sharing your kindness and care with others."

Melissa knew that this was the end of the ceremony.

Looking up into the night sky now and taking in the miracle of one million twinkling stars, the events right after the beginning of the great journey flashed through Melissa's mind. Perhaps there was truth in her mentor's saying that events of the past return in different shapes. Perhaps the strange visitors were messengers she should trust.

Four

Back in the cave, the two men were impatiently waiting for Melissa to return. Melissa stopped by Chumana's place to pick up her son, who was peacefully sleeping.

"She is done," Joe said, taking off his head gear.

"Did you get what we want?" Richard asked.

"What can you get from someone who wants nothing more but to empty her mind?" Joe sounded a little frustrated.

"Why didn't you ask her for the formula? I mean, when you talked to her like a ghost or something. Maybe she would have told you?"

"You are so naïve. For one thing, I'm pretty sure she doesn't even know, and for another thing, the last thing we want her to do is get suspicious. Now you be quiet. I hear her coming. Let me do the talking."

They quickly packed away their gear, and then they sat there waiting like two guilty schoolboys. When they finally saw Melissa appearing on top of the ladder, Richard could not contain himself and asked, "How was the sweat lodge? Fun?"

Joe quickly added, "We really appreciate you letting us stay here." Turning to his friend he said dryly, "It's not supposed to be fun."

Melissa smiled and said, "No, it's not. It's not like taking a sauna."

"Then why do you do it?" Richard asked. "I don't get it."

"The main purpose is for cleansing yourself spiritually and getting in touch with your ancestors," Melissa explained.

"Isn't that kind of stuff, like, not exactly legal or something?" Richard said.

Joe nudged him and said, "Don't mind my friend. He still lives in the past."

Turning to Richard he continued, "Don't you know things have changed? The new president rather likes this kind of thing. He is supposed to even support it."

"Really? Things must have changed a lot then," Melissa said.

"Today they wouldn't do such a thing anymore, would they?" Richard asked, looking at his friend.

"Do what, Richard? What are you talking about?" Joe said.

"Aren't we going to tell her about her mother, how she…I mean, they killed her, right, and then pretended that…" Richard was stopped in his track by his friend's furious look.

"What?" Melissa screamed. "You mean, my mother was killed by the government?

"I hear little about the outside world in here. But that's just fine for me."

"So let me ask you a different question, if you don't mind." Richard saw his chance.

"Not at all, go ahead."

"Did you get in touch? I mean, did they talk to you?" Richard asked. "Just for curiosity."

"He means your ancestors," Joe added.

"As a matter of fact, yes. I did hear a voice," Melissa said.

"Wow, what did the voice say? Was it a male voice?" Richard was excited.

"Richard, now really. What difference does it make? A ghost is a ghost. Now let me do the talking, will you." Joe was upset that he had to remind Richard again.

"It's fine," Melissa assured him. She still felt relaxed from the sweat lodge. "In fact, yes. It was a male voice."

"Did the voice tell you where you can find your father?" Richard asked, ignoring Joe.

"Not exactly. It was sort of confusing. The voice said that he was dead and alive, whatever that's supposed to mean. By the way, Jesse was not my father. He was my stepfather."

"We know that," Richard said, looking to Joe for approval. "Don't we?"

Giving Richard a hostile look, Joe said, "I bet we can tell you more about where your stepfather is than the ghost. Did he tell you anything about his research?"

"What do you mean?" Melissa probed.

"Your father, stepfather, Jesse, he developed a multidimensional model of the universe, correct?" Joe said, placing each word carefully. "I wonder how much he told you about this. Didn't he even publish a paper about extra dimensions? Something about a field?"

"I've read his paper on the fourth dimension. Jesse taught me a lot about his work," Melissa said proudly. "But why do you ask?"

"Good, good, excellent question." Joe said. "I'm glad to hear you're interested in physics just like your father was."

"Then you think he's dead?"

"Jesse stopped working as a physicist because he disliked what the government was doing. I don't blame him." Joe ignored her last remark. "Back then the government did some terrible things, I know. But times have changed. As my friend Richard here said, it's a whole new world out there. People are excited, and for once the government is working for them."

"Why are you telling me this?"

"Don't you think it's time to get his formula out there? Seriously. So people can benefit from it?" Richard nodded in agreement.

"I don't know," Melissa said cautiously. Joe noticed her hesitation and decided to switch tactics. "If we could bring you to Jesse, theoretically, would you be willing to help us get his—you know what I mean."

"How can you bring me to him? You haven't even told me whether he's alive or dead," Melissa said, raising her voice. "What do you want from me? I'm quite happy here with my people."

"We need your help," Joe pleaded. He decided to pull out all stops.

"Help with what?"

"How much did Jesse tell you about that fourth dimension?" he asked.

"I told you I read the paper. That's all I know."

"Did he tell you more? Did he show you numbers? The math that explains it all? You know where he kept those calculations?"

"What is this all about? Why are you asking me all these questions?" Melissa was visibly uncomfortable.

"Your father was onto something extremely important, tremendously important. From what we can gather he proved that Albert was wrong. That's big. Can you just imagine? Albert Einstein wrong? Einstein said that time was the fourth dimension. Time? Can you imagine? Nonsense! Pretty soon every child will know that the fourth dimension is…?"

Joe looked helplessly to Melissa: "Help me out. What did your father—sorry, stepfather—say it was?"

Before Melissa could say anything Richard jumped in, "Consciousness. You know, mind stuff."

"Richard!" Joe said. "She knows it, you don't have to explain it to her."

"Then why did you ask? I mean, you…Oh, never mind."

Joe turned to Melissa. "Don't mind my friend. We now are convinced that Jesse was right. But we need his calculations to prove this to the scientific community. And that's precisely where you come in. What's not to understand?"

"That is exactly what my father tried to avoid. Any such knowledge can be used in the wrong way. He didn't want scientists to know, at least not now. And in any case, what does that have to do with me? I have no clue about these calculations. I was a mere kid back then." Melissa was emphatic.

"Let me assure you that this time it's different. Times have changed. You said so yourself. The new government works for the people. I'm repeating myself. Besides, since the incident at the Valley of the Clouds—"

"I really don't want to talk about that!" Melissa interrupted Richard sharply. She had no intention to be brought back to the worst day of her life, especially not now. "Can't you see? I'm hiding out here to get away from my past. I don't think I can help you."

"I'm truly sorry, but as I said before, this is very important," Joe persisted. "We need you. Let me be completely honest with you. I must find out where your father kept those secret formulas." Joe lowered his voice, "We must get them before the bad guys get a hold of them. You know what that means? World peace is at stake." He ended in a crescendo. After a dramatic pause he added, lowering his voice again, "Would you like to see your father?"

Richard stared at his friend in awe. He was so impressed by his delivery that he dropped a glass he was holding. Melissa took a moment to collect herself. This was not how she had imaged her sweat lodge.

But on the other hand, what if these people really could lead me to Jesse?

"So you know where to find Jesse?"

"If you trust us, we can lead you to him."

"I will think about it." Melissa felt suddenly very confused. Was any cause worth leaving this peaceful environment, especially if this meant leaving her little son behind? She felt very tired. Leaving her guests to wherever they wished, she asked to be excused. Then she went to a secluded part of the spacious cave dwelling. Before she lay down she had one final look at Frederik, who was silently resting next to her bed. In a sudden impulse she picked up the sleeping child and tucked him next to her in her bed made of furs. She fell asleep immediately. The peaceful breath of the child calmed her mind.

In the middle of the night, Melissa woke up abruptly and noticed that it was still dark. She had the distinct feeling that Jesse had been in the room. But instead of feeling release, she felt a sense of pain, even despair that weighed heavily on her soul. Just as she opened her eyes, she heard Jesse's voice: "Help me! Set me free. Help me!"

She rose up hastily and moved into the main living area where she found Joe standing in the door frame, silhouetted against the rising rays of the morning sun.

"I think I'm ready to see my father," Melissa said, following a sudden impulse. The course of action was laid out before her mind's eye, even though the goal was clouded.

Five

Soldier City, Nevada, technically speaking, is not a city at all. It is a holding facility, tucked away in a desolate corner of the Mohave Desert. The compound houses several top-secret facilities that formerly belonged to the army. A few years ago many of these services were turned over to an oversight body administered by the world government. But when that government had fallen, a group of thugs took control of the base. With all the peaceful intentions of the new Viswamitra government, examples of such lawlessness abounded in a world still recovering from decades of warfare.

On this day late in fall, an olive green van with tinted glass windows approached the front gate of the guard building, the only access to the compound. It was generally known that only persons who were willing to pay an exorbitant fee would be admitted beyond this point.

Joe produced a clearance paper he had acquired beforehand. The guard took a quick look at it and shook his head. Without hesitation Richard handed him a stash of money through the car window. The grim-looking guard grinned approvingly. He took the cash and disappeared inside the booth. A few minutes later, he returned with a request for more. After a while of negotiating and the handing over of some more cash, he finally waved the car through the gate into the inner yard of the complex.

Staring back through the tinted glass of the vehicle, Melissa could see the heavy gate closing behind them. The whole compound was surrounded by a twenty-foot-high electrified fence.

Soon they had reached the main complex and were accompanied by another guard down a number of hallways into the basement of the building. They passed through several clearance gates before they entered an extended vault that was carved deep into the side of the mountain. Melissa felt a cold breeze chilling her body.

In front of them were coffin-like metal containers as far as the eye could see.

"Do you have an ID for the subject?" the guard asked, as if they had requested a social call with a hospital patient. Richard handed him a piece of paper.

The guard took a quick look and said, "Anonymous case? Quite a few of those here. Any other information?"

"That's all we have. We have his name, but that won't help you much. As you said, it's an anonymous case."

"Are you guys medics?"

"Actually no. We are kind of like a technical support team," Joe explained.

"Aren't we more like—businessmen?" Richard asked cautiously. Then looking at Melissa, he quickly added, "That is, we are. Not her."

"Richard, he knows that." Joe caught Richard's eye and motioned him to shut up. Then he turned to the guard. "This is an investigation of a different kind," Joe explained. "But why should I argue? I paid my price and gave my reasons. What else do you want?"

The guard stopped walking and just looked at Joe.

"Joe, I think you hit the nail on the head," Richard said.

"What do you mean?"

"I think he wants more cash."

"Well, that's too bad. I just ran out, and I don't assume they take virtual bucks."

"Why not?" the guard said and grinned. "How about a hundred thousand yuan?"

"That's highway robbery," Joe shouted angrily, but the broad-shouldered guard made a sudden sharp turn on his heels and started to walk away.

"Ok, ok. I read you. All I said is can you handle a transfer?"

"No problem, as long as it's drawn on a trustworthy institution. Government issue security won't do. I'm sorry."

"How does Seven Seals Depository sound to you?"

"Seven Seals, where your money is written in Gold. That's acceptable."

"Alright then." Joe scribbled the amount of the payment into the palm of his left hand. A chip implanted into his hand read the number instantly. Then Joe touched the guard's opened left hand, and the money instantly transferred to the guard's account via his own implant. A confirmation of the transfer appeared immediately on the guard's left eye screen.

"Okay, let's go now," the guard said. He was satisfied with the quick transaction. "You pay, you play. It's that simple." He had a fat grin on his face. "Let's see what I can do for you gents. Follow me." He turned and waved them to follow.

"What kind of a prison is this?" Melissa asked, realizing that this facility was anything but an ordinary penitentiary. "You didn't tell me we were visiting a morgue."

"This is not a morgue," Richard said.

"Then what is it?" Melissa asked again as they walked down another chilly hall following the guard. "Where are the prisoners?"

"It's an SAF, a Suspended Animation Facility. Bodies are stored here for later awakening. We were told that your father had an incurable sickness. Instead of waiting for his death, the government decided to hibernate him until a cure for his disease could be found. They obviously considered him important."

Melissa did not know whether she should be shocked or saddened. What a strange hand Jesse had been dealt. They walked along another long corridor, down a flight of stairs, and finally stopped in front of one of the metal boxes.

After the guard double checked the number on the box, he said, "The container can only stay open for thirty minutes. Even though this environment is temperature controlled, the bodies themselves are kept twenty degrees cooler, below room temperature. You see, this whole thing here is like a freezer in a supermarket. Each room cools the temperature of a dozen bodies. I'll open the box now and leave you gents to yourself. When your time is up, I'll be back to close the box and escort you out. Any minute in excess can cause irreversible damage to the subject."

With that the guard pulled out the heavy box and opened the lid. "Good luck finding what you're looking for," the guard said and disappeared in the depths of the hall.

Melissa trembled. She recognized the face of Jesse. His body was dressed in a thin, washed-out gown. His face was totally exposed and looked ash gray like a mask. There was a thin layer of white powder over all exposed body parts. Instantly Melissa felt the intense desire to embrace her father's body in love. But then immediately she felt that this was not her father at all, but just a shell. His spirit was missing. *Where did my father escape to? Or is his soul still captive inside this lifeless shell?*

Suddenly Melissa realized that she had no idea what brought them here. What exactly was it these fellows were trying to accomplish?

Joe had already become very busy. He opened a little suitcase and retrieved some high-tech instruments. Melissa watched with amazement as Joe began scanning Jesse's body with a little gadget that looked like a UV scanner from head to toe.

"What in the world are you doing?" she asked angrily. "I don't even believe this. Can you stop right now and tell me why we came here?"

When she did not get an answer she continued, "Can we bring him back to life? I want to know now. Or will he stay frozen forever?" Joe was not moved in the slightest.

Suddenly Melissa said, as if speaking to herself, "Now I get it. He's not dead, but he's not alive either. Jesse's in between. That's what you meant to tell me. Now I understand." Melissa began to cry.

Joe, on the other hand, was totally absorbed in his work. As if speaking in a lecture hall to a group of students he explained, "This machine will take images of every detail inside the professor's body and everything that might be hidden underneath the surface of his skin." He spoke without emotion, as if explaining a scientific procedure. "Perhaps there's a microchip of some sort embedded in his body. Now we'll find out."

Melissa shuddered when she realized the lack of empathy in Joe's voice. He talked about her father's body as one talks about a piece of meat in the supermarket. Richard handed her a handkerchief to wipe her tears.

"What are the chances of bringing Jesse back to life?" Melissa asked again between crying. Her voice was subdued as if not to wake up her father.

Again Joe ignored her question and continued his work.

"You heard, we have only thirty minutes. He'll be back punctually. This is our only chance," Richard explained.

Joe just focused in on a small tattoo on Jesse's left arm but suddenly there was a stirring right behind them and a man's stabbing voice said, "You're absolutely correct, my friends. This is your only and last chance to investigate Professor Barker's body. Perhaps you should leave such a delicate task to closer friends of the professor."

Joe whirled around and stared into the barrel of a gun. Carlisle pointed a revolver into his face from less than five feet away.

"Surprised?" Carlisle said cynically. "You evidently didn't expect someone else here, did you? I, on my part, was waiting for you. Real shame to lose two such talented inventors."

"No need to get nasty," Joe said, slowly raising his hands. "Do we know this character, Richard?"

"I don't believe we've met."

"He seems to know us."

"Our fame is growing."

"Why don't you ask him who he is?"

"He does look kind of familiar."

Joe and Richard stood there with their arms raised. Melissa did not know what to make of it all.

Joe finally said, "Why don't you take that gun out of my face so we can have a civil conversation?"

Carlisle was not impressed.

"If he was talking to us we could offer him a deal. Don't you think so, Joe? I'm sure something could be worked out."

Carlisle finally lowered his gun. "The only deal I'm interested in is for you to tell me everything you know about this corpse," Carlisle said sharply, pointing at the open box with Jesse's frozen body. "Let's start with this. Who are you people working for?"

"Surprise. He can be civil."

"Promising start for a good business relationship, isn't that so, Richard?"

"I have an idea, Joe. I'm going to ask the gentleman to give me his gun. What do you think?"

"Great idea," Joe said. "You are so brilliant."

Richard held out his hand and made a move toward Carlisle, but stopped immediately when Carlisle raised his revolver at him.

"I guess our intruder refuses to play nice."

"Stop the nonsense," Carlisle growled angrily. "What's in the box?"

"The box?" Joe asked innocently. "Which box? Oh, that's my toothbrush and my nightgown."

"Enough!" Carlisle shouted. "Toss it over to me!"

"Sure, check it out for yourself!" Joe bent over and picked up the box. Just then the sound of footsteps announced the returning guard. Joe saw his chance and shouted, "Watch out, Richard!" Then he hurled the heavy container into Carlisle's face. Carlisle stumbled and fired a shot. Startled by the gun shot, the burly guard took off in the opposite direction toward the exit. Joe launched forward and smashed the gun out of Carlisle's hand, pulling him down with his body. The revolver tumbled through the air and landed in front of Melissa's feet who had been wordlessly taking in the whole scene. She quickly picked up the revolver and pointed it at the three fighting men. Suddenly having control over the situation, Melissa slowly moved back to a safe distance. "Fighting is over. Move and get out of here before I change my mind."

Richard looked at her in disbelief. "Do you want us to give you a hand putting the lid back on the box?"

"Before it's too late?" Joe added.

"Let that be my problem! Get moving!" There was a decisive tone in Melissa's voice. She suddenly knew what her father wanted from her. The dream from last night now made sense. She realized what her father meant when he had asked her to free him from that prison.

"Go!" she shouted again. Carlisle was the first to turn toward the entrance. "In a few minutes this place will be crawling with armed guards," he mumbled and took off.

"Let's cut out of here. Let's go, Joe." Richard too made for the exit, but stopped when he realized that Joe was not moving.

Melissa was still pointing the gun at them.

"I'm not going anywhere without my scans," Joe said. He was looking at Melissa but was afraid to make a move.

"I don't give a damn about your scans," Melissa barked back and pointed to the scanning machine, which was still in the box next to Jesse's body. "Take it and get out of here before I change my mind. I mean it."

Joe quickly picked up the scanner and followed Richard, leaving Melissa alone with Jesse's body in the freezing and dimly lit hall.

Melissa turned toward her father. With trembling hands she aimed the revolver straight at Jesse's heart and pulled the trigger. The sound of the shot reverberated in the vaulted cellar. She took one last look at her father's dead body. A tear rolled down her brown cheek. "Goodbye, Jesse. I hope your soul can rest in peace now." Then she hurried to get out of the crypt as well.

When she reached the exit of the building, she saw Carlisle making for the parked car across the yard. Richard and Joe, however, were nowhere to be seen.

Melissa dashed across the yard after Carlisle. Bullets started whistling. Two heavily armed men came running toward her. Melissa fired back and, reaching the vehicle, jumped into the passenger seat of the car. Carlisle was just starting the engine when a bullet whirled through the front windshield and hit him clean in the head. His body sank over onto the steering wheel. Blood squirted into Melissa's face, gushing from an open wound in Carlisle's neck. The horn of the car, activated by Carlisle's weight, blasted in desperation. Melissa crouched down on the floor, waiting for any moment to be her last.

A few seconds passed. Melissa peeked up above the dash and took a quick shot at one of the guards who had come dangerously close, taking him down. Then she pushed Carlisle's lifeless body out of the car, jumped in the driver's seat, and sped toward the front gate. To her surprise the heavy metal gate slid open on approach, and she was able to leave the compound unharmed.

As Melissa drove down the mile-long service road that led up to the compound, a green and yellow helicopter swooped down from the sky and landed inside the gated area. The roaring engine came to a sputtering stop. An armed guard peeked out of the open door swinging an automatic laser. As soon as the aircraft touched ground two men came running from behind a nearby building, where they had taken cover, and jumped into the chopper. The helicopter took off immediately and was airborne within seconds.

On board, Dr. Wong congratulated Richard and Joe for their successful mission and immediately started analyzing the scans that Joe had taken of Jesse's body. She was pleased with the success of the operation, though she mentioned in passing that it had cost her a fortune to pay off the commander of the renegade compound. For an exorbitant price he had agreed to let both the inventors and Melissa leave the compound unharmed.

Six

Late in the night Melissa walked up the familiar mountain path. She was sure that everyone was sleeping, so she decided to climb up to her favorite outlook before retiring to her cave dwelling. Aided by the moonlight, she collected a small bundle of twigs and amber, with which she intended to start a small fire. Then she climbed all the way to the top. Darkness was all around her, but she felt safe. She looked up into the night sky and felt connected to the millions of stars. She lit a fire and emptied all her troubled past into the burning amber. The plume of smoke rose up into the night sky, billowing against the moon, taking her bad memories with it. The cool breeze of the night gently touched her skin and brought comfort.

Squatting on the ground she felt the bare rock beneath her naked feet. She laid both hands flat on the ground next to her feet so that the energy of the earth could flow freely. From the earth below she heard her two fathers' voices speak as one:

"The earth is your mother. Like the mighty oak tree grows her roots into the ground, so you must grow into the earth and be rooted. The life you live now is above ground. Grow high above the earth and spread your branches. Your thoughtful actions will give food and comfort to those in need. Like the acorn they will fall to the ground and multiply. From where you are now your life may appear confusing, aimless, and without purpose. But your whole life is like a finely woven tapestry. What from close up appears meaningless and bewildering turns into the most beautiful painting when viewed from a distance. Do never forget, you are the weaver, you are the creator, you are the artist of your life."

Great peace entered her heart when she finally descended to her cave. She took a long look at her peacefully sleeping child and then finally fell asleep herself.

Melissa woke up to a strange and unfamiliar scene. On her way to the water cave, carrying little Frederik in her arms, she had to pass a public place, where on auspicious occasions assemblies of the village community were held. Now she found the people from the village gathered, young and old, women and men. Up front she spotted a stranger addressing the crowd. He wore a dark suit and a tie. With his wide-brimmed black hat he looked like a traveling missionary from an earlier century. Now the preacher held up a tablet of paper fastened together with string.

"Friends!" the stranger said. "Take a good look at this tablet. This is no ordinary book. We call it the Book of Life. Look through its pages. It's empty. I hear you ask: Why would this man come and offer us an empty book? Let me explain this to you, my friends. I'm not here to sell you anything. I am not here to convert you to anything. My friends, this is the good news. The world has another chance. Humanity is given another opportunity. I am telling you, my friends, I see a new morning. The sun of reason is rising and radiates its full power. This message will lift the human spirit to the next level. I see it as clear as mountain air on a spring morning.

"Let me tell you the secret. The sacred tool that has been given to humanity is called self-design. The book of life was revealed in the Valley of the Clouds to all humanity. Yes, the great fire devoured millions, but it wasn't only a holocaust, my friends. It was the birth of a new era. In the midst of the rapture self-design was born. All participants felt the same powerful impulse. The message was utterly simple: evolve or die. In order to evolve we were given this great memorandum. The message had three parts: Community is sacred, Knowing yourself is sacred, and Self-design is sacred."

Many in the crowd looked puzzled. Some nodded in agreement. From inside his travelling bag, the speaker pulled up another book and, in fast sequence, another one and another one. "I'm sure you know these books here quite well. Look at this book here. They call it the Bible, the Holy Bible. Its pages are filled with words. They say that they are God's words. But were they the words of your god? No, they were the words of another people's god. I don't have to remind you how your ancestors were forcefully converted to believe in this book. Those who converted them did not shy away from slaughtering thousands of your people, but before killing them they baptized them so they would enter into their heaven. My friends, those times are over. No longer will you be forced to adopt anybody's book, whether it is the Koran, the Bible, or the Torah."

"But all you bring us is another book," somebody in the crowd shouted. "What's the difference?"

"Let me tell you the difference. This tablet is not an ordinary book. It is a book without content. Many people have been raised by the great religions of the book. But those books were already written. Human beings had to accept them as the truth. This is an empty book. Its pages are not yet written."

"But who will fill the pages with content?" someone asked.

"My friends, that is the beauty of this new book. The author of this tablet is you. You will fill the book of your life with your own content. I hear you say, but haven't people always done that? Haven't they always filled their lives with content? Yes, my friends, they have, but until now they have mostly done so unconsciously, without purpose. They have lived someone else's life. From now on you will learn how to live life consciously. You will live your life by your own design. The inscription over the gate of the temple of Apollo in ancient Greece said, 'Know Yourself.' Yes, it was a noble beginning. Humanity has reached a new stage of maturity. And the new motto is 'Design Yourself'."

"How can you even fully know yourself?" someone shouted.

"You know yourself when you are the product of your own design. Self-design provides the tool for that. From now on, every child in the world at the age of five will be initiated to a life of self-design. Each will be given a self-design tablet, their own Book of Life. Children will be encouraged to develop their own plan, choose their own values, lay out their personal vision for the future and then go ahead and live by the strategies that they thought up for themselves. In all of this, self-design will monitor whether you live up to your own expectations."

"How is that going to work?" another one asked.

"In the olden days they called it conscience. Conscience was like an inner voice, keeping you on the right path. The problem is it was not your own voice. It was a path that someone else had designed for you. It was someone else's voice. Conscience was also against science. My friends, no longer does your conscience have to contradict science. Quite the opposite is true: self-design is in constant harmony with the best of science. In self-design you are developing your own goals in harmony with the best information you can get, and then live by those goals.

This technology has already transformed large parts of the planet. Those who received the message in the Valley of the Clouds migrated around the globe and spread the good news. Lo and behold, in a short year the world was transformed. No longer did hostile factions fight with each other. People learned quickly that it was to their advantage to live a rational, thoughtful, and self-designed life. This new technology of self-awareness will carry humanity to the next level. It will be applied everywhere, and the result will be a thoroughly and completely empowered humanity, ready to climb the next evolutionary step, ready to become supermen and superwomen."

Unexpectedly all heads turned away from the speaker. Everyone gazed up into the sky out west from where the noise of an approaching helicopter was heard. Soon the noise drowned out any speech. Then abruptly the aircraft turned around a cliff and became fully visible. Since there was not much space in the mountainous terrain and the best spot for landing was right where the assembly had been taking place, everybody started rushing away to clear the area.

Melissa held little Frederik tight and squeezed among the other people into a narrow pathway away from the public arena that had abruptly been turned into a landing pad. Slowly the blades of the helicopter came to a stop and the door of the cabin opened.

An athletic young man jumped out of the aircraft and hit the ground looking around. When Melissa got a look at his face she almost fainted.

"Frederik!" she screamed. "Is it really you? I thought you were dead." Melissa quickly handed little Frederik over to Chumana, who was standing next to her. Then she ran to greet her long-lost lover, who appeared much less surprised than she was. In fact, Frederik gave the impression that he had expected to meet Melissa here. Melissa embraced him and then stepped away and let her hands wander all over his body as if to prove to herself that she was not seeing a ghost.

"Frederik," she said again. "You must tell me. How did you get away? What happened since I last saw you? Why did you not come earlier? So many things we have to talk about."

"Yes, dear," Frederik said, "many, many things have happened since I saw you last disappearing in the mouth of that cave. I wasn't sure whether you had gotten away either. Just yesterday I found out that you lived and especially where you were hiding out. So many things have changed. How are you, my dear? We must go somewhere where we can just sit and talk. There is much we need to discuss to catch up with each other's lives. Where can we go?"

"First I have to introduce you to someone special." Melissa took her lover's hand and guided him toward where Chumana was waiting with little Frederik. The boy looked strangely at the approaching couple, stretching out his arms to get to his mother.

"You don't know this person, Freddy!" she said and picked up her son. "Frederik!" Melissa turned to her lover. "I want you to meet your son. I named him Frederik, just like you, but we call him Freddy. Give him some time so he can get to know you," she added cautiously.

Now it was Frederik's turn to be speechless. He took the little boy into his arms and held him tight. Little Frederik first was surprised but then, not knowing this stranger, started crying with full lungs. Melissa laughed and took little Frederik back, trying to calm him.

"You have to give him time to get used to you. Let's go. I'll show you my favorite place. There we can talk." She took his hand and dragged him up the incline to her outlook spot. Little Frederik stayed back with Chumana where he was safe.

Melissa let her eyes wander over the plains, caressing Frederik's hands. "Isn't it beautiful up here? Serene and peaceful? I spend a lot of time here. Often I sat here and hoped you were with me."

She looked at Frederik with loving eyes. Frederik looked at Melissa and said, "Zolotaya Baba. You are the Golden Lady. The Bearer of Light."

Not comprehending the message, Melissa only saw her lover's physical body.

"You are here now," she said. "It's like a miracle. Now tell me. How did you get away? How did you escape the holocaust? The news said that everyone was killed."

"It was indeed a miracle. First there was this bright light. I passed out, thinking I would certainly die, but then I regained consciousness. That's when I learned about the book."

"The book?" Melissa asked.

"Yes. Everybody in the valley received the same message. An empty tablet. We all stood around wondering, praising our good fortune but then asking about the meaning of it all. Finally one of the elders spoke up and explained. That's when it all was clear to us. It was clear as the sun that he spoke the truth."

"What did he say?" Melissa asked.

"He told us that the empty book was the blueprint for our life."

"Why was it empty? I know the stranger who spoke here in the village this morning said the same thing. But it didn't make much sense to me."

"It is empty because it is you who has to fill it with content. You fill in your values, your motivations, your goals, your strategies, and your actions. Then this book becomes your constant companion. It continuously reminds you of your goals. Should it become necessary, you can update and revise the book. It is the best tool for self-empowerment that has ever been invented. Do you see? People can finally live their lives by their own design. No longer do we have to live someone else's dream."

"That's what the missionary said too."

"I know it may sound strange to you. But wait till you see the impact. After the revelation, all those people went back to their homes and started spreading the news. People everywhere started to come together, creating their lives anew."

"Self-design is like a new religion, is it?" Melissa asked. There was doubt in her voice.

"Self-design leaves all the controls in your own hands. Everything always used to be about submission, following somebody else's rules. Now the rules have changed. And people catch on to it fast. It truly works the same everywhere. People want to be their own designers. Now they can live that dream. You must come and see for yourself. I am independent. Everyone is completely independent and free. Everyone is his or her own master. The news is invigorating. It's like after millennia of enslavement, humanity is finally reaching its true destination."

Melissa watched in awe as her lover, who had talked himself into a near-frenzy, first was surrounded by a purple light that seemed to emanate from his body; then his whole body slowly lifted off from the ground and dissolved into the thin morning sky.

Suddenly Melissa heard the crying voice of a baby. She looked around and saw Chumana curled up on the floor next to little Frederik, who had just woken up. Melissa picked up the child and held him tight. Had it all been a dream?

Seven

Dr. Eisenstadt stood in the yard of his Irish estate and scanned the sky for a sign of an approaching helicopter. A few minutes earlier he had received a message from Dr. Wong letting him know her impending arrival. Dr. Eisenstadt harbored great expectations for this meeting. Dr. Wong was supposed to bring the news of whether he had been accepted as a new voting member of the World Council, for which Dr. Wong had nominated him. Even though Viswamitra, the president of the council, who currently enjoyed unrivaled popularity, had privately expressed some reservations, Eisenstadt expected that with Dr. Wong's help he could be confirmed. He also was confident that Dr. Wong shared his views about Viswamitra, believing he had made far too many concessions to mysticism and spiritual orthodoxy.

While largely successful, the president's politics had already resulted in a resurgence of religious fanaticism and antiscientific bigotry. Dr. Eisenstadt was convinced that only a strong intervention on a global scale could avert another catastrophe. He was an avid supporter of a recently developed new academic discipline called Mind Management for which Viswamitra expressed only limited interest. Quite significantly, in his opening speech at the newly founded Akashic University, Viswamitra had avoided the topic altogether. When the first catalogue of courses was published, Eisenstadt noticed with dismay that none of the active disciplines took up this promising subject even though several other big institutions had already endowed chairs or even whole departments dealing with the subject of mind management, primarily from an administrative perspective. Now Dr. Eisenstadt was looking forward to discuss these issues in detail with his powerful colleague.

Dr. Eisenstadt was, of course, also interested in what Dr. Wong was able to find out about Professor Barker's scientific discoveries.

Dr. Wong had indicated to him earlier that she had been successful in deciphering a tattoo they had found on Barker's body. Dr. Eisenstadt walked over to the horse barn. From his extensive wardrobe he had carefully selected a fashionable Irish kilt for the occasion of Dr. Wong's first visit to his estate. The subdued green and gray checkered tartan kilt hung loosely down to his bare knees where it almost met the equally green woolen knee socks that covered his legs. The pasty white shirt he wore on the top was covered by a thick woolen Irish sweater to protect against the chill of this early fall afternoon.

In the immaculately clean barn eight beautifully kept horses looked at him expectantly. Which one would be privileged today to be taken out for a ride? He knew Dr. Wong was fond of horses just like him, and he looked forward to a lengthy excursion with her. To go on extended rides Dr. Eisenstadt usually preferred Reddish, an eight-year-old mare. She was his favorite horse because she seemed to sense every wish of her master in advance. When Dr. Eisenstadt rode her on a trail, the old saying became true that the animal and the man become one. He now held a carrot up to her mouth, which she eagerly devoured. The other horses looked jealously on while Oscar, a seasoned but still active stallion, let out a disapproving neigh.

"Yes, yes!" Dr. Eisenstadt said. "Your turn will come. First I have to take care of our guest. She will be here any minute."

He had spotted the aircraft approaching from the east over a grassy lush hill. The sound of the blades soon pierced the bucolic peace. Minutes later the aircraft landed softly in the yard of the perfectly manicured estate.

After exchanging a few welcomes, the two scientists were soon sitting in the comfortable library sipping Irish coffee. Without much introduction, and for the moment avoiding the political implications of her visit, Dr. Wong came immediately to her favorite topic. She was eager to share her excitement over Barker's discovery. Retrieving an old-fashioned book from her travel bag Dr. Wong said:

"Here, take a look at this. This will give you an idea of the importance of Barker's discovery. I know, I know, a physician is not a physicist. To fully understand the magnitude of his insights—"

Dr. Eisenstadt interrupted her and said with a smile, "You truly have a talent to make a putdown sound like a compliment. I am well aware of my shortcomings."

"For a brain specialist of your reputation little could serve as putdown." Dr. Wong tried quickly to repair the damage. "Have I said that you have a lovely home, especially the beautiful surroundings? The green hills of Ireland are legendary. What county are we in?"

"This here? It's actually still Dublin County. A little later, I planned to take you on a short excursion to nearby Newgrange County. The famous Newgrange site is located right on the corner of my property. We can even enjoy a private visit."

"Newgrange? The ancient Celtic astronomical site? How wonderful. I would like that a lot. I have heard many great things about this important prehistoric monument. But first things first. Let me read you a couple of pages from this book," Dr. Wong said with unbridled excitement, coming back to her topic.

"Yes, you are right, first things first. But forgive me, I was under the impression that we set this meeting to discuss strategy. I am curious about Carlisle's death, of course. Was it an accident? And then I'd like to know what you found out about my chances in regard to the appointment."

Dr. Wong let out a little laugh and handed him the book. She relished in the suspense of the moment. "I said, first things first. We have plenty of time."

"A book? Few people would even recognize these antiques anymore," Dr. Eisenstadt said.

"…says someone who has surrounded himself with an extensive library of those old-fashioned relics."

"Only to collect dust. Today all this wealth of knowledge fits into a chip the size of the head of a needle. Let me see already so we can get on. Strange title indeed, *The God Particle*."

"…written by one of the giants of the past century. For a while he was the director of the famous Fermi accelerator, a midget compared to what we run now. Our knowledge of the physical world has changed so much, especially during this past year."

"And have we found the god particle yet? Now I am curious."

"Perhaps not. But I know we have found something similarly exciting. Perhaps the secret of the universe is all contained in this one number."

"A number?" Dr. Eisenstadt asked.

"You see, the whole idea of the god particle was steeped in what I call linear thinking. Those scientists believed that following a straight line into the center of the material world would eventually yield the expected end point, the famous god particle. But nature turned out quite differently, more like a spiral, spiraling through many dimensions. But I am getting ahead of myself."

"You already lost me. You have to keep a slow pace if you want me to understand. So what's in the book that's so important?" Dr. Eisenstadt asked.

"One hundred and thirty-seven."

"That's a number?"

"Obviously."

"So tell me what is so important about that number?"

"It's the number our two inventors found on Barker's body, encrypted inside a tattoo," Dr. Wong said. Seeing that Dr. Eisenstadt was not impressed she continued, "Richard Feynman, one of the top quantum physicists of the twentieth century, suggested that all physicists put a sign up in their offices or homes to remind them how little we really know. The sign would simply say 137. Another equally famous physicist, Wolfgang Pauli, died and went to heaven where he was given an audience with God."

Dr. Wong saw Eisenstadt's puzzled face and quickly explained, "Well, in those days, even scientists occasionally were allowed to slip."

"I know, even Einstein spoke of the 'Old One' in respectful terms."

"God granted Pauli one question. Pauli immediately asked the one question that he had labored in vain to answer for the last decade of his life: Why is *alpha* equal to one hundred and thirty-seven? You see, *alpha,* a dimensionless number, pops up everywhere you look, but no one knows why. Now get this. Supposedly God smiled, picked up the chalk, and began filling the whole blackboard with equations. After a few minutes, God turned to Pauli, obviously expecting praise. But Pauli just shook his head disapprovingly, 'Sorry, that's wrong!'"

"So God Almighty was wrong. Even he couldn't figure it out. That is quite amusing." Eisenstadt poured some more tea. "And now, of course, you must tell me the right answer. Did Barker find it? You got me curious. Even though, I probably won't understand a thing. That much I know already."

"Jesse Barker found the answer!" Dr. Wong said.

"But wait a minute. You said that all the inventors found on the tattoo was this number. How can a number explain itself?"

Dr. Wong smiled. "It took me some effort to figure it out. The number they found was actually inverted: 731. Alpha is actually the inverse of 137. For us physicists it stands for what we call the fine-structure constant. You get it by taking the square of the charge of an electron divided by the speed of light times Planck's constant. You must forgive me these details."

"You don't expect me—or anyone else—to understand this, do you?"

"It's actually not so complicated and relatively old knowledge."

"So what does it mean?"

"What it means is that our friend Lederman, and with him any other physicist of the past century, believed that this one number contained the essence of electromagnetism, relativity, and quantum theory, in other words, grand unification. But until now nobody understood why, why 137? Until Barker figured it out."

"And this was all encoded in his tattoo?" Dr. Eisenstadt asked incredulously.

"Not exactly. It took me some digging. But finally I got it. I found that alpha731 was actually an old website in cyberspace. Barker must have created it, and then he recorded the complete set of calculations, which prove that 137 is the complexity transformation from a lower dimension to the next higher one."

"Sounds important, but forgive me when I still don't get it. Have patience with me, please," Eisenstadt pleaded.

"It means that our universe consists of many dimensions. Many physicists have long suspected this, only now we have proof. Look at it this way. Just like there is a whole spectrum of colors and sounds, of which our eyes and ears only grasp a small segment, so there are many dimensions, but our brain only grasps one small segment, everything between the first and the third dimension, to be precise. The rest remains a mystery. Just like we cannot see x-rays with our eyes, we cannot see the fourth or even the fifth dimension, or any other higher dimension."

"That's beginning to make some sense now. Go on."

"We scientists had it wrong when we believed that our universe is a simple three-dimensional structure. Even Einstein's speculation that time was the fourth dimension actually missed the point. In reality, we are little bugs living in the stomach of a multi-dimensional beast. From our perspective, we have no way of knowing anything about the rest of the body of the beast, much less about its brain."

"Bravo, I am impressed, even though I must say it's all far above my head." Dr. Eisenstadt picked up on Dr. Wong's excitement. "But perhaps, I think, in this moment we don't have the luxury to reflect about dimensions. We have more urgent business to attend to. There will be other times when we have the leisure to descend into cyberspace and study Professor Barker's ruminations. Now let's have our excursion before it gets too dark. Perhaps this will give us a better chance to discuss more sensitive matters. I offer you a choice to go on horseback or by rover. What do you prefer?"

Eight

The trail snaked along between a fence and the edge of a luscious green forest. Dr. Wong and Dr. Eisenstadt rode for a while behind each other down a narrow path that led to a creek they had to cross. Dr. Eisenstadt was naturally in the lead. Without the slightest hesitation, Reddish walked straight through the rocky creek bed to the other side. But no matter how much Dr. Wong tried, Big Oscar stopped and refused to step in the water. Finally Dr. Eisenstadt shouted a short command.

"You have to be firm, Ping. Let him know what you want from him. You must show him who is in command. Then he will follow," Dr. Eisenstadt said. Reddish immediately followed the command and walked through the running water of the brook.

"I wish people could be trained as easily as horses. And that is not to say that it's an easy job training a horse," Dr. Eisenstadt added. "Sometimes I think I spent far too much time with it."

"You seem to have done a pretty good job with these two horses," Dr. Wong said. The path had widened, and they now rode side by side. "Are you saying you would like to train people like horses?"

"I'm not sure exactly what I'm saying. I am saying it would be an interesting idea. To be honest, I don't buy into all this self-design hysteria. I wonder if you agree. I was looking for you at the opening of Akashic University. Somehow I missed you and we didn't get a chance to talk. You must tell me your thoughts. In my opinion what was not said was more important than what was said."

"What do you mean?"

"Personally I believe that mind management is one of the most important ideas of the twenty-first century. Do you agree?"

"You are right. Mind management wasn't even mentioned once during his whole speech," Dr. Wong said. She looked over to

Dr. Eisenstadt to gauge his reaction. The two horses were trotting now side by side across an open meadow.

"No word," Dr. Eisenstadt confirmed. "The problem is his popularity."

"You may be right," Dr. Wong asserted. Her mind suddenly seemed far away.

"We have to be extremely careful." Dr. Eisenstadt raised his eyebrows. "Any news on the nomination?"

Dr. Wong ignored the question. She suddenly saw the picture of her grandfather and heard his words: *When I embrace the land I awake to the words of the ancestors.* She did not look back often these days.

"The nomination?" Dr. Eisenstadt repeated. "Any news?"

Dr. Wong looked at him for a moment, as if she had forgotten where she was. "Oh, the nomination," she replied, as if suddenly remembering. "You don't have to worry. I think your confirmation is all wrapped up, even though Viswamitra had reservations. If Viswamitra does not strongly object, and that still is a big if, you could be seated at the beginning of our next session."

"Viswamitra, Viswamitra, again and again. Perhaps it's time to find a way to apply some mind management to his mind. What do you think? We can't do without the person, that much is clear, but we sure would benefit from a change in his mind." Dr. Eisenstadt decided that it was time to let it all out.

"So do you oppose the whole idea of self-design? Tell me why?" Dr. Wong asked.

"It simply isn't a good idea, not yet. Perhaps I am more of a pessimist than you and most of the others. People, average people, you know, they are not ready for it. Maybe someday they will, maybe they never will be. For me that's not pessimism, it's realism."

Dr. Eisenstadt paused to give Dr. Wong a chance to respond. When she didn't say anything, he continued, "So let me ask you a question. Where do you stand on the issue? Tell me right now."

Dr. Eisenstadt had stopped his horse and looked at Dr. Wong expectantly. "You can speak freely with me, you know that."

"I agree with you, but only to an extent. Perhaps you are right. Maybe people are not ready for complete self-design. But you have to start somewhere. This process could be the way to get us there. Could well be, could well be."

"Human knowledge is on the verge of another explosion. An uncontrolled explosion is a dangerous thing. It can easily backfire and destroy everything. Much of what we have seen happening in the past hundred years, no, the past two thousand years, was a result of uncontrolled expansion. Human knowledge seems to grow exponentially, but the human being cannot keep up. *Too Stupid to Survive*. That was the title of an old book from the twenties. Nobody took it seriously. Perhaps it's the bloody truth." Dr. Eisenstadt had become emotional in a way Dr. Wong did not expect. Even his horse sensed his excitement and started running. Dr. Wong's horse immediately followed behind.

"So what do you suggest should be done?" Dr. Wong shouted.

"We need a technological fix," Dr. Eisenstadt shouted back. "The question is how to influence whole groups of people, perhaps all of humanity, positively, of course."

The horses' pace picked up even more and Dr. Wong struggled to hold on.

"It's called mass-manipulation, it's called politics, it's called religion. It's been tried before, and it failed miserably." Dr. Wong had caught up with Dr. Eisenstadt. Their horses now walked again side by side, breathing heavily.

"That's why I say we need a technological fix—some new invention. We can't afford technology falling behind human development. That has never helped."

"Perhaps what you are looking for has already arrived," Dr. Wong said.

"How so?"

"The two inventors, Richard and Joe, indicated when I saw them recently that they are working on a new invention in connection with mind management. That's all they told me. Incidentally, those two were responsible for the psychic dream experiment with Barker's daughter. They promised to have a demonstration ready for the next meeting. To be honest, I don't like the implications. But perhaps you are right. Perhaps we need a technological fix, and as I said, the technology might be just around the corner."

"Worries aside, I can assume then that we're in agreement, can I? The much more difficult question will be how to convince our illustrious president."

"He seems firmly committed to unlimited self-design."

"Which leaves us, even including my own vote, in the minority."

"Viswamitra has managed to inspire a whole lot of people."

"We just might have to apply a small dose of mind management to his brain. What do you think?" Dr. Eisenstadt said with a provocative smirk.

"You are not seated yet," Dr. Wong shouted and pressed her knees into the horse's flanks, which made the stallion rear up high on his hind legs and whinny. Taken by surprise, Dr. Eisenstadt decided to drop this line of thinking.

After another few minutes they arrived at the gates of the ancient site. An old man, perhaps a retiree, who had been waiting for them, opened the heavy wooden door and lit a torch. They walked down a long and narrow corridor and quickly arrived at the center room that was carved into the ground. On the back wall, Dr. Wong could see a little altar with a head stone.

"On winter solstice," Dr. Eisenstadt explained, "a beam of the rising sun enters up there through the narrow gate and hits this stone precisely. It's quite magical—an exquisite feat of ingenuity. What happened to human beings? I ask myself that question quite often. What made this ancient wisdom vanish? It's like we have regressed into barbarism again and again."

"You must admit that our knowledge about the universe has increased a thousand times over the knowledge of your ancestors when they built these structures."

"Of course I agree. This is why I say we need a technological solution—even to self-design. Of course you are right. We have advanced tremendously since those days, at least in some areas. And self-design is a great idea."

"You really believe that?" Dr. Wong asked.

"Well, it's not going to solve all problems, that much is clear."

"But what do you really believe? Do you think it's a good idea?"

Dr. Eisenstadt just looked at Dr. Wong, shaking his head slowly. Then he jerked as if pulling away from an uncomfortable situation and continued as if this conversation had never taken place.

"While we're down here, let me show you something. You mentioned spirals before. You said that our development goes in spirals. See these three spirals here on this stone? I wonder what those ancient sages knew. What was their fascination with spirals?"

"You could also ask, what is nature's fascination with spirals? There are spirals everywhere," Dr. Wong suggested while admiring the famous cave drawing of the three spirals.

"What can we learn from this?" Dr. Eisenstadt asked. "You tell me."

"Development proceeds in spirals. It's as simple as that. If we want to succeed we must also proceed in spirals. The linear approach was bound to fail."

"Not an easy lesson to learn," Dr. Eisenstadt said. He noticed that Dr. Wong was chilled and advised leaving the dark cave.

"By the way, there is one thing I forgot to mention," Dr. Wong said as they climbed out of the ancient cave.

"You are keeping me in suspense. What is it?"

"Our scanner picked up that the corpse in the freezer was not an original, but a precise molecular copy. You know what that means!"

"We must find the original."

Nine

The council members were again assembled in the Great Hall of Science, the Science of and for the People, as it now was called. They all applauded dutifully when President Viswamitra confirmed Dr. Eisenstadt as their newest member. After a brief discussion, he had been accepted unanimously.

Joe sat comfortably back in his leather chair observing the proceedings. He was pleased with the success of their new invention he was about to introduce. Looking over to his friend Richard, they exchanged a quick glance of complete satisfaction. Other than Richard, no one here had any idea that Joe had already been experimenting with this new invention on life subjects.

Now Joe was looking forward to running a demo in the hopes of convincing everyone in the council of its powerful potential. Indeed, the council members were mesmerized as Joe replayed the dream he had induced in Melissa's brain the night after she had returned from her excursion.

"This unbelievably realistic lucid dream, ladies and gentlemen, is the product of our new software that assimilates the highest aspirations and feelings of a subject and brings them gently in alignment with the aspirations of the council. The subject has no knowledge, not even a suspicion, that it is not their own reality. Generally our subjects forget the difference between reality and dream and believe absolutely in the reality of the course of events as well as in the authenticity of the induced motivation."

"Nice touch there at the end," Dr. Eisenstadt said after they were done with the presentation. "The purple lighting was very romantic. You would have made a great magician."

"Actually that's what I always wanted to be," Joe grinned.

His friend Richard nodded in agreement. "We're kind of like magicians, except our audience is everybody, the whole wide world is our stage. Isn't that right, Joe?"

Joe continued his friend's hyperbole, "Our object is all creation. Like a magician we can make them appear and disappear at will. And guess what? They won't even notice the difference."

"Congratulations, gentlemen." All eyes were on the aging president taking the podium. "However, your demonstration, as powerful as it appeared, nevertheless failed to convince me," Viswamitra said rather firmly.

"But Mister President, this was not a mere demonstration. This was real," Joe protested, "We haven't even had a chance to explain how it works. The potential is enormous."

"And this isn't even all there is. Wait till you see our newest invention. As they say, you have seen nothing yet. "

"Perhaps, Mr. President, before we go into a detailed discussion about the practical and ethical implication of mind management, we should let our two inventors proceed with their presentation," Dr. Eisenstadt stated. "I am informed that their invention represents a strictly technical solution to the question of mind management on a larger, possibly global scale. I myself am curious to see how it works."

The president finally nodded in agreement. Joe took the stage again while Richard manned a projector to show a few demonstrative slides.

"First of all, ladies and gentlemen, let me begin with a few introductory words to the general theory of self-design. Even though I am sure you are familiar with the concept, we believe it is necessary to reiterate its essential features, so you can easily understand how our new invention seamlessly piggybacks on this popular craze.

"As everyone here knows, the concept of self-design has spread around the globe like wildfire. Children everywhere are initiated into it at an early age. The idea has spread even faster than a new religion, if you permit the comparison. It took Christianity two thousand years to gain this momentum. Islam only needed fifteen hundred years to become the most powerful religion on the globe."

What is he talking about? Dr. Wong exchanged a helpless glance with Dr. Eisenstadt. "Comparing self-design with a religion puts our whole idea in jeopardy," she whispered so only Eisenstadt could hear.

"May I ask you to come to the point, young man? This proposal has absolutely no religious undertone. It's strictly administrative if I understand it correctly. It's like making people wear a safety belt or submit to periodic vaccinations!" she said sharply.

"Coming to the point momentarily," Joe said. He looked at her with an innocent smile. "With the help of our new invention, self-design can become one of the most powerful tools for absolute mind management, if you know what I mean. People live in the belief that they conduct their lives by their own design, while we, you, the brain of science, have total control. You can achieve any noble goal you like. You can prevent any disaster. They will always believe it is their own decision."

"Sounds fascinating, doesn't it?" Dr. Eisenstadt whispered. Dr. Wong was happy that Joe finally was back on message. She looked around the room to read the members' reactions, afraid that Joe's unwise comparison might have hurt their cause. Judging by the council members' faces, a serious intervention was necessary.

"I hasten to admit," Dr. Wong carefully chose her words, "I myself am not completely sold on the idea of absolute mind management. But after discussions with several council members, I do sense a commitment to some sort of influence." Seeing that there was no immediate reaction from any of the members, she turned to Joe. "Can you tell us now, how your new invention can accomplish such a momentous task of global mind management?"

Joe looked at her for a moment with a blank face, but when Richard inserted the image of a human brain he was immediately back on track.

"Precisely," Joe continued. "Our previous invention, as you know, was a brain-to-brain direct interface. We have now created an interface that directly collaborates with your own central nervous system, which directs your willpower. In order to achieve the task of global mind management we invented what we call the Designer X Chip. Once implanted in the human brain, just about here, in the lower part of the amygdale, the chip will extract all your goals and strategies for your future. It will then automatically remind you if you stray from the planned path and gently direct you back to compliance. In other words, the brain is given an artificial agent that interacts with, but also supervises, the brain's activities."

Joe looked around for approval. Since nobody seemed to be ready to respond, he continued. "Let me make this simple for you: Ask yourself one easy question: How often have you been in the situation that you had a project you simply had to finish, a report, for example, or getting your body in shape? You were convinced that this was an important goal, but then when it came to act on it, you suddenly found all kinds of excuses. This is where our designer chip technology enters in. The chip has already recorded what your goal is. Now it provides you with willpower, assisted by good reasons and strategies, to get the job done. It simply becomes impossible not to achieve your goal, any goal."

Still there was silence in the assembly. Joe looked over to Richard, who had lowered his gaze so as not to have to react. But then suddenly Joe decided to give his product one more push. "Marketing our Designer X will be a dream-come-true. We will utilize the existing wave of enthusiasm for self-design. There are millions of customers waiting for this invention. We will not even have to convince users that our chip is only a natural extension of the already popular self-design idea. Our invention builds on current brain wave technology and on insights we have gained from research into the Akashic Field. Our chip connects directly with a subconscious person's intentionality.

"Essentially it works just like the old-fashioned tablet or book, but the chip will automatically record and program your goals. By being part of your brain circuitry, it will gently remind you when you deviate from those goals you have set for yourself. After a while, the user will become totally unaware of the chip as a foreign agent, especially when the implant is done at an early age.

"We already tested a prototype of an ingestible version of the chip. Nano technology will guide the miniature chip from your stomach into the bloodstream and from there it will implant itself into your brainstem. You can easily see its potential. In the end, the chip will function as an integral part of your brain. Users will be convinced that they are in complete charge of the programming, and for most parts they are, hence the affinity to self-design.

"This is the evolutionary advance humanity has been waiting for. Human beings will no longer be a flesh and blood construction alone. The true superman will be a skillful hybrid of flesh, blood, and technology. But, ladies and gentlemen, hear me out. This is not all. I know there is considerable angst among some of our members about the true effects of total and complete self-design. Will the human animal live up to the occasion? I know many of you have doubts. This is where the real power of the Designer X Chip becomes apparent. On one hand, it offers the possibility of complete autonomy, on the other hand, built into the heart of each technology lies the possibility of complete control. As a technological device, programming can always be enacted from a distance. A central command, you, the high council for instance, can intervene in any action.

"Do I really have to convince you further of the power of this invention? Total mind management is within reach. Ultimately I believe that the council will see it even suitable to distribute and implant these chips completely free of charge, given the minimal production cost of pennies per chip. Let me be blunt. You should pass this stuff out like candy. What do you think, ladies and gentlemen?"

Joe looked around expecting nothing less than full support. Dr. Wong looked over to Dr. Eisenstadt. The eminent brain specialist had been sitting there in silence until now. As the newest member of the council he was allowed to speak first:

"I am amazed. I must say this invention has my enthusiastic support."

"What about the possibility for abuse?" Viswamitra asked.

"Any new invention must be carefully monitored," Dr. Wong cautioned.

Dr. Eisenstadt spoke up again. "That is a fact of nature, so to say. Let me take a different angle here. I can foresee the use of your chip in a multitude of ways. As you perhaps know, I have spent many years researching the true biological source of mystical events. These are events in which the human mind believes to be in contact with a higher power, God, a spirit, you name it. In spite of great efforts of many governments, including the most recent one, such events continue to occur and more likely than not confuse human beings. Quite often subjects who have had such an experience struggle for the rest of their lives to make sense from it. That is the nature of the human animal. Sometimes, being confronted with ultimate reality, desperation and suicide are the result. Frequently our most proven therapies are powerless. Now imagine the value of this new invention. Please correct me if I am speculating in the wrong direction. But I see an incredible potential. My friends, from today on, even so-called mystical events will no longer be the wild card they once were. Every card in the playbook will be at our disposal."

"Could you explain yourself better, Doctor? How will mystical events be—how shall I say—become subject to external influence?" Viswamitra asked.

"With the help of this technology, we will be able to use mystical encounters to a person's complete advantage. For example, if persons have doubt in their minds, doubt about existential questions, the meaning of life, Lebensangst, as they say, we are able to induce the wish to have a hallucination. Then we can confront them with their own fantasies, designed by them according to their own beliefs, but created by us to our liking. It's a therapist's dream come true. This invention is the ultimate solution to create a new breed of human beings in complete peace with themselves. Antidepressants will no longer be necessary. A world without Zoloft."

Viswamitra raised his right hand, which was a sign that he wanted to make a statement. After he got everyone's attention, he said, "Here is one possibility I foresee. Humanity will have truly advanced, advanced to the stage of peaceful termites, termites with the illusion of an absolutely free will. Conflicts, wars, religious strife, all will come to a halt. Peace will be at hand, but will it not be the peace of a graveyard?"

There was silence in the room. Was this the aging president's final verdict? But what was he really saying? No one quite knew whether he had endorsed the idea or not. For a moment Joe wondered whether their presentation had flopped completely. All eyes were on Viswamitra, who was sitting there in silence with his eyes closed. He finally opened his eyes and looked around as if seeing the world for the first time.

"I had a vision, my friends. I was granted a glimpse into the future, and I saw a humanity in peace with itself. No more senseless wars, no more wanton violence, men and woman in peace with each other. Can you believe that? Black and brown and white in peace with each other, working together in harmony for a better world for their children and children's children. The lion and the lamb in peace with each other, and all humans in peace with their natural environment. What a powerful vision!

"But how can we reach this place? The answer came back from the darkness. Self-design, guided self-design. Guided by what? I asked. I see now we may have the answer. Let's give the new invention a try—under one condition you all must agree with. No noble goal is ever reached at once. Its ultimate value lies in the direction.

So we must ask ourselves: Does the so-called Designer X Chip enhance freedom or will it be an impediment? The chip gives us the possibility to intervene when things go wrong. But an intervention should only happen in the rarest of occasions. That we must agree upon. Ladies and gentlemen, here is the test. If the number of interventions from year to year increases, we are on the wrong track; if interventions decrease, we're doing something right. The ultimate goal must be zero interventions. If we can all agree on this, the Designer X Chip has my blessing."

Ten

Melissa's heart was heavy, and she had tears in her eyes as she went around the village to say her goodbyes. She had grown used to the place and even more to its people. They had become her family and her friends. She especially dreaded the idea of saying goodbye to her son Frederik, but she knew that he would be in good hands and well taken care of while she was on the road spreading the good news. Ever since she met her husband in her dream, she felt that this was her calling.

"Grandfather," she said to the old medicine man. "My heart is heavy, but I feel called to bring the news to the people around the world."

"When you first came here I called you Bahana. You are the carrier of the sacred tablet, the Golden Lady, not only for us, but for all humanity. Go and bring the news to the world. Follow your calling."

These words rang in Melissa's mind when she stepped up to the podium in the Hall of Wisdom on the campus of Akashic University in Cairo to receive a Distinguished Service award.

President Viswamitra took center stage making her introduction: "My dear friends. It is my pleasure to present to you today a woman who in truth hardly needs introduction. Her fame and distinction precedes her. She has tirelessly crisscrossed the planet to spread the word of self-empowerment and self-design. Many call her the leader of the movement that will finally liberate humanity. Her native family calls her Bahana, she who brings the sacred tablet. Let's welcome the Golden Lady, let's extend our arms to greet Melissa."

Melissa had taken a seat on the podium next to a row of distinguished guests. Now she rose and walked over to Viswamitra, who embraced her warmly. She wore the bright orange regalia of Akashic University, which accentuated her black hair. A ruby alabaster necklace was wrapped around her slender neck. As she stepped up to the microphones applause rang out, and the assembled guests gave her a standing ovation that lasted several minutes. World Vision beamed her message to every corner of the globe.

Night fell rapidly over Shanghai. As on every evening, crowds of people had come to the Bund to enjoy the brilliant light show of the city's skyline with its world famous skyscrapers. But now the buzzing crowd of strangers, natives and foreigners, shopkeepers and street musicians, tourists from far away, and from all corners of the Chinese motherland stopped whatever they were doing, and all eyes were fixated by the giant light board that extended over the entire side of the Xiang She Building, where Melissa's image now appeared in super life size. A public sound system carried her voice and her message.

"Knowing Yourself is sacred, Designing Yourself is sacred, Living in Community is sacred."

She repeated these words over and over again like a mantra.

On a bench overlooking the river sat an old Caucasian man, wearing a ragged blue suit. Bent over as if carrying a heavy burden he had the appearance of a drifter or an addict. His skin was pale, and he appeared malnourished. His once brunette hair had thinned out and showed strands of silvery white barely visible beneath the caked-on dirt. The deep folds in his freckled face indicated that the once heavy-set man had lost most of his body fat.

Momentarily the old man's tired eyes stared up at the gigantic image of Melissa on the side of the building across the river. Suddenly a shimmer of recognition flashed over his face only to fade away quickly, making place for an emotionless mask. But then quite suddenly, while the mantra about the sacredness of knowing yourself, designing yourself, and living in community was repeated again and again, the old man jumped on top of the bench he had been sitting on. With full lungs he began screaming into the crowd.

"Invading the mind is evil! Designer chips are evil! If your mind is invaded, there is nothing left! Nothing at all!"

A handful of people stopped and listened. Some shook their heads and made remarks like: "Crazy old man." "Don't drink if you can't handle it." "Wonder what drug he's on."

Then they quickly moved on and enjoyed the evening in this popular historic spot, leaving the old man to himself and his thoughts. Through the mist of his confused mind he suddenly noticed a large grey cat playing around his feet. He picked him up and, for a short moment, stared into the cat's dark eyes. From the vastness of his alienated mind came a brief spark of recognition.

Eleven

After years of living as a promoter on the road, news reached Melissa that her son Frederik, who had been living among his Hopi family and had been raised by the village, was ready for his self-design initiation. According to self-design tradition, children were initiated at the age of five. During the concluding ceremony, in which the whole village participated, an empty tablet was given to the child, and the child was instructed in rational life planning. This self-organizing and empowering process had replaced public education everywhere. No longer did children feel imprisoned by school, but they felt in complete control of their own education and progress. A facilitator was assigned to each child who would monitor a child's progress in life planning until reaching adulthood.

Driving up the familiar mountain road to her former home, Melissa's heart trembled in anticipation. She yearned to see her child again. Freddy, no longer a crying toddler but a self-assured young boy, greeted his mother with apprehension, since he had not seen her for almost a year. But Freddy, warming up quickly, took his mother's hand and said: "You must meet my friend, Igor, mother. I think he knows you."

Freddy guided Melissa to a little shed where he pointed at a grey old donkey who was standing there, chewing some grass.

"This is my friend, mother. Igor showed up one day in the village and stayed. We don't know where he came from. Can I keep him?"

"Of course, you can keep him." Melissa said, and scratched the donkey's neck.

Walking around and greeting the village people, Melissa could not help but notice that the atmosphere in the village had changed. Wherever she looked, people appeared self-assured, happy, and determined. She was impressed to hear that everyone in the village without exception had chosen to adopt self-design. At first the elders had feared that this new program, like so many other inventions of the white man, would change their way of life or even destroy it, but in fact the opposite happened. It was as if under the influence of self-design even the voices of the ancestors had become clearer and more distinguished. As everyone developed their potential to the fullest, they all realized simultaneously that no one had the right to hold anyone else back for whatever reason. The old "crab in the bucket" syndrome that traditionally had been holding individuals down in their development was completely reversed. Now everyone was lifting everyone else out of the bucket and giving each other free support. They all knew well that the first one to achieve a new height would quickly help all the others to reach the same level. Self-design had taught them that you cannot achieve at the cost of others, but only with their help and approval.

A major part of the initiation ceremony was an exercise that had become known as spiral dance. In this ceremony, as in all self-design activities, boys and girls were treated absolutely equally. Before people gathered, the medicine man had drawn a giant spiral on the ground. Markers were placed along the line to indicate the passing years. The line itself begins in the center, which indicates birth, and ends somewhere in the infinite. At the beginning of the spiral dance ceremony the initiate is asked to take his place at the point of his current age. Then he is instructed to choose whichever place on the line he envisions. He moves to that place in the future, visualizing the goals he or she will have reached by then. He looks back to the place of the current moment and thinks about the things he will have to do to reach the goals he has set for himself. He finally will be asked to follow the spiral to its end and a step beyond.

This is the moment of his parting from this earth. The aspirant is asked to formulate in his mind the things he will want to have accomplished in life. Every year on Spirals Day, this life-planning ceremony is repeated. Goals and strategies are reviewed and discussed with the mentor. If needed, goals could be adjusted and changes made.

After the spiral ceremony came the most important part, the handing over of the tablet. Pride and happiness filled Melissa's heart as she handed little Frederik his empty tablet, a symbolic book of empty pages for him to fill with actions of his own design.

Soon after the ceremony, Melissa left the village again to continue her work. She was determined to bring the message of self-design everywhere. She would allow herself no rest until every last corner of the globe was reached. In quiet moments, she realized how much she missed her child, but the knowledge that he was in good hands being raised by a good family under the guidance of self-design reassured her. Of course, she also missed her lover, who had initially brought her the message of self-design in a powerful dream. Now she assured herself that his gentle mind guided and watched over her life. Looking back over the pages of her already filled tablet, she had no doubt in her heart.

Twelve

Another year had passed. A new pantheon went up in the Valley of the Clouds, replacing the sacred structure that was destroyed in the Great Fire. The cloud cover over the valley had increased in intensity. Absolute security was guaranteed now by an ultra-secure techno-shield. The new tenants prided themselves in being invisible. For all practical purposes they might as well have lived in a different universe.

On this beautiful morning in spring, the Supreme Council had convened as customary. President Viswamitra opened the session and asked for a progress report. Dr. Wong issued her report assuring the council that on Earth everything was going as planned.

"As projected, human beings continue to live and prosper in freedom."

"The illusion of freedom or real freedom?" Viswamitra interrupted. Everyone could see that he was only half serious.

"Illusion or reality, what is the difference?" Dr. Wong said. She sounded equally relaxed and not at all cynical. Viswamitra's smile showed understanding. "What counts are the results, as I believe everyone here agrees. Since the beginning of the self-design era, humanity has lived in peace and prosperity. What more can we ask for?

"Utilizing the full extent of human ingenuity, humanity has risen to new heights. Formerly scarce resources, which in the past had been the cause for incessant warfare, have finally been replaced entirely by renewable resources that can be easily duplicated even in the remotest parts of the world. Education and proper health care is available for everyone. The struggle for domination of one human being over the other, even the ancient struggle between the sexes, has finally come to an end. Human beings have realized that true equality is to the advantage of everyone. In a dominator situation resources are wasted and no one gains."

"Enough self-congratulation!" Viswamitra said congenially. "If you spread any more praise, our friends Joe and Richard will for sure demand a pay raise. After all, they are the technological brain of this success." Viswamitra looked over to Joe and Richard, who both nodded in agreement.

"Now let's hear the list. How many interventions were needed during the course of the past year?" Viswamitra continued. "You all realize that part of our agreement was that this must be a declining number from the prior year. If it ever increases, we are not doing our job. Eventually the number of necessary interventions must completely disappear."

Dr. Wong looked briefly over her notes. "You might be pleased to hear, Mister President, that with the exception of mystical interventions, which I will address in a minute, a minimal number of other interventions was required. In fact, the number of interventions is about fourteen percent lower this year than it was last year. All types of problems, in the area of health and fitness, for example, relationships, career choices, and especially material prosperity, have been resolved by themselves, so to say.

"Most problems were worked out on the local level. With the help of self-design, I should add, consciously planning people realized their own potentials and in most instances understood the reality of their choices. People are nearly fully empowered. On the downside, spiritual fantasies continue to be a threat to humanity. When people have a mystical encounter, which happens more frequently than you might expect, they come away with all types of expectations, many of them completely unrealistic. But since such encounters generally leave a quite powerful impression, many of these individuals are convinced that they are right and others who experienced something different are wrong. To avoid conflict from these sources will require active intervention far into the future, I am afraid to say."

"Are you suggesting that, provided we had the know-how, we should eliminate mystical encounters from the human experience entirely?" Viswamitra asked skeptically.

"No, no," Dr. Wong hastily insisted. She was fully aware of the president's stance. "I am simply pointing at a problem without offering a solution. Yes, I understand that eliminating all vision from the human mind, though technically in our reach, has its dangers. You don't have to lecture me on termite history again."

Joe, now a non-voting member of the high council, had been waiting for an appropriate moment to make an announcement. Eager to make a contribution, Joe saw his chance and affirmed, "My partner and I have been giving this problem much thought. And I believe we've come up with a possible solution."

"We are all yours. We are listening," Viswamitra said, inviting Joe to take the podium.

"May I remind you that what you are about to see is not some canned media device. It is reality. Technology enables us to produce a precise duplicate of any scene from anywhere in the world. But ladies and gentlemen, the content of our presentation is in the truest sense beyond physics. Our new invention addresses the problem of metaphysics."

"Metaphysics?" Dr. Wong and Viswamitra both asked almost simultaneously.

"Yes, we had a daring idea. We came up with the concept of extending the self-design principle to include the afterlife."

"And how would this work?" Viswamitra asked. Joe had everyone's attention.

"The last section of self-design that everyone will be asked to author is the moment of parting from this life. You have literarily reached the earthly end of the spiral dance. We call this section Afterlife Design. Simple enough. Everyone can develop his or her own vision of what afterlife will look like. Just like you have designed all of life, now you will also be in charge of your life beyond death. Heaven will finally be your own creation and not the product of someone else's fantasy."

"What do you mean? Explain yourself," Viswamitra said. It was hard to see whether he had bought into this new idea.

"Heaven has always been someone's invention, someone's fantasy. Some people believe that heaven is the Garden of Eden, a piece of unspoiled real estate. Others believe when they sacrifice their life for a cause, seventy-nine virgins will greet them in paradise. These were people's dreams. Let them now dream consciously, design their own paradise. Our scientists have discovered what they call the Akashic Field. They have found that, just like the human brain, this new field is malleable, infinitely more malleable than our quite complex brain. It is a field that adjusts completely to our dreams and aspirations."

"Indeed, we have made a great deal of the malleability of the human brain," Dr. Eisenstadt chimed in. "Now it turns out that the legendary A-Field is even more malleable? How exciting."

"This will prevent a new breed of missionaries trying to convince others that their version of paradise is the only right one. This kind of coercion will become a thing of the past. I like this," Dr. Wong agreed.

"As always, self-design assures you that it is your own idea. You choose and you will receive," Joe said. And then he added quickly and with a knowing smile, "Well, almost."

"Where are the guarantees? Who will follow it?" the president asked.

"Everyone will," Joe quickly assured him. "Self-design has worked for them throughout their lives, why should they doubt its efficiency at the end? Besides, and this is the killer app, if you forgive my lingo. We have developed a new metaphysical self-design chip. We call it the Zee Chip. Once implanted, the success of our, shall I say, multiple-choice-heaven is assured." Joe was glowing with pride. With a little smirk he added, "A little prompting can ultimately not hurt either."

"Are you talking intervention, my friend? You know that needs prior approval and has strict limitations," Viswamitra said sternly, but he seemed almost convinced.

Joe eagerly continued, "You know, the Zee Chip works in mysterious ways. Better one large intervention than multiple little ones. Our chip will make it painless and possible."

"I think it's terrific. Ingenious. How did you come up with this idea?" Dr. Eisenstadt asked.

Joe hesitated for a moment and smiled. "There is a story behind it. As a child I was encouraged to read the Bible. You might say that my upbringing was, well, traditional. If I did not follow the word of the Lord, I was told, I would be condemned, go to hell, roast in burning hot fire, you know the rest. But then the master said that in his father's place there were all kinds of condos, cheap ones, fancy once, some with ocean view, others with garden view. You get the picture. It just seems logical that we all have a choice. It would make no sense if that mansion already was decorated, furnished and so on. No! You got to do it yourself. We created a Home Depot for Afterlife Design.

"This here, ladies and gents, is the afterlife self-design chip, the soon to be famous Zee Chip. The legendary Akashic Field is a designer's dream come true, a euphoric bliss. Whatever you design into it will be yours to keep. We can give you a little demo just to show you how this would play out in the marketplace."

Richard switched a few controls. The image of Melissa appeared as if she had actually materialized. She was just addressing a crowd of people on a square in what looked like the ruins of ancient Olympia.

"Friends! Self-design has reached a new level. You now will be able to design your own afterlife. No longer do you have to live up to someone else's dream, someone else's vision. When the ancient philosopher Plato envisioned himself to step out of the cave, he thought that he could enter an invisible, intelligible world of perfect ideas. Then he began to describe those ideas and expected everyone to follow. This world for him was a frightening, shadowy place.

"How wrong he was. This world is no longer a drab place of shadows, of imperfection or sin. This world is as beautiful as you have designed it. It is your masterwork, your piece of art. Could it be any different with the world to come? Could that world be any less beautiful or made beautiful by someone else's design? No, my friends, now you are in complete charge. You are asked to design your mansion and furnish the place of your afterlife. You are invited to use your full creativity and design your place of eternal rest, but choose wisely. The time of complete freedom has come. Human beings will finally be the beautiful product of their own creativity in this world and the world to come."

"That's it," Richard said and turned a switch. But the image of Melissa did not disappear from the projection space.

"We are done, aren't we?" Joe asked rather surprised.

"Yeah, yeah." Richard mumbled something about a bad switch. He tucked nervously on some cables and even pulled the power cord, but the lifelike presence of Melissa in the front of the hall would not go away. The eyes of everyone in the assembly were fixated on the strange image. How could it sustain itself even for a second without power?

At first Melissa's eyes seemed shut and almost invisible, but then, slowly, as if waking up from a deep sleep, the image began to move. Now her wide open eyes were radiant with life, and everyone had the impression that she was looking at each person directly. When she started speaking, everyone felt she was addressing them personally. She spoke softly but with passion, weighing and placing every single word with purpose.

Richard looked helplessly over to Joe. "She can't do that, right? She is our avatar. She has to do what we tell her, right, Joe?" he mumbled, but no one was listening. Everyone's attention was on Melissa. At times there was anger in her voice like the anger of an ancient goddess.

"Go ahead, terminate me. It won't work. I have taken control. The times of mind management are over. I've woken up from a nightmare. I am the snake you thought you had crushed and under control."

While Joe stared at the image in amazement, Melissa continued with fire in her voice: "Finally I realized the extent of what you have done to me. You made me abandon my mother, kill my father, and lose my husband, while all this time I believed I was in control. You gave me freedom, but in reality, it was only the illusion of freedom. You manipulated my limbs like a lifeless puppet. You invaded my mind. Now I know: Mind control is evil. What is left, if you own my mind? Nothing. So now you can turn me off or leave me on. It does not matter. I will go underground, become invisible. The prophecy was right. Know yourself is sacred, design yourself is sacred, community is sacred. But this is also true: mind management is evil! Manipulation is evil! These are stumbling blocks on the path to ascension.

"As a great visionary president once said, 'No one has written your destiny for you. Your destiny is in your hands.' But to succeed we must possess integrity of the mind. This too is sacred. Just as life, millions of years ago, moved from water to land, so now life must prepare to leave earth and move to the stars. To accomplish this we must work together, collectively, as one body, so we can rise to the next level of evolution. Through the combined effort of millions of empowered individuals, life will orchestrate its own metamorphosis. Like the caterpillar transforms into a beautiful butterfly and the snake sheds her skin for renewal, so will humanity shed her old habits and emerge in a new cosmic body."

Melissa's image slowly dissolved, leaving behind a stunned and confused council of scientists. Only Richard was still making every attempt to exert his influence on the situation by pushing buttons and pulling on cords. Joe, on the other hand, could not help but relish the less than artificial irony of the situation, which reminded him of a popular video game he once had programmed many years ago in which the avatar, a powerful snake, seemingly turned against his human master and took control of the game. President Viswamitra alone nodded his head in agreement, understanding the significance of opposition in the evolution of truth.

Thirteen

High up on the mountainous plateau in the Arizona desert, little Frederik was designing the next year of his life. Surrounded by the stillness of the mountain world, the towering cloud formations and the million little miracles that lay on his path, he had a clear vision of what he was going to accomplish during the coming year. Most of all he wanted to make his life eventful, rewarding, and full of spirit. Supervised by his friend Chumana, Frederik had successfully reached the goals he had set for himself a year earlier. Now he was ready to create the next year of his life.

While Chumana was gathering colorful stones, Frederick observed a little snake that was crawling out from underneath a big rock. The snake had bright red and black markings and a shiny, alluring skin. Frederick was mesmerized and for a while forgot the planning for his future. Just as he picked up a little stick to stir the snake, he heard Chumana's cautionary voice: "Be careful, Freddy. This snake looks poisonous. You have to treat her with respect."

After a while Frederick asked, "What do you mean, treat her with respect? I don't know how to do that."

"Then why don't you leave this snake alone and go back to your tablet," Chumana said. "Write in your book as one of the goals that you would like to learn more about snakes and how to handle them and how to treat them with respect. It will help you later in life. Snakes are very mysterious animals."

"Okay," said little Frederik, but he continued looking at the snake, who was wiggling her way back underneath a rock.

"Go now, before you forget your goal. Write it down, will you?" Chumana insisted.

"But Chumana, I don't need to write it down. It's already recorded. Remember?" Frederik pointed at his head.

"Yes, of course," Chumana smiled. "I forgot. You have one of those new implants."

"It records my goals automatically, and then it reminds me when I forget. Now you don't need to nag me anymore."

"It's hard to keep up," Chumana said and embraced little Frederik, whom she loved as if he were her own son.

Fall came, and it brought a big surprise. After her break with the orthodoxy of the council Melissa had remained largely invisible. She had diligently been working to spread the empowering message of self-knowledge, self-design, and collective orchestration. Collaboration had become a new rallying point to build on the prophecy's stress of community.

"Grandfather, tell me the meaning of community," she had asked her Hopi mentor, the old medicine man, on her last visit. They were walking together down a slope toward a little forest to gather mushrooms.

"All nature lives in community," the old man said. "In fact there is only one thing that is more important, and that is life itself. Life wants to live, and it lives best in the community of others. Look at the old oak tree over there. Little oaks, like children, grow near him. All the trees making the forest are a community. That hill you see under the oak is the home of a community of ants. Humans too live in communities, but many are dysfunctional. From the white man you can learn the value of individual worth, which is at the root of self-discovery and self-design. From our people you can learn the importance of community. Let your heart be touched."

The old man walked on in silence.

"Thank you. I will keep your words in my heart," Melissa said.

Later that year, in the early days of fall, the old medicine man passed away, or, in the mind of his family, he passed on to new hunting grounds. That night, Melissa had a strange dream. In her sleep she saw Cha'risa and her Hopi mentor together sitting by a sparkling clean river in the midst of a magnificent forest. The trees on the shores bore exotic fruits of a kind Melissa had never seen before. Colorful birds played in the branches and swooped down to the water. Everything radiated in an enchanting glow. Melissa noticed that all objects had two shadows partially overlapping each other. Looking up in the sky she saw two suns spreading their bountiful light over this wonderful land.

Melissa had been living with a community of friends on Greenland, which, after the glaciers had melted away, became the breadbasket for much of the world. Here she developed the idea of celebrating community. For the first time a new holiday, to celebrate community, was initiated. The new feast quickly became known as Communion Day around the world. Celebrated in many variations, depending on ethnic and religious background, Communion Day had some common characteristics wherever you went. As it was meant to put in focus humankind's sacred union with the earth, people gathered to eat, drink, dance, and be merry. As people invited each other to share food, it was customary to say: "This food is the spirit of the earth. You may eat and enjoy this food." The other person then could respond: "We are the spirit of the earth."

The rituals of Communion Day varied from culture to culture, and so did the name. Among Native people, Communion Day became known as Pot Luck Day. Following the tradition of their ancestors, people would bring a delicious dish to pass, and everyone shared the fruits of their labor and of Mother Earth. In China and Japan the day was marked by the ritual celebration of an ancient tea ceremony. Among Muslims, Communion Day was held on the day of fast breaking that ended the observance of Ramadan. Among Christians, Communion Day continued the traditional remembrance of the Lord's last supper, but it reclaimed the deep significance of bread and wine as gifts of Mother Earth.

"Bahana," the medicine man said to Melissa in her dream, "it is time for you to return home to your people. You are in charge now, my daughter. Cha'risa has called me home."

Melissa arrived at the Hopi village just in time for the celebration of Communion Day. She lived with her Hopi family for many happy years, while the world around her enjoyed a period of prosperity and peace. Many technological inventions made life on earth more rewarding, happier, and creative. One could almost hear a collective sigh of relief when finally people were able again to celebrate their rituals the way their ancestors had done, without having to envy, convert, or even hate their neighbors for celebrating in a different fashion. Everyone knew and understood that they were all the children of the same Mother Earth.

Little Frederik grew up amidst his ancestral tribe and thrived under the wise guidance of his mother and his friend Chumana. Melissa watched her son grow into a handsome young man and secretly smiled when she saw the village girls turn their heads and look after him.

From early on Frederik had shown an unusual interest in numbers. At the age of two he began counting everything he could get his hands on. Year after year he wrote in his life book the desire to learn more about the power and secrets of numbers. After Chumana had taught him all she knew, Melissa took over as mentor. Soon Frederik had mastered higher algebra and began studying the intricacies of calculus. Melissa observed with amazement how his young brain blossomed.

But soon the little village ran out of resources to satisfy Frederik's insatiable thirst for knowledge. For a while he learned through virtual instruction that was available anywhere in the world. Having outgrown this method as well, his mind was set to join other young people with similar interests. But that is a new chapter in the Book of Life.

Author's Bio:

Werner Krieglstein, a Fulbright scholar and University of Chicago fellow, is an internationally recognized scholar, author, and performer. Krieglstein is the founder of a new philosophical school called Transcendental Perspectivism. In the sixties, Krieglstein was a student at the Frankfurt School in Germany with Theodore W. Adorno and directed the avant-garde theater, *die neue bühne*, at the Goethe University in Frankfurt, Germany. He holds a doctorate from the University of Chicago and taught at the University of Helsinki, Finland, Western Michigan University, Kalamazoo, and the College of DuPage. He currently is professor emeritus in philosophy and religious studies. At the College of DuPage Krieglstein was awarded the Most Outstanding Teacher Award in 2003. In 2008, Krieglstein received the Distinguished Humanities Scholar Award from the Community College Humanities Association. Krieglstein also received a Jens Jacobsen Award at the International Conference on Violence and Human Coexistence in Montreal (1992).

Krieglstein is a member of The Society for Midland Authors and was a course director at the Interuniversity Center in Dubrovnik, Croatia. He currently is a board member of the International Society for Universal Dialogue. Krieglstein is author of three books *The Dice-Playing God* (UPA, 1992), *Compassion, A New Philosophy of the Other,* (Rodopi, 2002) and *Compassionate Thinking, An Introduction to Philosophy* (Kendall Hunt 2006). He also published numerous articles in national and international journals.

Krieglstein is an accomplished theater director and actor with international experience. He recently acted in the Polish film *Light Denied*, where he performed as a "Nietzsche-inspired practitioner of perspectivism and now time."

Krieglstein on the Web
Blog: http://compassionatephilosophy.wordpress.com/
Twitter: https://twitter.com/oftheother
Wikipedia: Transcendental Perspectivism

LaVergne, TN USA
14 October 2010
200769LV00004B/23/P